Praise for the novels of *New York Times* and *USA TODAY* bestselling author DIANA PALMER

"The popular Palmer has penned another winning novel, a perfect blend of romance and suspense."
—*Booklist* on *Lawman*

"Diana Palmer is a mesmerizing storyteller who captures the essence of what a romance should be."
—*Affaire de Coeur*

"Readers will be moved by this tale of revenge and justice, grief and healing."
—*Booklist* on *Dangerous*

"Diana Palmer is one of those authors whose books are always enjoyable. She throws in romance, suspense and a good storyline."
—*The Romance Reader* on *Before Sunrise*

"Lots of passion, thrills, and plenty of suspense… *Protector* is a top-notch read!"
—*Romance Reviews Today* on *Protector*

"A delightful romance with interesting new characters and many familiar faces. It's nice to have a hero who is not picture-perfect in looks or instincts, and a heroine who accepts her privileged life yet is willing to work for the future she wants."
—*RT Book Reviews* on *Wyoming Tough*

**For a complete list of titles
available by Diana Palmer,
please visit www.dianapalmer.com.**

And don't miss DEFENDER, coming soon!

DIANA PALMER

WYOMING
STRONG

HQN™

Recycling programs
for this product may
not exist in your area.

ISBN-13: 978-0-373-60286-5

Wyoming Strong

This edition published by arrangement with Harlequin Books S.A.

For questions and comments about the quality of this book, please contact us at CustomerService@Harlequin.com.

www.Harlequin.com

Printed in U.S.A.

Dear Reader,

I am plagued with insomnia. It seems to run in my family. Some nights I don't sleep. One morning at 3:00 a.m. when I was wide-awake, I saw a young man with dark eyes and beautiful long hair in a shot on YouTube, auditioning in 2012 for *Britain's Got Talent*. Beside him was a lovely young woman. The caption was something about a shy boy captivating the judges. So I clicked on it. Mr. Antoine was picked on in school. This video is every hurt child's triumph.

I bawled the first time I heard it. To date, I have watched it at least fifteen times (along with forty-eight million other people). The young man's name is Jonathan Antoine. His partner was Charlotte Jaconelli, a fellow music student. They auditioned as Charlotte and Jonathan on *Britain's Got Talent* in 2012. Both have recording contracts now. I sincerely hope that Mr. Antoine has the attention of the Metropolitan Opera. I have never in my life heard such a voice.

This book you are about to read is one that virtually wrote itself. It is about two very damaged people who grow together out of their own tragedies. Wolf Patterson and Sara Brandon were introduced in *Texas Born*, my Harlequin Special Edition, where he accused her of harboring flying monkeys and using a broom for transport. Unknown to each, they play "World of Warcraft" together and are friends there, but enemies in real life. When Wolf is targeted by a psychotic former lover, Sara is drawn into the crosshairs with him.

I am indebted to all of you who read my books. I am still your biggest fan.

Love,

Diana Palmer

To Becky Hambrick, a dear woman
who never missed a signing. She crocheted
little scrubbers for my sink, which I still have.
I think of her every time I use them.

And to J.L. Smith, who served Cornelia, Georgia, for
many years as a police officer. James went to school
with him. He was a good and kind man.
And he was our friend.

CHAPTER ONE

It wasn't the long line so much as the company in it that was irritating Sara Brandon. Not only the company, but the way she was being watched, too.

He was lounging back against the nearby counter at the Jacobsville pharmacy, arrogant and amused, watching her with those icy Arctic-blue eyes that seemed to see right through her. As if he knew exactly what was under her clothing. As if he could see her creamy skin. As if...

She cleared her throat and glared at him.

That amused him even more. "Am I disturbing you, Ms. Brandon?" he drawled.

He was elegant. Devastating, physically. Lean-hipped, tanned, broad-shouldered, with big, beautiful hands and big feet. His Stetson was pulled low over his eyes, so that only their pale glitter was visible under the brim. His long, powerful legs in designer jeans were crossed, just the feet of his expensive tan boots peering out from under the denim. His chambray shirt was open at the throat. Thick, black, curling hair was exposed in the narrow vee.

The beast knew he was...stimulating. That's why he did that, why he left those top buttons unbuttoned, she just knew it. She couldn't completely hide her reaction to him, and he knew that, too. It drove her mad.

"You don't disturb me, Mr. Patterson," she said, her voice sounding a little choked as she tried to keep it steady.

Those eyes slid down her slender, elegant body in narrow black slacks topped by a black turtleneck sweater. His smile widened as she pulled her black leather coat closer and buttoned it, so that her sweater didn't show. Her long, thick black hair dropped to her waist in back, waving around her exquisite face. Perfect, pouting lips led up to a straight nose and wide-spaced black eyes. She was a beauty. She wasn't conceited about it. She hated her looks. She hated the attention she drew.

She crossed her arms against her breasts over the coat and averted her eyes.

"Oh, I wonder about that," he drawled in his deep, slow voice. "You don't look at all calm to me."

"Do tell me what I do look like, then."

He shouldered away from the counter and joined her. He was tall. He moved a little closer, as if to force her to look up and see how much he towered over her. She retreated a step, nervously.

"You look like a young filly, just taking her first steps out into the pasture," he said quietly.

"I've been out in the pasture for a long time, Mr. Patterson, and I'm not nervous."

He just cocked an eyebrow. He pursed his sensuous lips. "Well, you look nervous to me. Left the flying monkeys at home, did we?"

Her mouth flew open. "You listen here…!" She winced at the sudden turning of heads and quickly lowered her voice. "I do not keep…flying monkeys at my house!"

"Oh, I know that. You probably have them hidden out in the woods. Along with the broom."

She ground her teeth together.

"Miss Brandon?" Bonnie called from the cash register. "I have your refill."

"Thanks," Sara said, and quickly moved away from the tall threat of Wofford Patterson's body. They called him Wolf as a nickname. She could see why. He was really predatory. And it was something of a bit of luck that he didn't like her.

She paid for her acid reflux medicine, smiled at Bonnie, glared at Wofford Patterson and started for the front door.

"Fly at a safe speed now," he cautioned in a good-natured tone.

She whirled, her long black hair whipping. "If I really had flying monkeys, I'd have them drop you in the biggest manure lagoon in the whole state of Texas, and then I'd throw a match in it!" she flashed at him.

Everybody started laughing, especially Wofford Patterson. Red-faced, Sara almost ran out of the building.

"I WILL HAVE him shot," she muttered to herself as she stalked to her white Jaguar. "I will have him shot, and then I'll have them dismember him, and then…"

"Talking to yourself. Tsk, tsk," she heard behind her. He was following her.

She turned around. "You are the most obnoxious, unbearable, tedious, irritating, vicious man I have ever known in my life!" she raged at him.

He shrugged. "I doubt that. You do inspire people to dislike you."

Her small fists were clenched at her sides, the paper

pharmacy bag gripped in one of them. She was almost on fire with anger.

She glanced beside her and saw Cash Grier, the Jacobsville, Texas, police chief, just coming up on the sidewalk. "I want him arrested!" she yelled, pointing at Wofford.

"Now, what did I do?" Wofford asked with a straight face. "I was only asking you to drive safely, because I worry about your health." He gave her an angelic smile.

She was nearly shaking with anger.

Cash tried to hide a grin. "Now, Ms. Brandon," he began gently.

"What exactly is a Miz?" Wolf wondered aloud. "Is it like a Mr. Woman sort of thing?"

She threw the bag of pills at him.

"She assaulted me!" Wolf exclaimed. "Assault is a felony, right?"

"Oh, I'd love to assault you," she muttered under her breath.

"You really would, honey," he drawled as he watched her come back up with the sack of pills. "I am a legend in my own time." He even smiled.

She drew back a little foot in a pretty shoe.

"If you kick him, I really will have to enforce the law, Sara," Cash reminded her.

She looked as exasperated as she felt. "Couldn't you just…well, wound him?" she asked plaintively. "A little?"

Cash tried not to laugh and failed. "If I shoot him, I'll have to arrest myself. Think how that would look."

"You should go home," Wolf told her with mock concern. "I'll bet you haven't fed the flying monkeys all day."

She stamped her foot. "You pig!"

"Last week I was a snake. Is this a promotion?" he wondered aloud.

She took a step toward him. Cash got in between them. "Sara, go home. Right now. Please?" he added.

She blew a tendril of hair out of her face and turned back to the Jaguar. "I should have moved to hell. It would have been more peaceful."

"The flying monkeys would have felt at home, too," Wolf mused.

"One day," she said, raising a fist.

"I am always at home," he pointed out with a grin. "Come on over. I'll find some boxing gloves."

"Will they stop a bullet?" she asked hotly. She added a few choice words in Farsi. In fact, she added a lot of them, in a high, provoked, angry tone. She stamped her foot to emphasize that she meant them.

"Your brother would be shocked, shocked I tell you, to hear such language coming out of his baby sister's mouth," Wolf said haughtily. He glanced at Cash. "You speak Farsi. Can't you arrest her for calling people in my family names like that?"

Cash was looking hunted.

"I'm going home," Sara said furiously.

"I noticed," Wolf replied lazily.

She told him what he could do in Farsi.

"Oh, it takes two for that," he replied in the same tongue, and his pale eyes absolutely howled.

She got into the car, revved it up and roared off down the street.

"One day," Cash told Wolf, "she'll kill you, and I'll have to appear at her trial to say it was justified self-defense."

Wolf just laughed.

SARA BROKE SPEED LIMITS. She was still shaking when she pulled up outside the house her brother, Gabriel, had bought in Comanche Wells, just down the road from Jacobsville. She wished Michelle was home from college, if only briefly. Michelle would listen and commiserate with her. She would understand. She knew more about Sara than local people did.

Michelle knew that Sara's stepfather had assaulted her, almost to the point of rape when Gabriel had all but broken her bedroom door to get to him. Sara had to testify at the trial that sent her stepfather to prison, sit in the witness chair and tell total strangers exactly what the animal had done to her. And about the disgusting things he'd said while he was doing it. She couldn't force herself to tell it all.

The defense attorney had been eloquent about Sara, a young girl teasing an older man and getting him so worked up that he had to have her. It wasn't that way, but she was sure some people on the jury listened.

Her stepfather had gone to prison. He'd died when he got out. Sara shivered violently, remembering how and why. Sara and Gabriel's mother had shoved them out the door after the conviction and left them on the streets. One of the public defenders who was in Sara's corner at a second trial, when her stepfather was shot by police, had a maiden aunt who took them in, spoiled them rotten and left them most of her enormous estate.

She was worth millions, and the public defender refused to hear a word about Sara and Gabriel turning down the inheritance. They still thought of him as family. He'd been kind to them when the world turned against them.

The Brandons' mother moved away, grieved herself to death over her second husband and refused to have any contact afterward with either of her children. It had been devastating, especially to Sara, who felt responsible.

The experience had sickened her, turned her into a recluse. Sara was twenty-four, beautiful and all alone. She didn't date anybody. Ever.

The way Wolf Patterson looked at her, though; that was new and unsettling. She…liked it. But she couldn't afford to let him know. If he pursued her, if things heated up, he'd figure out her secret. She couldn't hide her reactions to any sort of physical intimacy. She'd tried once, just once, with a boy she liked at school. It had ended with her in tears and him leaving in a temper, calling her a stupid tease. So much for dating.

She locked the door behind her, tossed her purse onto the side table and went upstairs. She'd had a light lunch before she left for the pharmacy, so the rest of the day was hers to do as she pleased. She was rich. She didn't have to work. But she had no social life. At least, not in the real world. In the virtual world, however…

SHE TURNED ON her state-of-the-art gaming computer and pulled up the World of Warcraft website. Sara was a secret gamer. She didn't tell anybody about her habit. Gabriel knew, but nobody else did. She had a beautiful Blood Elf Horde toon, a character with almost white-blond hair and blue eyes—sort of a reverse Sara, she liked to think, chuckling. It was a world away from the black-haired brunette that she really was.

She pulled up her character, Casalese, a powerful warlock, and walked into the game. The minute she came online, she was whispered.

Want to do a raid with me? he asked. "He" was a level 90 Blood Elf death knight named Rednacht. The two had met at an in-game holiday event, started talking and had been online friends for a year or so. They didn't do the Real ID thing, so she had no idea who he really was. She didn't want a lover. She only wanted a friend. But they did friend each other, using the generic ID she used for her account, so she knew when he was online. And vice versa. They'd both turned level 90 at the same time. They'd celebrated at an in-game inn with cake and juice, and shot off the fireworks they were gifted with out in the countryside of the new area, Pandaria.

It had been a magical night. Rednacht was fun to be around. He never made really personal remarks, but he did mention things that were going on in his life from time to time. So did she. But only in a generic way. Sara had real issues with her privacy. Because of Gabriel's profession, she had to be especially careful.

Most people didn't know what her brother did for a living. He was an independent military contractor who worked frequently for Eb Scott. He was a skilled mercenary. Sara worried about him, because they only had each other. But she understood that he couldn't give up the excitement. Not yet, anyway. She did wonder how that might change when Michelle, who had become their ward with the sudden death of her stepmother, graduated from college. But that was sometime in the future.

I feel more like a battleground, she typed. Rough morning.

He typed back lol, laughing out loud. Same here. Okay. Shall we slay Alliance until our blades are no longer thirsty?

She laughed back. That sounds very nice.

A COUPLE OF hours of play, and she felt like a new woman. She signed off, told her friend good-night, had a light dinner and went to bed. She knew that she was hiding from life in her virtual playground, but it was at least some sort of social life. In the real world, she had nothing.

SARA LOVED OPERA. The local opera house in San Antonio had been closed earlier in the year, although a new opera company was being founded. However, she had to have her opera fix. The only remaining one within reach was in Houston. It was a long drive, but the Houston Grand Opera was performing *A Little Night Music*. One of the songs was "Send in the Clowns," her absolute favorite. She was a grown woman. She had a good car. There was no reason that she couldn't make the drive.

So she got in the Jaguar and took off, in plenty of time to make the curtain. She'd worry about coming home in the dark later.

She loved anything in the arts, including theater and symphony and ballet. She had tickets to the San Antonio Symphony and the San Antonio Ballet companies for the season. But tonight she was treating herself to this out-of-town spectacular performance.

She was looking at her program when she felt movement. She turned as a newcomer sat down, and she looked up into the pale, laughing eyes of her worst enemy in the world.

Oh, darn, was what she should have said. What she did say was far less conventional, and in Farsi.

"Potty mouth," he returned under his breath in the same language.

She ground her teeth together, waiting for his next

remark. She'd stomp on his big booted foot and march right out of the building if he said even one word.

But he was diverted by his beautiful companion before he could say anything else. Like the other woman Sara had seen him with, at another performance, this one was a gorgeous blonde. He didn't seem to like brunettes, which was certainly to Sara's advantage.

Why in the world did he always have to sit next to her? She almost groaned. She bought her tickets weeks in advance. Presumably so did he. So how did they manage to sit together, not only in San Antonio at every single event she attended, but in Houston, too? Next time, she promised herself, she'd wait to see where he was sitting before she sat down. Since the seats were numbered, however, that might pose a problem.

The orchestra began tuning its instruments. Minutes later, the curtain rose. As the brilliant Stephen Sondheim score progressed, and dancers performing majestic waltzes floated across the stage, Sara thought she'd landed in heaven. She remembered waltzes like this at an event in Austria. She'd danced with a silver-haired gentleman, an acquaintance of their tour guide, who waltzed divinely. Although she traveled alone, she'd shared sights like this with other people, most of them elderly. Sara didn't do singles tours, because she wanted nothing to do with men. She'd seen the world, but with Gabriel or senior citizens.

She drank in the exquisite score, her eyes closed as she enjoyed the song that was one of the most beautiful ever written, "Send in the Clowns."

INTERMISSION CAME, BUT she didn't budge. Wolf's companion left, but he didn't.

"You like opera, don't you?" he asked her, his eyes

suddenly intent on her, drinking in her long black hair and the black dress that fit her like a glove with its discreet bodice and cape sleeves. Her leather coat was behind her in the seat, because the theater was warm.

"Yes," she said, waiting with gritted teeth for what she expected to follow.

"The baritone is quite good," he added, crossing one long leg. "He came here from the Met. He said New York City was getting to him. He wanted to live somewhere with less traffic."

"Yes, I read that."

His eyes were on her hands. She had them in her lap, with a death grip on her small purse, her nails digging into the leather. She didn't seem to have a care in the world, but she was wired like floodlights.

"You came alone?"

She just nodded.

"It's a long way to Houston, and it's night."

"I did notice."

"Last time, in San Antonio, it was with your brother and your ward," he recalled. His eyes narrowed. "No men. Ever?"

She didn't reply. In her hands, the purse was taking a beating.

To her shock, one big, beautiful, lean hand went to her long fingers and smoothed over them gently.

"Don't," he said tersely.

She bit her lip and looked up at him unguardedly, with the anguish of years past in her beautiful dark eyes.

He caught his breath. "What the hell happened to you?" he asked under his breath.

She jerked her hands away, got to her feet, put on her coat and walked out the door. She was in tears by the time she reached her car.

IT WAS SO UNFAIR. She hadn't had a flat tire in years. She had to have one tonight, of all nights, on a dark street in a strange city many miles from her San Antonio apartment. When Gabriel and Michelle were gone, she didn't like staying by herself on the small property in Comanche Wells. It was remote, and dangerous, if any of Gabriel's enemies ever set themselves on retaliation. It had happened once in the past. Fortunately, Gabriel had been at home.

She'd already called for a tow truck, but the account she used was briefly tied up. It would be just a few minutes, they promised. She hung up and smiled ruefully.

A car approached from the direction of the theater, slowed and then whipped in just in front of where she was parked. A tall man got out and came back to her window.

She froze until she realized who it was. She powered the window down.

"This is a hell of a place to be sitting with a flat tire," Wolf Patterson said shortly. "Come on. I'll drive you home."

"But I have to stay with the car. I've called the tow truck, and they will be here in a few minutes."

"We'll wait for the wrecker in my car," he said firmly. "I'm not leaving you out here alone."

She was grateful. She didn't want to have to say so.

He chuckled softly as he got a glimpse of her expression when he opened the door of her car. "Accepting help from the enemy won't cause you to break out in hives."

"Want to bet?" she asked. But with a resigned sigh, she got into his car.

IT WAS A MERCEDES. She'd never driven one, but she knew a lot of people who did. They were almost indestructible, and they lasted forever.

She was curious about the windows. They looked odd. So did the construction of the doors.

He saw her curiosity. "Armor plating," he said easily. "Bulletproof glass."

She stared at him. "You have a lot of people using rocket launchers against you, do you?"

He just smiled.

She wondered about him. He spoke several impossible languages. He wasn't well-known locally, although he'd lived in Jacobs County for several years. Of all the spare tidbits of information she'd been able to gather about him, he'd once worked for the elite FBI Hostage Rescue Unit. But apparently, he was involved in other activities since then, none of which were ever spoken about.

Gabriel found him amusing. He only said that Wolf had moved to Jacobsville because he was looking for a little peace and quiet. Nothing more.

"My brother knows you."

"Yes."

She glanced at him. He was looking at his cell phone, pushing through screens, apparently sending emails to someone.

She averted her eyes. He was probably talking to his date, maybe apologizing for keeping her waiting.

She wanted to tell him he could go, she'd wait for the wrecker alone; she wouldn't mind. But she did mind. She was afraid of the dark, of men who might show up when she was helpless. She hated her own fear.

He glanced at her hands. She was worrying the purse again.

He put away the cell phone. "I don't bite."

She actually jumped. She swallowed. "Sorry."

His eyes narrowed. He'd been deliberately provoking her for a long time, ever since she ran into him with her car and then accused him of causing the accident. She was aggressive in her way. But alone with him, she was afraid. Very much afraid. Such a beautiful woman, with so many hang-ups.

"Why are you so nervous?" he asked quietly.

She forced a smile. "I'm not nervous," she said. She looked around for car lights.

His eyes were narrow, assessing. "There was a pileup just outside the downtown loop," he told her. "That's what I was checking for on my phone. The wrecker should be here shortly."

She nodded. "Thanks," she said jerkily.

He lifted an eyebrow. "Do you really think you're that attractive?" he asked in a cool drawl.

Her shocked eyes went up to meet his. "Excuse me?"

There was something ice-cold in his look, in his manner. She was bringing back memories he hated, memories of another beautiful brunette, provocative, coy, manipulative. "You're sitting there tied in knots. You look as if you expect me to leap on you." His sensual lips pulled up into a cold smile. "You'd be lucky," he added provocatively. "I'm very selective about women. You wouldn't even make the first cut."

She stopped twisting the purse. "Lucky me," she said with an icy smile. "Because I wouldn't have you on toast!"

His eyes flashed. He wanted to throw things. He

couldn't leave her here alone, but he wanted to. She made him furious.

She started to get out of the car.

He locked the door from a control panel. "You're not going anywhere until the wrecker gets here." He leaned toward her abruptly, without warning.

She shot back against the door, suddenly trembling. Her eyes were wide and frightened. Her body was like taut rope. She just looked at him, shivering.

He cursed under his breath.

She swallowed. Swallowed again. She couldn't even look at him. She hated showing that weakness. Aggression always provoked it. She'd never dealt with her past. She couldn't get over it, get through it.

Headlights came up from behind and slowed. "It's the tow truck," Sara said. "Please let me out," she choked out.

He unlocked the door. She scrambled out and ran to the vehicle's driver.

He got out, too, cursing himself for that look on her face. She'd done nothing to cause him to attack her, nothing except show fear. It wasn't like him to attack women, to threaten them. He was disturbed by his own response to her.

"Thank you for staying with me," she told Wolf in a hunted tone. "He's going to drop me off at my apartment and take the car to the dealership," she choked out, indicating the elderly driver. "Good night."

She ran to the wrecker and climbed up into the passenger seat while the driver worked at securing her car.

Wolf was still standing beside his car when the tow truck left. Sara didn't even turn her head.

GABRIEL WAS HOME for a few days. Sara went to Comanche Wells to cook for him.

He noticed her subdued attitude. "What's wrong, honey?" he asked softly as they drank coffee at the kitchen table.

She grimaced. "I had a flat tire, coming home from Houston after the opera."

"At night?" he asked, surprised. "Why did you drive? Why not take a limo?"

She bit her lower lip. "I'm trying to…grow up a little," she said, managing a shaky smile. "Or I was."

"I hate to think of you sitting in the dark waiting for a wrecker," he said.

"Mr. Patterson saw me there and stopped. I sat in his car while the wrecker got to me."

"Mr. Patterson?" he mused. "Wolf was in Houston, too?"

"Apparently, he likes opera, too, and there isn't a company here right now," she said through her teeth.

"I see."

Her expression was tormented. "He…he didn't even do anything. He just turned in his seat and leaned toward me. I…reacted like a crazy person," she bit off. "Made him mad."

"We've had this discussion before," he began.

"I hate therapists," she said hotly. "The last one said I wanted people to feel sorry for me, and I probably overreacted at what happened!"

"He what?" he burst out. "You never told me!"

"I was afraid you'd hit him and end up in jail," she returned.

"I would have," he said harshly.

She drew in a breath and sipped coffee. "Anyway, it

wasn't helping." She closed her eyes. "I can't get past it. I just can't."

"There are nice men in the world," he pointed out. "Some even live right here in Jacobsville."

Her smile was world-weary. "It wouldn't matter."

He knew what she'd gone through. He hadn't known that the rape attempt wasn't the first one, that their stepfather had spent months making suggestive comments, trying to touch her, trying to get her into bed long before he used force. That, combined with the court trial, had warped Sara in ways that made Gabriel despair for her future. What a hell of a thing to happen to a girl at the age of thirteen.

"You love children," he said quietly. "You're dooming yourself to a life all alone."

"I have my entertainments."

"You live in that virtual world," he said irritably. "It's no replacement for a social life."

"I can't cope with a social life," she replied. "I have never been more sure of anything." She got up and bent to kiss his forehead. "Leave me to my prudish pursuits. I'll make you an apple pie."

"Bribery."

She laughed. "Bribery."

GABRIEL WAS AT the feed store the next Friday when Wolf Patterson came in. He was scowling even before he saw Gabriel.

"Is she with you?" Wolf asked.

Gabriel knew who he meant at once. He shook his head.

"Is she crazy?" he asked. "Honest to God, I stayed

with her in my car until the wrecker came, and she acted as if I was bent on assault!"

"I'm grateful for what you did," Gabriel said, side-stepping the question. "She should have taken a limo to Houston. I'll make sure she does next time."

Wolf calmed down, but only a little. He shoved his hands deep into the pockets of his expensive jeans. "She ran into me with the car, you know. Then she blamed me for it. That started the whole thing. I hate aggressive women," he added shortly.

"She tends to overreact," Gabriel said noncommittally.

"I don't even like brunettes," he said curtly. His pale eyes flashed. "She's not my type."

"You're certainly not hers," the younger man pointed out with a grin.

"Who is?" Wolf asked. "One of those tofu-eating tree huggers?"

"Sara…doesn't like men."

Wolf raised an eyebrow. "She likes women?"

"No."

Wolf's eyes narrowed. "You're not telling me anything."

"That's exactly right," Gabriel replied. He pursed his lips. "But I'll tell you this. If she ever showed any interest in you, I'd get her out of the country by the quickest means available."

Wolf glared at him.

"You know what I mean," Gabriel added quietly. "I wouldn't wish you on any woman alive, much less my baby sister. You still haven't dealt with your past, after all this time."

Wolf's teeth were clenched.

Gabriel put a hand on his shoulder. "Wolf, not all women are like Ysera," he said softly.

Wolf jerked away from him.

Gabriel knew when he was licked. He smiled. "So, how's the wargaming?"

It was a carrot, and Wolf bit. "New expansion coming out," he said, and smiled. "I'm looking forward to it, now that I've got somebody to run dungeons with."

"Your mysterious woman." Gabriel chuckled.

"I assume she's a woman," he replied, shrugging. "People aren't usually what they seem in these games. I was complimenting a guildie on his mature playing style, and he informed me that he was twelve years old." He laughed. "You never know who you're playing with."

"Your woman could be a man. Or a child. Or a real woman."

Wolf nodded. "I'm not looking for relationships in a video game," he replied easily.

"Wise man." Gabriel didn't tell him what Sara did for amusement. It really wouldn't do to sell her out to the enemy. He hesitated and glanced toward the street. "There's a rumor going around."

Wolf turned his head. "What rumor?"

"Ysera got away," he reminded the other man. "We've searched for over a year, you know. One of Eb's men thinks he saw her, at a small farm outside Buenos Aires. With a man we both remember from the old days."

Wolf's face tightened as if he'd been shot. "Any intel on why she's there?"

Gabriel nodded grimly. "Revenge," he said simply. His eyes narrowed. "You need to hire on a couple of extra men. She'd have your throat slit if she could."

"I'd return the favor if I could do it legally," Wolf returned with faint venom.

Gabriel slid his hands into his jeans pockets. "So would the rest of us. But you're the one in danger, if she really is still alive."

Wolf didn't like remembering the woman, or the things he'd done because of her lies. He still had nightmares. His eyes had a cold, faraway look. "I thought she was dead. I hoped…" he confessed quietly.

"It's hard to kill a big snake," the other man said flatly. "Just…be careful."

"Watch your own back," Wolf replied.

"I always do." He wanted to tell the other man about Sara, to warn him off, to avert a tragedy in the making. But his friend didn't seem really interested in Sara, and he was reluctant to share intimate details of Sara's past with her worst enemy. It was a decision that would have consequences. He didn't realize how many, at the time.

CHAPTER TWO

GABRIEL WENT BACK to work, and Sara had a weekend jaunt to the Wyoming ranch with Michelle during spring break. Then Michelle went back to school, and Sara went shopping in downtown San Antonio.

Sara shopped for spring clothes and then tried on mantillas in the huge Mercado in San Antonio, enjoying the sounds and smells of the market. A few minutes later, she took her purchases to the River Walk and sat down at a small table, watching the boats go by. It was April. The weather was warm and dry, and flowers were appearing in the planters all around the café. It was one of her favorite places.

She put her purse under the table and leaned back, her beautiful hair rippling with the movement. She had on black slacks and loafers and a candy-pink blouse that emphasized her exquisite complexion. Her black eyes danced as she listened to a strolling mariachi band.

She moved her chair to accommodate two men sitting down behind her. One of them was Wolf Patterson. Her heart jumped. She rushed to finish her cappuccino, gathered her bags and went to pay for it at the counter.

"Running away?" a silky, deep voice asked at the back of her head.

"I was finished with my coffee," she said stiffly,

smiling and thanking the clerk as she was handed her change.

When she turned, he was blocking the way out. His pale eyes were flashing with hostility. He looked as if he'd have liked to fry her on a griddle.

She swallowed down the nervousness that always assailed her when he was close. She tried to step back, but there was no place to go. Her huge, beautiful eyes widened with apprehension.

"When does your brother get back?" he asked.

"I'm not sure," she said. "He thinks maybe by the weekend."

He nodded. His eyes narrowed on her face. "What are you afraid of?" he asked half under his breath.

"Not a thing, Mr. Patterson," she replied. "Because I'm not your type."

"Damned straight."

She was ready to try to push past him, frustrated beyond rational behavior, when one of his companions called to him.

While he was diverted, she slipped to the side of him, and went out of the area at a dead run. She didn't even care if people stared.

THERE WAS A ballet later in the week. She loved the ballet. She loved the color, the costumes, the lighting, all of it. She'd studied the art in her childhood. At one time, she'd dreamed of being a prima ballerina. But the long years of training and the sacrifices the role demanded were too much for a young girl just discovering life.

Those had been good days. Her father had still been alive. Her mother had been kind, if distant. She remembered the happy times they'd had together with a bittersweet smile. How different her life might have been if their father had lived.

But looking back served no real purpose, she told herself. Such as her life was, she had to try to cope.

She sat down in her seat near the front of the concert hall, smiling as she looked at the program. The prima ballerina was an acquaintance of hers, a sweet girl who loved her job and didn't mind the long hours and sacrifice that went along with it. Lisette was pretty, too, blonde and tall as a beanpole, with eyes as big and dark as chestnuts.

The ballet was *Swan Lake*, one of her absolute favorites. The costumes were eye-catching, the performers exquisite, the music almost enchanted. She smiled, her heart swelling as she anticipated the delightful performance.

She heard movement nearby and almost had a coronary when she saw Wolf Patterson and yet another beautiful blonde moving into the seats beside hers. She actually groaned.

The woman stopped to speak to someone she knew. Wolf dropped down into the seat next to Sara's and gave her conservative black dress and leather coat a brief scrutiny. His glare could have stopped a charging bull. "Are you following me around?" he asked.

She counted to ten. In her hand, the program was twisting into large confetti.

"I mean, just a couple of weeks ago, there you were at the opera in Houston, and here you are tonight at the ballet in San Antonio, with seats right next to mine," he mused. "If I were a conceited man..." he added in a deep, slow drawl.

She turned her black eyes up to his and made a

comment in Farsi that made his hair stand on end. He snapped back at her in the same language, his eyes biting into her face.

"What in the world sort of language is that?" his blonde companion asked with a laugh.

Wolf clenched down on more words as Sara turned her head and tried to concentrate on the stage curtain. The orchestra began tuning up.

"Aren't you going to introduce me?" the blonde woman persisted, glancing at Sara's discomfort with an honestly worried expression.

"I am not," Wolf said, enunciating every word. "Curtain's going up," he added shortly.

SARA WANTED TO get up and walk out. She almost did. But she couldn't bear to give him the satisfaction. So she lost herself in the color and beauty of *Swan Lake*, her heart in her throat as the preliminary dancers gave way to the title role, and Lisette came on stage.

Her friend's exquisite beauty was apparent even at a distance. She twirled and pirouetted, making the leaps with precision and grace. Sara envied her that talent. Once upon a time, she'd seen herself on the stage in a costume like that beautiful confection Lisette was wearing.

Of course, reality had put paid to that sad dream. She couldn't imagine standing in front of a lot of people, having them all look at her, without flinching. Not after the trial.

Her face grew taut as she remembered the trial, the taunting of the defense attorney, the fury in her stepfather's face, the anguish in her mother's.

She didn't realize that she'd crumbled the program in her slender fingers, or that the tragic look on her face was drawing all too much reluctant interest from her acquaintance in the next seat.

Wolf Patterson had seen that look before, many times, in combat zones. It was akin to what was called the "thousand-yard stare," familiar to combat veterans, a blank expression with terrible eyes that recalled things no mortal should ever have to witness. But Sara Brandon was pampered and rich and beautiful. What reason would a woman like that have to act tormented?

He laughed silently to himself, faint contempt on his hard features. Pretty little Sara, tempting men, ridiculing them in passion, making them plead for satisfaction and then laughing when they achieved it. Laughing with contempt and disgust. Saying things...

A soft hand touched his. The mature blonde woman beside him was frowning.

He shook himself mentally and dragged his eyes away from Sara. He managed a reassuring smile at his companion, but it was a lie. Sara unsettled him. She reminded him of things past, things deadly, things unbearable. She was everything he hated in a woman.

But he wanted her. The sight of her lithe, elegant body made him ache. It had been a long time. He hadn't been able to trust another woman after Ysera, want another woman.

In the back of his mind was the ridicule and the laughter. He hadn't been able to control his desire, and Ysera thought it was funny. She loved manipulating him, tormenting him. And when she'd had her fill of humiliating him in bed, she'd sent him off on a chore of personal vengeance with a lie.

He closed his eyes. A shudder ran through his powerful frame. He couldn't escape the past. It tormented him still. There had been no consequences, but there should have been. Ysera at least should have been held accountable, but she was out of the country before she could be arrested. For over a year there had been no word of her. He'd thought she'd finally gotten what she deserved—that she was dead. Now she was back, still alive, still haunting him. He would never know peace for the rest of his life.

"Wolf," the blonde woman whispered urgently. She wrapped her hand around his clenched fist. "Wolf!"

Sara realized, belatedly, that something was going on beside her. She turned her head in time to see an expression of such anguish on the tall man's hard face that concern replaced her usual resentment.

His fist was clenched on his chair arm. The blonde woman was trying to calm him. He looked like a drawn cord.

"Mr. Patterson," Sara said, her voice very soft so that it didn't carry. "Are you all right?"

He looked down at her, coming out of the past with the pain still in his eyes. They narrowed, and he looked at her as if he hated her. "What the hell do you care?" he gritted.

She bit her lower lip almost through. He looked coiled, ready to strike, dangerous. She forced her attention back to the stage, a deathly pallor in her cheeks. *More fool me, for caring*, she thought.

He was trying to cope with memories that were killing him. Sara reminded him too much of things he only wanted to forget. He cursed under his breath in Farsi, got to his feet and walked out of the theater. The blonde woman looked at Sara with a grimace, as if she wanted to explain, to apologize. Then she just smiled sadly and followed him out.

THAT TORMENTED LOOK on Wolf Patterson's face haunted Sara for the rest of the week. She couldn't get it out of her mind. He'd stared at her as if he hated her in those few seconds. She began to realize that it wasn't necessarily her whom he hated. Perhaps it was someone she reminded him of. She smiled sadly to herself. Just her luck, to feel the stirrings of attraction to a man for the first time in her life, and have him turn out to be someone who hated her because she reminded him of another woman. An old flame, perhaps, someone he'd loved and lost.

Well, it was hopeless to look in that direction anyway, she consoled herself. She'd only really been alone with him once, and look how she'd embarrassed herself when he came too close. She still flushed, remembering how she'd run from him after her flat tire. He wouldn't understand why she'd reacted that way. And she couldn't tell him.

SHE CLIMBED INTO her pajamas late that night and pulled up her game on the computer, setting the laptop on a board across her lap as she propped up in bed.

Her friend was on. Hi, she whispered.

Hi, he whispered back.

He was usually more wordy than that. In the middle of something? she queried.

No. Bad memories, he said after a minute.

I know all about that, she wrote sadly.

There was a brief pause. Want to talk about it? he asked.

She smiled to herself. Talking doesn't help. How about a battleground?

He wrote lol on the screen, invited her to a group and queued them for a battleground.

Why does life have to be so hard? she wrote while they waited.

I don't know.

I can't get away from the past, she wrote. She couldn't tell him everything, but she could talk a little. He was the only real friend she had. Lisette was kind and sweet, but she had so little free time just to talk.

Neither can I, he wrote after a minute. Do you have nightmares? he asked suddenly.

She grimaced and wrote, All the time.

Me, too. There was a hesitation. Damaged people, he wrote.

Yes.

Holding each other together, he added, with another lol.

She returned the laugh, and smiled to herself. BRB, she wrote, gamer's slang for "be right back." I need coffee.

Good idea. I'll make some and email you a cup, he wrote.

She chuckled to herself. He was good company. She wondered who he was in real life, if he was a man or a woman or even a child. Whatever, it was nice to have someone to talk to, even if they only talked in single syllables.

He was back before the queue popped. We should

get one of those chat programs like Ventriloquist, he commented, so that we can talk instead of type.

Her heart almost stopped. No.

Why?

She bit her lower lip. How could she tell him that it would interfere with the fantasy if she brought real life into it? That she didn't want to know if he was young or old or female.

You're frightened, he wrote.

She hesitated, her hands over the keyboard. Yes.

I see.

No, you don't, she replied. I have a hard time with people. With most people. I don't... I don't like letting people get close to me.

Join the club.

So in a game, it's sort of different, she tried to explain.

Yes. There was a hesitation. Are you female?

Yes.

Young?

Yes. She paused. Are you male?

There was no hesitation at all. Definitely.

She hesitated again. Married?

No. And never likely to be. Another pause. You?

No. And never likely to be, she replied, adding a smile.

Do you work?

And now, time for the lies. I cut hair, she lied. What do you do?

There was a hesitation. Dangerous things.

Her heart skipped. Law enforcement? she typed.

There was a howl of laughter. How did you get there?

I don't know. You seem very honest. You never try to ninja the loot when we do dungeons. You'll stop to help other players if they get in trouble. You're forever using in-game skills to make things for lower level players. Stuff like that.

There was a long hesitation. You're describing yourself, as well.

She smiled to herself. Thanks.

Damaged people, he mused. Holding each other together.

She nodded. She typed, It feels...sort of nice.

Doesn't it?

There was a new warmth in the screen. Of course, they could both be lying. She didn't work, she didn't have to, and he might not be in law enforcement. But it didn't matter, since they were never likely to meet in person. She wouldn't dare try. She'd had too many false starts in her young life, trying to escape the past.

She would never be able to do it. This was all she could hope for—a relationship online with a man who might not even like her in the real world. But it was strangely almost enough.

Time to go, he said, as the Join Battle tag came up.

After you, she typed back. Which was a joke; since they were a group, they entered together.

SHE WAS SITTING in the park, feeding the pigeons. It was a stupid thing to do, the birds were a nuisance. But she had bread left over from a solitary lunch, and the birds were comfortable, cooing around her feet as she scattered crumbs.

She was wearing a green V-necked pullover sweater with jeans and ankle boots. She looked very young with her long hair in a braid down her back and her face clean of makeup except for the lightest touch of lipstick.

Wolf Patterson stared at her with more conflicting emotions than he'd ever felt in his life. She was two different people. One was fiery and temperamental and brilliant. The other was beautiful and damaged and afraid. He wasn't sure which one was the real Sara.

He'd felt guilty at the way he'd snapped at her at the ballet. He hadn't meant to. The memories had eaten at him until he felt only half-alive. Just knowing Ysera was out there, still plotting, made him uneasy. With the memory of her came others, sickening ones, that Sara reminded him of.

She felt eyes on her and turned her head, just slightly. There he was, a few feet away, standing with his hands in his pockets, scowling.

It fascinated him to see the way she reacted. Her lithe body froze in position with crumbs half in and half out

of the bag she was holding. She just looked at him, her
great black eyes wide with apprehension.

He moved closer. "A deer I shot once looked just
like that," he remarked quietly. "Waiting for the bullet."

She flushed and dropped her eyes.

"I don't hunt much anymore," he remarked, standing
beside her. "I hunted men. It ruins your taste for blood."

She bit her lower lip, hard.

"Don't do that," he said in the softest voice she'd ever
heard him use. "I won't hurt you."

She actually trembled. She managed a faint laugh.
How many times in her life had she heard that from
men who wanted her, hunted her.

He went down on one knee right in front of her and
forced her to meet his eyes. "I mean that," he said quietly. "We've had our differences. But physically, you
have absolutely nothing to fear from me."

She swallowed. Hard. Her eyes when they met his
were full of remembered fear and pain.

His Arctic-blue eyes narrowed. It had been a shot
in the dark, but he watched it hit home. "Someone hurt
you. A man."

She tried and failed to make words come out of her
mouth. On the bag, her hands were clenched so tightly
that the knuckles went white.

Her very vulnerability hurt him. "I can't imagine a
man brutal enough to try to hurt something so beautiful," he said very softly.

Her lower lip trembled. A tear she couldn't help
trickled out of the corner of her eye.

"Oh, God, I'm sorry," he said roughly.

She caught her breath and swiped at the tear, as if it

made her angry. "Should you be giving aid and assistance to the enemy?" she asked in a choked tone.

He smiled. Antagonism was much preferable to those silent tears. They hurt him. "Truce?"

She looked into his pale eyes. "Truce?"

He nodded. "We don't want to scare away the pigeons. They're obviously starving. You're upsetting them."

She was upsetting him, too, but he didn't want to admit it. He felt guilty at the things he'd said to her. He hadn't realized that she was damaged. She had such a strong, brave spirit that he hadn't expected this vulnerability.

She straightened a little and tossed more crumbs at the birds. They gathered around them, cooing.

"I expect if the police see me, I'll be arrested. Nobody loves pigeons."

He got up and dropped lightly onto the bench beside her, just far away enough not to make her nervous. "I do," he corrected. "If they're cooked right."

A tiny little laugh jumped out of her throat, and her black eyes lit up like fires in the night.

"I had them in Morocco, when I was there on a case once," he remarked.

"I did, too. In this beautiful hotel on a hill in Tangier," she began.

"El Minzah," he said without thinking.

Her hand stilled in the bag. "Why, yes," she stammered.

"They had a driver named Mustapha and a big Mercedes sedan," he continued, grinning.

She laughed. It changed her whole appearance, made

her even more beautiful. "He took me to the caves outside the city, where the Barbary pirates hid their loot."

"You? Alone?" he probed gently.

"Yes."

"You're always alone," he said thoughtfully.

She hesitated. Then she nodded. She turned back to the pigeons. "I don't...mix well with people," she confessed.

"Neither do I," he said gruffly.

She tossed another handful of crumbs to the birds. "You have that look."

"Excuse me?"

"My brother has it, too," she said without glancing at him. "They call it the thousand-yard stare."

He cocked his head and narrowed his pale eyes as he stared at what he could see of her face. He didn't say a word.

She lifted her eyes and winced. "Sorry," she said, flushing. "I always put my foot in my mouth around you." She shifted restlessly. "You make me nervous."

He let out a short laugh. "Me and the Russian Army maybe," he mused.

She turned her face toward him. She didn't understand.

He searched her black eyes slowly, and for longer than he meant to. "You stand your ground," he explained. "You fight back. I admire spirit."

She averted her eyes. "You fight back, too."

"Long-standing habit."

She tossed some more crumbs. She was running out. "You don't really like women, do you?" she blurted out, and then flushed and grimaced. "Sorry! I didn't mean..."

"No," he interrupted, and his eyes grew cold. "I don't like women. Especially brunettes."

"That was awful of me," she apologized without looking at him. "I told you I don't mix well with people. I don't know how to be diplomatic."

"I don't mind blunt speaking," he said surprisingly. "So it's my turn now." He waited until she looked at him to continue. "You were hurt, badly and physically, by a man somewhere in your past."

The bag went flying. She wrapped her arms around herself and shivered.

He wanted to draw her close and hold her, comfort her. But he moved toward her, and she shot to her feet, her head lowered.

"God, Sara, what happened to you?" he asked through his teeth.

She swallowed. Swallowed again. "I can't…talk about it."

He was going to find out from Gabriel. He had no right to be curious, but she was too beautiful to go through life locked up inside like that. He stood up, too, but he didn't move closer. "You should be in therapy," he said softly. "This is no sort of life."

"I should be in therapy?" she returned with a short laugh. "What about you?"

His face shuttered. "What about me?"

"At the ballet," she said. "You have no idea how you looked…"

His chin lifted. His pale eyes flashed. "We were talking about you."

"Something happened to you, too," she said doggedly. "I thought you hated me because I ran into you with the car. But that wasn't it at all, was it? You hate me because I look like her, because I remind you of her."

His face was like stone. Beside him, one big hand clenched.

"You...loved her," she guessed.

His eyes fragmented, like icy shards cutting into her face. "Damn you," he whispered in a vicious undertone. He turned and walked away.

Sara, watching him, wasn't even offended. She began to understand him, just a little. There was something traumatic in his past, too. Something that tied him up in knots, that left him no peace. He'd loved the woman. She saw it in his eyes.

Perhaps she'd died. Or left him for another man. Whatever the reason, he was still tied to it, wrapped up in it. He couldn't get past it, any more than Sara could forget what had been done to her.

Damaged people, she thought, and smiled sadly. She picked up her bag, tossed it in a nearby trash receptacle and went back to her apartment.

GABRIEL CAME HOME that weekend. He looked tired, and he wasn't smiling.

"Bad week?" Sara asked. They were at the ranch in Comanche Wells. She only stayed there when he was at home. She was nervous of being so far out of town on her own.

"Very bad," he said. "We're having some problems over the oil fields. Terrorists, kidnappings, the usual," he added with a smile. "How are you?"

It was a throwaway remark, except that his eyes were very intent on her face as he waited for the answer.

"I'm...the same. Why do you ask?"

"Because Wolf Patterson called me and asked what had happened to you that made you back away from him if he came too close."

Her heart jumped. "He had no right," she began furiously.

"He reminded me that he waited for a tow truck with you one night after an opera in Houston, when you had a flat, and that you almost ran to get into the wrecker with the driver. Then he told me about a conversation you had in the park. He said you were afraid of him when he moved close to you."

"Only because he was being sarcastic and obnoxious," she shot back. "I can't abide the man!"

His eyes narrowed. "I know you too well to believe that," he said. "You find him attractive."

She flushed.

He drew in a long breath. "He went through hell because of a woman who resembles you," he said after a minute. "He's not an evil man. He wouldn't hurt you deliberately. But he might not be able to help it. He's carrying scars. Bad ones."

"Can you tell me why?"

He shook his head. "It's much too personal."

"I see."

"He's had some very hard knocks from women. His mother hated him."

"What?"

"She didn't want a child, but her husband did. When he died, she farmed Wolf out to one set of friends after another. In one of those households, the father was an alcoholic. He beat Wolf until he was old enough to fight back. His mother thought it was funny when the authorities tried to make her take him back. She said that she had no use for a sniveling little brat that she didn't want in the first place."

Sara sat down. She was getting a very sick picture of the man's background.

"But he ended up in law enforcement. He was with the FBI," she recalled, having heard him say that.

Gabriel almost bit his tongue off not replying. "He was a cop in San Antonio for a while. He went into other work, and they farmed him out to various agencies over the years. But he left the old life behind when he came here and bought the ranch."

"He seems an odd fit for a small town," she said slowly.

"It's not the usual small town," he replied. "He has enemies. Jacobsville is overflowing with mercs and ex-military, and he has friends here. Including me."

She frowned. "He has enemies?"

"Deadly ones," he replied. "There's already been one attempt."

"Someone tried to kill him?" she asked, shocked, hating her own reaction to those words, because it mattered to her that someone had tried to kill him.

Gabriel saw that. "Yes. Which makes him a moving target, along with anyone who gets close to him." He put his big hand over hers. "You've had enough tragedy and trauma in your life. I don't want you around him."

She gnawed her lower lip.

"Sara, whatever you think you feel," he said, choosing his words, "it wouldn't end well. He hasn't faced his past any more than you've faced yours. The two of you could damage each other, badly."

"I see."

"He's not the man for you to cut your teeth on. I can't

tell him what happened to you, and I know for a fact that you won't. He's aggressive with women he wants. You can't afford to let him want you. Do you understand?"

She swallowed. "Yes."

"I'm sorry."

She drew in a breath, forced a smile and changed the subject. "How about a slice of cake? I made you a chocolate one."

He smiled back. "That would be nice."

CHAPTER THREE

SARA FELT GRIEF like a living thing when she remembered what Gabriel had said about Wolf Patterson. Until then, she hadn't realized how her attitude toward him was changing. When he'd knelt in front of her in the park, spoken to her in that gentle tone, her heart had started to melt. But she knew Gabriel was right. She couldn't afford to encourage a man like that.

Aggressive with women he wanted, Gabriel had said. So her brother knew things about him, knew that he had women.

It shouldn't have surprised her. Wolf was an attractive man. When he wasn't baiting her and being sarcastic, he was charming. Those blonde women she'd seen him with were certainly charmed, she thought bitterly. Blonde. Always blonde. He hated brunettes. Sara was a brunette…

The more she thought about it, the more it hurt. She'd buried herself in her studies for years, learned languages, traveled, done anything she could to force the horrible memories out of her mind. She succeeded for whole days at a time, although the nightmares came frequently, and she woke up screaming.

In the daytime there was a remedy. She could ride. She loved horses, and she was an accomplished rider. The freedom of sailing across the pastures on the back of Black Silk, the fastest of Gabriel's geldings, was a thrill beyond description. It blew away the pain. It gave her peace.

Black Silk had a wild, free spirit, much like Sara herself. She tossed the saddle onto his back, checked the bindings and swung gracefully up onto his back. She pushed him into a full gallop across the pasture. Laughing, with her lithe body clinging to the saddle, her long black hair flying behind her, she made a picture that an artist would have loved.

But the man driving along the road, watching her, was filled with horror. She could break her neck like that!

He drove hell for leather down the road to the end of the pasture, swung the Mercedes up to the fence and slammed out of it seconds after he cut off the engine.

Sara, shocked, saw him and pulled Black Silk up at the fence, patting him to ease his nervousness. She let him walk to the watering trough and sat still while he drank, and a furious Wolf Patterson came right over the fence toward her.

"Get down," he said in a tone that could have curdled milk.

Speechless, she just sat and looked at him.

He reached up and pulled her off the horse's back as if she weighed nothing. He stood there, holding her in his arms off the ground, and glared into her shocked black eyes.

"You crazy little fool, you could have killed yourself!" he ground out.

"But...I always ride...like that," she began.

His hard face was pale. His eyes were flashing like fireworks. His eyes fell to her beautiful face, to her wide black eyes, to her soft bow of a mouth. He groaned, almost shivering with hunger, and suddenly brought his mouth right down over Sara's soft lips without one single sign of hesitation.

He felt her body go stiff. His mouth insisted, but the harder he kissed her, the more she stiffened. After a few seconds, he realized that she was frightened of him.

He forced himself to slow down, although her mouth was the sweetest nectar he'd tasted in years. He smoothed his lips tenderly over her top lip, teasing it, toying with it, in a silence broken only by the raspy sound of his own breathing and the quick rhythm of hers.

"I won't hurt you," he whispered. "Don't fight me. Open your mouth under mine. Let me taste you…"

She'd never felt anything quite like it. Her hands had a death grip on his neck, cold and tremulous as she let him kiss her. It had been years since she'd even tolerated a kiss. His mouth was sensuous, firm, very expert. She didn't know what to do, but she did relax just a little. It felt good. It felt…wonderful. Nothing like the man in her nightmares…

He lifted his head a few seconds later and looked into her wide, curious black eyes. "You don't know how to do this," he said in a deep, almost shocked tone.

She swallowed. She could taste him on her mouth, tasted coffee and something like mint.

He was fascinated. He bent to her mouth again, drew his ever so softly over it, smiling faintly, because she wasn't resisting him.

"Like this," he whispered, and taught her the brushing little caresses that were tender and slow and arousing.

She followed his lead, her heart racing. He was her

worst enemy in the world, and she was letting him kiss her. Not only that. She was…kissing him back. He tasted like honey…

"That's it, baby," he whispered. "Yes. Just like that…"

His arms contracted and his mouth opened, pressing her lips apart. His body was hardening as he held her. He hadn't felt anything so powerful for a very long time. Her mouth was the sweetest honey he'd ever had.

She felt the strength in his hard arms, the warmth of his muscular chest against her breasts. She moaned softly as sensations she'd never felt in her life lanced through her.

He heard the soft moan and suddenly ground her breasts against him as the fever began to burn in him. That was when he felt her go stiff.

He forced himself to lift his head. Her eyes were wide and shocked, and now there was fear in them. His eyes narrowed as he realized why. Her nipples were hard, like little stones pressing into his chest. Did she know why they were hard? he wondered. Because she acted like a woman with her first man.

His chin lifted as he looked at her. He felt arrogant. "Have you ever had a man?" he asked in a deep, rough whisper.

Her reaction shocked him. She made a sound like a sob deep in her throat and pushed at him, frantically. "Let me down. Let me down, please!"

He put her on her feet. She looked up at him with anguish.

The reaction set him off. He hadn't meant to touch her. The way she was riding had frightened him, God knew why. He was only trying to keep her safe. But she backed away as if he'd done something unspeakable.

His pale eyes narrowed. "Your love life is none of my business," he said shortly. "But it's a good act."

Her tongue felt thick. "Act?"

His mouth pulled up into a cold, sarcastic smile. "The frightened virgin bit," he explained. He slid his hands into his pockets, and hateful memories flooded his mind, of another brunette, coy and teasing and innocent. Except that she wasn't innocent. She'd tormented him, shattered his life. It had started just like this.

She wrapped her arms around her chest. She felt cold all over. Technically, she was still a virgin. But that was only due to a physical barrier that had stopped her stepfather long enough for Gabriel to break in the door.

She closed her eyes, and a wave of pure nausea swept over her. She was back in that time, in that space, in her room, screaming for help that she never expected to come. Her mother had gone shopping. Gabriel was in school. Except that he'd left class early. Thank God he had!

She shivered.

Wolf, watching her, was torn by conflicting emotions. Part of him was ablaze with a monstrous desire to push her down in the grass and have her right there. Another, saner, part was certain that it was an act. A woman who traveled, was sophisticated and was of her age was afraid of kisses? She'd been putting on an act. In his car, after the opera, in the park and now here. Tempt him, pretend to be afraid to make him vulnerable. And then the knives would come out of hiding. Exactly as they had with Ysera.

Ysera. His eyes closed on a silent groan. He'd loved her. What she'd done to him was beyond cruelty.

Sara had turned away. She climbed back into the saddle. She didn't look at Wolf Patterson.

"I've been riding horses since I was three years old," she said through her teeth. "When I was younger, I did rodeo. I know how to handle horses."

"And now I know that, don't I?" he said. He smiled at her. It wasn't a nice smile. It was demeaning, arrogant. "Just for the record, I don't like brunettes. You might have noticed that the women I date are blonde."

She didn't answer him.

"The frightened virgin bit won't work again," he added. "You'll have to think of something a little more original. I'm an old fox, honey. I know women."

She felt a chill run down her spine. She lifted her chin. "Whatever you may think, I'm not in the mood for a torrid love affair, Mr. Patterson," she said haughtily. "Least of all with you."

He only smiled. "You'd be lucky," he drawled.

She fought the memory of how gentle he'd been, how very tender. She didn't want to remember. Her hand tightened on the reins. Then, involuntarily, she remembered what Gabriel had told her about Wolf's mother, and she winced inwardly. The woman had done untold damage. No doubt there was some other woman, as well, more recently, who'd added to his scars. He was the most mistrustful person she'd ever known. She didn't trust people, either, but she couldn't talk to him. He disliked her. But why had he kissed her? She couldn't understand the way he went from hot to cold and back again with her.

He was studying the horse closely.

"Something on your mind?" she asked coolly.

"Couldn't get the broom cranked?"

Her black eyes flashed like lightning. "If I had a broom, I'd hit you with it!"

"And you know what I'd do when you did, don't you?" His voice was deep and caressing. His eyes were sensuous, like that firm, chiseled mouth, smiling at her as if he knew everything she was feeling. She could see in her mind what he was thinking, see him take the broom away and jerk her into his arms, and bend his head…

She swallowed, hard, and fought down a new and disturbing hunger.

"I have to go home." She turned the horse with easy skill.

"Time to feed the flying monkeys?"

She started to say something, bit her tongue instead and galloped away, red-faced.

GABRIEL DIDN'T LIKE parties as a rule, but there was always the one exception. Jacobsville had holiday events to benefit the local animal shelter. There was a dance at the civic center, and everybody attended. It was one of several throughout the year. This one was for spring.

Sara went with her brother. Michelle was coming home soon, but she'd had a job interview in San Antonio, and she wanted to stay there over the weekend in Sara's apartment. So it was just Sara and Gabriel at the dance.

Sara let her hair fall naturally, thick and black and down to her waist in back. She wore an off-white ankle-length dress that complemented her soft, pale olive skin, while emphasizing her black eyes, her beauty. She wore only a string of pearls and stud earrings with it.

She looked exquisitely beautiful.

Wolf Patterson hated her on sight in that dress. He remembered Ysera wearing one like it when they went nightclubbing in Berlin. At the end of the evening, he'd removed it. Ysera had vamped him, seduced him, whispered how much she loved him, how much she wanted him. Then she'd ridiculed him, laughed at him, made him feel like a fool.

Sara caught that expression on his face and couldn't understand it. She averted her eyes and smiled at an elderly cattleman who seemed to have come to the benefit alone.

"Pretty young woman like you shouldn't be hanging out with an outlaw like me," he teased. "You should get out there and dance."

She smiled sadly as she nursed a soft drink. "I don't dance." She did, but she couldn't abide being that close to a man. Not anymore.

"Now that's a pity. You should get our police chief to teach you." He chuckled, indicating Cash Grier, who was out on the dance floor with his beautiful redheaded wife, Tippy, doing a masterful waltz.

"I'd just trip over my feet and kill somebody." Sara laughed softly.

"Hi, Sara," one of Eb Scott's men called to her. She knew him. Gabriel had invited him to the house a couple of times. He was tall and dark, very handsome, with flashing green eyes. "How about dancing with me?"

"Sorry," she declined with a smile. "I don't dance…"

"That's silly. I can teach you. Here." He took the soft drink away and caught her hand.

She reacted badly. She jerked back, flushed. "Ted, don't," she said in a curt undertone, tugging at her hand.

He'd had at least one drink too many. He didn't realize what he was doing to her. "Oh, come on, it's just a dance!"

Wolf Patterson caught him by the collar and almost threw him away from Sara.

"She said she didn't want to dance," he told the man, and his posture was dangerous enough to sober the other man up. Fortunately, they were in an alcove, and they didn't draw attention. Sara was embarrassed enough already.

"Gosh. Sorry, Sara," Ted told her, flustered, as he glanced at Wolf Patterson, whose eyes were glittering like fresh ice.

"It's okay," she said in a husky undertone. But her hands were shaking.

Ted grimaced, nodded at Wolf and made himself scarce.

Sara swallowed, then swallowed again. She was shaking. Any sort of aggression from a man, even slight, was enough to set her off.

"Come with me," Wolf said quietly. He stood aside, indicating the side door.

She followed him out into the night. It was cold, and her coat was in the hall with all the others.

Wolf took off his jacket and slid it over her soft, bare shoulders. It was warm from his body. It smelled of masculine spice.

"You'll get cold," she protested.

He stuck his hands into his pockets and shrugged. "I don't feel the cold much."

They stared out over the long pasture that led to a

wooded area around the community center. The night was quiet, except for the distant sound of dogs howling. There was a crescent moon that gave just enough light to let them see each other.

"Thanks," she bit off, not looking at him.

He drew in a long breath. "He was drinking. He'll apologize the next time he sees you."

"Yes."

"You have some real issues with men," he said after a minute.

"No, I..."

He turned quickly toward her. She jerked backward helplessly.

He laughed coldly. "No?"

She bit her lower lip and lowered her eyes. "You think you can get over things," she said in a dull tone. "But the past is portable. You can't run from it, no matter how fast you go, how far you go."

"You can cash checks on that," he agreed bitterly.

"I'm sorry I set you off, at the house," she began.

"You remind me of her," he bit off. "She was beautiful, too. Brunette, black eyes, olive complexion. In the right light..." He hesitated. "Do I remind you of the man who hurt you?" he asked abruptly.

"He was blond," she said unsteadily.

"I see."

She closed her eyes.

"Gabriel won't tell me a damned thing about you."

"We're even. He won't tell me about you, either."

He managed a faint laugh. "Curious about me, are you?"

"Not...that way," she said under her breath.

"Really?" He turned and moved just a step closer. "You were kissing me back in the pasture."

She flushed. "You caught me...off guard."

"Just how experienced are you?" he asked bluntly. "Is that innocence real, or is it an act? Something to disarm a man and make him feel protective?"

She wrapped his jacket closer around her thin shoulders. "I live inside myself," she said after a minute. "I don't...need other people."

"I feel that way, too, most of the time. But then there are the long, empty nights when I have to have a woman just to get through them."

Her face flamed. "Lucky women," she drawled.

His hand came up, very slowly, and pushed back a long strand of silky black hair from her face. "Yes, they are. I'm a tender lover," he said softly.

She stepped back, nervously. She didn't like the mental pictures that were forming in her mind.

"Sara, are you all right?" Gabriel asked from the doorway.

They both turned to look at him. "Yes," she said.

He gave Wolf a speaking look. "You should come back in. It's cold."

"I'll be there in just a minute," she promised.

Gabriel nodded and went inside, but with obvious reluctance.

"Your brother doesn't want me anywhere near you," Wolf told her.

"Yes. He told me that you're..." She flushed as she recalled what Gabriel had said, that Wolf was aggressive with women he wanted. "He said that you have a past that you haven't dealt with."

"Like you," he returned.

She nodded. "He said we could hurt each other badly."

"He's right," he replied with narrow, dark eyes. "Past a certain point, I wouldn't be tender. And I think aggression is what frightens you the most."

"I can't...do that," she said, her voice curt.

"Do what?"

"Sleep...with anyone."

His face hardened. "Then you shouldn't send out signals that you're available. Should you?"

"I haven't!"

"You lay in my arms like a silken doll and let me have your mouth," he said under his breath, his voice deep and soft and sensuous. He leaned toward her conspiratorially. "That's a signal."

"I was surprised," she shot back. "Caught off guard."

"You don't like men close to you," he said, thinking out loud. "You were frightened of Ted. But you like it when I touch you, Sara."

"I...don't!"

His forefinger went to her soft bow mouth and traced around its outline in a slow, sensuous appraisal that made it tremble.

He moved a step closer, watching her face lift helplessly, feeling the quick, involuntary whip of her breath.

"Your brother was right," he whispered as he bent. His mouth shivered over her parted lips, barely touching, tracing, tempting. "I'm much more dangerous than I look."

She wanted to move away. She really did. But the feel of him so close to her, the smell of him, familiar and dear, the hard warmth of his mouth teasing hers, made her reckless. She'd never really wanted a man to kiss her. But she loved it when Wolf did. He made the bad memories go away.

His fingers were tracing up and down her long neck, making sensuous little patterns while his mouth smoothed over her lips.

"You could become an addiction," he whispered. "That would be the worst thing I could do to you."

Her eyes opened wide on his face, seeing it harden, seeing his eyes glitter.

"I mean it," he said roughly. "I hate brunettes. I wouldn't mean to take out old vendettas on you, but I might not be able to help it." His mouth crushed down on hers briefly and then lifted. "She liked to make me crazy in bed, then she laughed at me when I lost control and went over the edge."

She caught her breath at the images that flashed through her mind.

"I don't think she ever felt a damned thing. But she pretended that she did, at first. She told me she was a virgin. She even acted like one..."

He jerked away from Sara. His pale eyes were glittery on her face. "Just like you," he said in a rough undertone. "Backing away to make me come close then pretending that I got through her defenses, that I wasn't like the other men who frightened her."

She began to understand what Gabriel meant. She felt a sense of loss. This man was far more damaged even than she was.

"Have you ever had therapy?" she asked sadly.

"Therapy." He laughed out loud. "I had two years of a woman ridiculing me every time I lay in her arms, making me beg for satisfaction. Can damned therapy fix that?" he asked in a rasping tone.

She winced.

"So I date blondes. They don't come with bad memories, and I can make them lose control, make them beg me." He smiled coldly. "Payback."

She had a sick feeling deep inside. He would do that to her, if they ever became involved. He would make her pay for those scars the other woman had given him. She hadn't realized until then that she felt different with him than she ever had with other men.

"Have I shocked you?" he asked sarcastically.

"Yes," she replied softly. "I...haven't ever... Well, that's not quite true." She lowered her eyes. "My stepfather tried to have me. He was brutal and vulgar and there was a trial... I had to testify against him. He went to prison."

"Did you tease him?" he asked coldly. "Drive him crazy until he had to do something about it?"

Why had she thought he might feel differently than other men had? She laughed softly to herself. She took off his jacket and handed it to him. "I'm sure that's what I did," she replied. "It must have been my fault."

He couldn't see her face. He didn't realize that she was being sarcastic. "Poor damned fool," he bit off. "Just don't think you'll ever get the opportunity to try it out on me."

"Mr. Patterson," she said with ragged pride, "it would never occur to me that you'd be that stupid. Excuse me."

She brushed by him and went into the civic center. She found Gabriel standing by the punch bowl. She was poised, but very pale.

"I'd like to go home, please," she said in a haunted tone.

Gabriel looked over her head at Wolf Patterson's cold

expression. He glared at his friend, but Sara looked as if she couldn't take any more.

"Yes," he told her. "Come on."

SHE MADE COFFEE. They sat at the kitchen table and drank it.

"What did he say to you?"

"The usual things." She sighed. "But he did tell me about the woman…"

"Ysera?"

She looked up. "Is that her name?"

He nodded. His face was grim. "We hated her. We knew what she was doing to him, but you can't drag a man away from a woman he thinks he's in love with. She damned near destroyed him." He frowned. "He's never spoken of it to anyone. Not even to me. I know about it from a girl who worked with her. She thought Ysera was warped, mentally. I have to agree."

"He told me about her to warn me off," she said. She shook her head. "I can't imagine a man putting up with that."

"He loved her," he said simply.

She drew in a breath and sipped coffee. "He said that he didn't think therapy could do anything for him." She flushed.

"What else did he say?"

She laughed hollowly. "That I must have teased our stepfather until he went crazy to have me."

"I'll break his damned neck!"

"You will not," she said, pulling his shirtsleeve to make him sit back down. "He doesn't know a thing about me. It's what even one of my friends thought."

"You were thirteen!"

She winced. "Maybe I wore shorts too much…"

"Oh, God, don't do that to yourself!" he burst out. "You were a child, far more innocent than most girls your age. He'd been after you for months."

"I didn't tell you that!" she exclaimed, embarrassed.

"The prosecutor told me," he replied. "He was livid. He said they should have the death penalty for cases like yours."

She lowered her eyes to the table. "I have no peace. I have nightmares." She smiled sadly. "There's this man I play WoW with," she recalled. "He says he has nightmares, too. Of course, he could be a woman or a man or a child, I don't really know, but he...he gives me peace. We get along so well together. He said that he couldn't get away from the past. I know how that feels."

He didn't dare tell her that her WoW friend was none other than Wolf Patterson. The player was the only real confidant she had, besides Gabriel. It was one of the only happy things in her sad life, that game. Perhaps it was the only thing Wolf had, as well.

"Do you know who he is in the real world?" he asked conversationally.

"Oh, no. I don't want to," she added. "The game isn't like real life. We just have fun playing together, like children." She laughed. "It's so funny. I don't have friends, you know. But I have a friend in him. I can talk to him. Not that we go into specifics. But he's a compassionate person."

"So are you."

She smiled. "I try to be."

"Sara, do you understand now why I told you that you can't afford to let Wolf get close to you?"

She nodded.

"Someone said that Ted got insistent about dancing with you," he said abruptly.

"Yes. He tried to drag me out onto the dance floor," she replied uneasily. "Mr. Patterson caught him by the collar and almost threw him into a wall." She shivered. "He's scary when he loses his temper."

"Only because he never loses it," Gabriel replied. "That's one man you don't ever want to make mad. Well, if you're a man, that is. I've never known him to hurt a woman." He studied her. "He was aggressive with Ted?"

"Yes."

He didn't want to make the obvious assumption, but it presented itself just the same. Ted was trying to put the make on Sara, and Wolf was protective of her. Jealous over her? Possibly.

"It wouldn't end well," he said, thinking out loud.

"Don't you think I know that?" she asked. "He even told me that he...gets even for what the brunette did to him, with other women." She flushed.

"He doesn't talk about it, to anyone," he repeated. "Why did he tell you?"

"I don't understand why, either," she replied. "He hates brunettes."

"You have to make sure he doesn't develop a taste for you," he said firmly.

She nodded. She was remembering how it felt to kiss him, to be in his arms, and she didn't want to. She didn't dare tell Gabriel how things had already gotten physical between them.

"Don't worry," she said gently, and smiled. "I'm not suicidal."

A FEW DAYS LATER, she had occasion to remember those words.

CHAPTER FOUR

SARA WAS DRIVING past Wolf Patterson's ranch on a Sunday afternoon, on her way home from picking up a loaf of bread at the Sav-A-Lot Grocery Store, when she noticed a big black form in the middle of the road.

She slammed on the brakes just in time to avoid hitting what was on the road, a huge Rottweiler. It had blood all over it.

She parked her car in the middle of the road. There was no traffic, darn the luck, so she couldn't wave down anyone to help her. She approached the big dog. It was whining. There was blood on its side, and one leg was turned at an odd angle.

"Oh, dear." She ran to the car, pulled an afghan out of the backseat and put it in the front seat. Then she went back to the dog. It was enormous, but maybe she could lift it. If she could get it into her car, she could find a vet. She hoped it wouldn't bite her, but she couldn't stand by and do nothing. She reached down, talking gently to it, smoothing over its head. "Poor, poor thing," she whispered, and slid her arms under it.

She was wearing a yellow sweater and black slacks. Blood saturated her sweater as she struggled to pick up the huge animal. She heard a vehicle approaching and eased the dog to the ground. She ran toward the truck, waving her arms frantically.

"What the hell…!" Wolf Patterson exclaimed when he slammed out of the truck. She was covered in blood. He felt a jolt of fear. Had she been injured? "Sara!"

That was when he spotted Hellscream, lying on the road.

"What happened?" he bit off. "She's my dog."

"I don't know," she groaned. "I almost hit her before I saw her lying on the road. Somebody must have run over her and just left! Damn the coldhearted idiot who did this! I tried to lift her and put her into my car to take her to the vet, but she's so heavy!"

"I'll get her to the vet," he said. He looked at Sara with narrow, shocked eyes. "Your sweater is soaked with blood."

"It will wash," she said. "Oh, hurry, she's in so much pain!"

He turned and put the big dog on the seat beside him and sped away.

SARA HAD A SHOWER and washed her clothes. She hoped the dog would be all right. Gabriel had gone to see Eb Scott. She wished he was home, so that she could get him to call Wolf and ask about the dog. She was too intimidated by the big man to do it herself.

She was sitting at the kitchen table drinking coffee when she heard a car drive up.

She went to the door, peering out through the security port, and saw Wolf Patterson striding up to the porch.

He was wearing ranch clothes, denim jeans and a chambray shirt with a battered black Stetson and tan boots that had seen better days. Tan batwing chaps flapped when he walked.

She opened the door before he could knock.

"How is she?" she asked.

He nodded. "She'll be fine. It's Sunday and the staff was off, so I had to help Dr. Rydel hold her while he cleaned the wounds and stitched her up. He set the break in her leg. She's pretty sick, but he says she'll mend." He hesitated. "Thank you for stopping."

"I could never leave an animal hurt on the road."

"Someone did. And I'll find out who," he added coldly.

Looking into those piercing pale eyes, she was glad she wasn't the person who left his dog bleeding on the highway.

"Would you...like coffee?" she asked.

"Yes. Is Gabe here?"

"He went over to Eb Scott's, but he should be back soon. Did you need to see him?"

"Yes. I'll wait, if I may."

"Of course."

She poured black coffee into a mug while he straddled a chair at the kitchen table. He watched her move around the room, gathering up cream and sugar to put on the table.

"Do you cook?" he asked suddenly.

She laughed softly. "Yes."

He was looking at the rack of cookbooks on the counter. "French cuisine?"

"I like French pastries," she said. "We never lived close enough to a city to buy them, so I learned to make them. My father loved éclairs," she recalled with a sad smile.

"Did your mother cook?"

Her face closed up. "Do you take cream or sugar in your coffee?" she asked instead.

His eyes narrowed on her suddenly pale face. He shook his head. "Your mother blamed you for what happened."

She sat down and wrapped her hands around her mug. "Yes."

"She saw you as a rival, I gather."

He made it sound as if Sara had been grown when it happened. But it was too painful to discuss. "I don't know how she saw me. She hated me. I never saw her again, after the trial. She died some time back."

He lifted the mug to his lips and raised an eyebrow. "You could float a horseshoe in this," he pointed out.

She managed a smile. "I like strong coffee."

"So do I." He sipped it again. "My mother turned me out when I was about four. She hated my father. I had the misfortune to look like him."

She didn't betray that Gabriel had already told her about this part of Wolf's past. "I'm sorry," she said. "I wouldn't know what a sweet mother was. Gabriel and I never had much love from ours."

He turned the cup in his hands. "Neither did I."

"Is she still alive?"

His eyes were terrible to look into. "I don't know. I don't give a damn."

She sighed. "I would feel the same, if mine was still alive."

He sipped coffee. "That was one damned expensive sweater you had on," he said after a minute. "You didn't even hesitate to lift Hellie."

"Is that her name? Hellie?" she asked with a smile.

He nodded. He didn't add that it was short for

Hellscream. She wouldn't understand the reference, anyway. Hellscream was a male orc in his video game, and he thought the name was amusing for a female dog. He hated Hellscream as leader of the Horde forces.

"I bought her when I moved here. She's three years old. My best girl," he added with a smile, one of the few genuine smiles she'd ever seen on his hard face.

She was studying the backs of his hands. There were fine scars on them.

He raised an eyebrow. "Something you want to say?" he mused.

"You said that you got scars on your hands from rappelling from helicopters in the FBI," she said.

"Yes?"

"How do you get scars on the backs of your hands when you're rappelling? You wear gloves, don't you?"

His eyes had an odd expression. "You're perceptive."

She studied his face. "That means you aren't telling me a thing, Mr. Patterson."

He searched her eyes and then averted his. She was so formal with him. Well, she was young and he wasn't. Thirty-seven to her twentysomething. It made him feel cold inside, those years that stood between them. Even if he was tempted, and he was, she was far too young for a man with his jaded past. Not to mention he was friends with her brother. He couldn't afford to get involved with her. She was mysterious in her way, and she'd tempted her stepfather away from her mother. She might pretend to be innocent, but was she? Ysera had tried that trick on him. He didn't trust women. Lying seductresses, the lot of them.

"You never stay down here on the ranch when Gabe's

out of town, do you?" he asked, for something to break the uncomfortable silence.

"No," she said. "I'm…nervous if I'm alone at night."

"You have an apartment in San Antonio, don't you? You're alone there."

"I have neighbors that I know," she replied. "Out here, there's just me." She swallowed. "Gabriel has enemies. One of them targeted me, in the past. I was very lucky that he was home at the time."

He scowled. He hadn't considered that Gabe's line of work would put her in danger. But of course it would. He had enemies of his own. One had tried to kill him, although he wondered now if Ysera hadn't sent the man after him. She'd sworn bloody vengeance when he turned her over to the authorities.

His eyes went to the silky blue blouse she was wearing. It had fine pearl buttons all the way down the front. Under it, he could see the outline of her breasts, firm and tip-tilted. They made him ache.

"Could you…not do that, please?" she asked, folding her arms across her blouse.

He leaned back in his chair and just looked at her. There was a world of sensual wisdom in his pale eyes. "You seem like two people sometimes," he remarked. "One brash and hot-tempered, the other nervous and vulnerable."

"We all have different sides to our personalities, I think. More coffee?" she asked, for something to say.

He nodded. His eyes were calculating, but she didn't notice until it was too late. As she reached for his cup, he reached for her, and pulled her gently down onto his lap.

"Nothing heavy," he promised, his voice deep and

soft, like velvet. His big hand spread across her cheek, holding her face so that he could see her black velvet eyes. They were huge in her beautiful face, sad and apprehensive. "Your brother will be home any minute," he reminded her.

Yes. But she worried about what could happen in the meantime. She put her hand on his broad chest, and it encountered the thick hair where the shirt was open at his throat. She caught her breath and tried to jerk her hand back.

He spread it into the opening, watching her face as he pressed her long, cold fingers into the thick hair. She shivered a little at the feel of him, so intimate. There was warm, hard muscle under the hair. His heart was beating heavily, like hers. She really should protest and get up.

But just as she thought about it, his thumb brushed over her full lower lip and teased it away from the upper one. He felt her shiver.

It was obvious that she hadn't had a lover who knew what to do with her. He shouldn't be touching her, of course. He was only going to make things worse.

While he was considering that, his head was bending. He brushed his open mouth over hers, tenderly parting her lips. It was like that day in the pasture when he'd pulled her off the horse, terrified that she was going to kill herself. He hadn't been able to get her shy response out of his mind. It haunted him.

He reminded himself that innocence could be faked. Ysera had taught him that.

His fingers stroked up and down her long throat, making her breath jerk, while his mouth gently explored her soft lips.

He was damaged. So was she, in some sort of way. Perhaps the man she'd taken away from her mother had been rough with her. He scowled, remembering that she'd sent a man to prison for being intimate with her. It disturbed him.

He lifted his head and looked into her wide, fascinated eyes. His own narrowed as the heat began to build in him. It had been a long time. Too long. He wanted her. He hated himself for it.

His big hand slid down over her breast and cupped it, teasing the nipple with a forefinger until it went hard, and her body stiffened.

That was when he lost it. His mouth crushed down over hers in a fever of hunger. She tasted like honey. Her body was warm and soft in his arms. He turned her, so that her breasts were crushed against his shirt. He groaned, on fire to have her.

She wanted to protest. But the feel of his mouth on hers was drugging her. She clung to him, whimpering softly as she felt her body begin to swell. She'd never felt anything like this, never wanted so much to have a man's mouth on hers, demanding and insistent. She wasn't even afraid. That was a first.

He stood up, with her in his arms, and his eyes were flashing like blue lightning. He couldn't think past relief. He could put her down on the sofa in the next room, smooth his aching body on top of hers. He could jerk those tight jeans off and go into her, hard and fast, make her scream with pleasure.

Except that it was broad daylight, and he could see Ysera's face, mocking, laughing. He was a weakling, she taunted while he died in her arms, a weakling who couldn't control his desire, who looked ridiculous when his face went rigid, when his body corded over hers as he drove for satisfaction...

He shuddered.

Sara saw nightmares in his pale eyes. She'd been uneasy when he picked her up, afraid of what he might intend. They were alone, and she wasn't really sure when Gabriel might come home. She'd never tried to be intimate with anyone. There were reasons why she might not be able to at all, and one was very physical, a reason she was too shy to speak of, especially to a man like Wolf Patterson.

But her nervousness left her when she looked up into his eyes. He looked tormented. He smelled so good, clean and manly, as if he'd showered before he came here. He must have, because he picked up the dog, and it had been covered in blood. His face was corded with anguish.

"It's all right," she said softly. She lifted her hand and traced down his hard cheek. "It's all right," she whispered.

He shivered. His face clenched. "Damn it!" he bit off.

He put her down on the chair and walked out of the house. She heard the door slam. But she didn't hear his car start up.

She didn't understand her own reactions to him. She felt such a kinship with him, as if they shared secrets that they could never share with other people. She knew he wasn't going to leave. She wasn't sure how she knew it, but she did.

Sure enough, a minute later he came back in. His hat was jerked low over his eyes. He looked ice-cold.

He walked back into the kitchen and stood over her.

"I don't need pity or compassion or anything else from you," he said coldly.

"I know that," she replied gently. Her eyes were soft with compassion. She understood anger and pain; she'd lived with both for long enough to be intimate with them. "Sit down. I poured more coffee."

"You knew I'd be back?" he drawled with biting sarcasm.

She drew in a long breath. "Sometimes the most terrible part of being so damaged is not being able to tell anybody," she said, her eyes on her own coffee cup. "Even Gabriel doesn't know everything. I...couldn't tell him."

He felt a kinship with her that had nothing to do with blood. He took off his hat, tossed it into a vacant chair and straddled the one next to his coffee. He held the cup with his elbows resting on the back of the chair. His eyes were brilliant with subdued pain.

"How long did you know her?" she asked, giving him an opening, if he wanted to talk.

He sipped coffee. "For three years, on and off," he said quietly. "She was going with another man in my unit. But she threw him over for me. I was flattered at first. She was...extraordinarily beautiful. She could play the piano, speak several languages, even sing. I'd had women. But she was sophisticated. She knew more than I did. I'd never been with anyone who was so uninhibited."

It hurt her to hear that. She was shocked, but she managed to hide it.

"At first, it was intoxicating," he said, not looking at her. "I went in headfirst. She was all I could think about. I fell in love. I was sure she felt the same way.

She was always doing things for me, giving me things, and in bed she was any man's most erotic dream." He drew in a slow breath. "I'd never done it with the lights on," he said through his teeth. "I had inhibitions. A couple of the foster homes I lived in were deeply religious. They schooled me in things that a man never did. Sensual pleasure was a sin. It belonged in marriage. So I thought that way. Ysera was a very guilty pleasure."

She searched his face. It grew harder as the memories washed him in misery.

"She wanted to watch me come, she said." He glanced at Sara and had to stifle laughter at her expression. "Too blunt, Sara?" he asked softly.

She swallowed. She flushed, but she shook her head. "You can't talk about this to anybody else, can you?"

"No," he said through his teeth.

"It's all right," she said. "I'm not... I don't know a lot about that. But I can listen."

He wondered just how much she did know. She seemed honestly embarrassed, but he averted his eyes. He needed to talk about it. Inside, the past festered like a wound.

"So I turned on the lights. She watched me. Then she started to laugh." His hands clenched around the coffee cup. "The hotter I got, the more insulting she got. When I lost it, she laughed like a demon and said that I looked ridiculous..."

She winced.

He saw that. He sipped coffee, and it burned his mouth, but he hardly noticed. "Of course, she apologized. She was innocent, she told me, and she didn't realize how it might have hurt me that she laughed. She promised that she wouldn't do it again. But she did.

Over and over again. She'd arouse me to the point of madness and then turn on the lights and make fun of me when I was the most vulnerable." His eyes closed. He was oblivious to the sympathy on Sara's pale face. "Ironically, the more she hurt me, the more I wanted her. She could turn me on faster than any woman I ever knew. I can't tell you what it felt like." He drew in a breath and sipped more coffee. His face was rigid with remembered pain. "A man's ego is his soft spot. None of us like to be vulnerable, even at the best of times. I grew to hate her. But I couldn't let go. I couldn't stop wanting her. Then…"

He hesitated.

Her soft hand slid over one of his.

He put down the coffee cup. His fingers tangled with hers. The unexpected comfort made it easier to speak of it.

"We were in a dangerous area, just outside a compound in a war-torn African nation. We'd gathered intel on a rebel leader who was torturing young women. Ysera said she knew who he was. She drew a map and had one of her informants lead us right to his door." His eyes closed. He shivered. "She told us that he was heavily armed and that he knew we were coming. She said if we didn't go in hot, we'd be dead. So we went in. Hot."

His fingers were crushing hers, but she didn't say a word. She just waited.

"We killed a man and his wife…and his three-year-old son."

She gasped.

"It was vengeance. He was a handsome man and she'd wanted him, but he wouldn't have anything to do with her. He said his wife was worth ten of her. It made her angry. She got even."

His expression was terrible. She got up out of her chair and pulled his head to her breasts, holding his cheek there, rocking him, kissing his dark hair.

"I'm sorry," she whispered. "I'm sorry. I'm so sorry!"

He shuddered. His arms went around her and held her, crushed her. He'd never told a soul. Only the men in his small unit had known. It was the greatest shame of his life. It was why he'd come back here, left the unit, shunned the world.

"How long ago?" she whispered.

"A year. Almost two now." He groaned. "It was an honest mistake on our part, and the house had been used as a safe house for insurgents. There were no charges pressed, and the media never got wind of it. But we had to live with it. One of my men couldn't. He killed himself. The other became an alcoholic."

She laid her cheek against his cool, thick hair. "It's why you came to live here."

"No. I moved here three years ago. There were other memories, not as terrible, but disturbing. I wanted a change of place, a change of scenery. I thought it would help."

She drew in a breath. "But the memories are portable," she said aloud, reminding him of what she'd told him earlier. "You can't leave them behind. They go with you."

"I know that. I have…nightmares."

"So do I," she whispered.

His head burrowed closer to her breasts. He turned it, and his mouth found one soft breast, exploring it through the soft fabric.

She shivered.

"Let me," he said roughly when she stiffened. "Oh, God, let me!"

She felt him stand up, lift her. His mouth covered hers, and he shivered as he carried her into the living room. He slid her onto the sofa and followed her down, his heavy body covering hers, his mouth devouring on her soft lips.

"I haven't touched a woman since then," he whispered against her mouth. "I haven't trusted a woman since then. But I'm so...damned...hungry!"

The words ended on a groan. One long leg inserted itself between both of hers. He pushed between them. She gasped and pushed at his chest, really frightened.

He lifted his head. His mouth was swollen. His pale eyes glittered, narrowed. "Are you really that innocent?" he asked through his teeth. "Or are you teasing, like she did?"

She swallowed, hard. She licked her lips and tasted him on them. "Do you know...what an imperforate hymen is?" she asked, flushing even as she said it.

He stilled on her body. His eyes were the only things alive in the sudden stone of his face. "Yes," he said after a minute.

"I...can't," she managed. Her lips trembled. She averted her eyes. "It was the only thing that saved me, when he tried to..." She swallowed. "Gabriel broke a door down to get to him." Tears welled in her eyes.

He didn't say what he was thinking, that her body would have tempted a saint, and that the poor man was probably out of his mind, the way Wolf had been out of his mind with Ysera. But he didn't want to hurt her. She had her own scars. She'd been kind to him. Kinder than he deserved. She'd listened without judging. She'd given him the first comfort he'd ever had.

He rolled over onto his back and drew her beside him, shuddering. He was aroused and hurting.

She slid her hand onto his chest. He caught it roughly and stilled it.

"Don't do that," he snapped.

"Wh-what?"

"Oh, God, are you really that naive?" he groaned. Without thinking, he carried her hand down below his belt and pressed it there.

She jerked back as if she'd touched a snake. Her eyes, shocked and wild, saw what she'd touched. She threw herself off the sofa and almost fell getting to her feet. She was remembering. That was what her stepfather had done, that night. He'd said things, vulgar things, about his condition and what he wanted her to do to him. He'd forced her down onto the bed and torn her clothes out of his way. She was screaming…

"Sara!"

She shivered. Her eyes were wild. Great, huge black orbs in a face like rice paper. He was standing over her, stunned at her reaction.

That didn't look like an act. She seemed genuinely afraid of intimacy. His pale eyes narrowed. "I'm not going to force you," he said quietly. "I would never do that. I swear it!"

She wrapped her arms around her chest and lowered her eyes to the floor. "I wish I would die," she said unsteadily.

"Sara!"

She turned and ran back into the kitchen. She saw a cloud of dust in the distance and recognized the black truck coming down the road. "It's Gabriel," she choked out, aware of Wolf's presence behind her.

He caught her hand gently and led her to a chair. "Sit down. I'll make another pot of coffee."

She bit her lower lip. "I'm sorry," she choked out.

"No. I'm sorry for repaying honest compassion with lust," he bit off. "I'm ashamed of what I did to you."

She looked up, surprised.

He searched her pale face. "Next time," he said quietly, "it's your turn to talk."

"I...don't think I can."

"I told you things I never dreamed I could say to another person, much less to a woman," he said, averting his face as he moved to fill the coffeepot with water.

"I'm sorry for what she did to you," she said quietly. "I must lead a sheltered life. I didn't know, I didn't dream, that there were people like that in the world." She swallowed. "With the lights on... I could never...!"

He wondered who she'd done it with since her bad experience, and how many times. He wanted to know. It shouldn't have mattered. But it did. He turned his attention to making coffee. He really hoped that Gabriel wouldn't notice the way they both looked.

GABRIEL WAS PERCEPTIVE, but they both looked so miserable that he didn't comment. Sara excused herself after a minute and went upstairs.

Gabriel gave his friend a speaking look.

"It isn't what you think," Wolf said quietly. "She... listened."

The other man was surprised. "You told her?"

He nodded. He sipped coffee. "I've never been able

to talk about it. She's a good listener." He managed a faint smile. "I shocked her."

"She's not very worldly," Gabriel said quietly. "In many ways, she's still a child."

Wolf's pale eyes narrowed. "She said you broke down a door to get to her."

Gabriel's face closed up.

"Why won't you tell me?" he asked.

"Because it's Sara's secret, not mine," Gabriel replied quietly. "She wakes up screaming sometimes, late at night. I don't know if she sleeps more than a couple of hours at a stretch."

Wolf was wondering what in the world a man could do to a woman to cause that sort of reaction. Sara wasn't totally innocent. She certainly knew what passion was like. Until he'd made her touch him intimately, she'd seemed to enjoy what he did to her.

"She should be in therapy," Wolf said.

"Pot."

"Excuse me?"

"Pot calling the kettle black," Gabriel expounded. "You need it more than she does. You've never dealt with what happened."

"How do you deal with innocent deaths?" Wolf asked through his teeth.

"The way we deal with all deaths," came the stoic reply. "It goes with the business we're in. People die. That's war."

"It was a child!"

Gabriel grasped the other man's wrist, hard. "Intent is everything in law," he said. "You would never harm a child. Never!"

Wolf's eyes were glittery with feeling. "But I did."

"Because of that lying, sick tramp," Gabriel said shortly. "And that brings me to something we have to discuss."

"What?"

"Eb's got a contact in Buenos Aires. He had a positive ID on Ysera."

"It really is her?"

Gabriel nodded grimly. "She's up to her old tricks. She's formed a new insurgent group, and the 411 is that she's headed back to Africa with it. She's still a high-level intel agent for the Red Scar."

The Red Scar was one of the more brutal organizations founded along religious lines to foment rebellion in African provinces where precious natural resources were at stake. The unit had dealt with it before. Ysera had been part and parcel of it, but none of Gabriel or Wolf's men had known of her connection until it was too late.

"So what now?" Wolf asked.

"Now we do all we can to get an organized group watching your back," Gabriel said quietly. "She's been in hiding since it happened, with Interpol on her tail. But now she feels safe, and she's put the word out that she wants you dead for betraying her. She's got a new boyfriend. This one is a Brazilian millionaire. So she's got the money now, thanks to her new boyfriend, to get the job done!"

CHAPTER FIVE

"WELL," WOLF TOLD Gabriel heavily, "I guess I knew it would come down to that one day. I've had attempts before."

"One serious one," Gabriel recalled. His black eyes narrowed. "But Ysera wasn't behind it. If she tries, we could have real problems. I worry about Sara," he added. "Someone thought she was here alone last year and made an attempt on her, because of an enemy I made. I was home at the time."

"Luckily," came the grim reply.

Gabriel sipped coffee. "If Ysera targets you, she could also hit anybody you're with."

"I would never let anyone hurt Sara," he said in a tone that drew the other man's eyes. He grimaced. "I know. We could hurt each other. But she…gives me peace," he bit off, hating to admit it.

"A rare thing, in our line of work," the other man replied. He stared into his coffee cup. "Try not to hurt her. She's had a hell of a life."

"I wonder sometimes if there are any people in the world who are genuinely free of bad memories."

"I seriously doubt it."

He finished his coffee. His pale eyes met the other man's. "She's amazingly fragile," he said after a minute. "How old is she?"

"Twenty-four."

"And she doesn't date."

Gabriel bit down on a harsh reply. "There are reasons."

Wolf had a good idea what they were. He wondered if her stepfather had been the love of her life, if she'd been crushed when he went to jail because of her testimony.

"You won't tell me what they are, will you?" Wolf mused.

Gabriel shook his head. "That's Sara's business."

"All right."

"You watch your back," Gabriel said, rising. "Ysera was dangerous enough when she lost everything and went into hiding. But now, with a bankroll, she could become your worst enemy. I wish to God we'd put her down while we had the chance."

"The authorities let her slip by," Wolf said coldly.

"Money changed hands," Gabriel replied. "It cost her everything she had, but it got her out of the country just a jump ahead of the militia."

"What a damned shame," was the reply.

Gabriel nodded. "How's your game life going?" he teased.

He shrugged. "My friend the warlock and I are the terror of battlegrounds everywhere." He chuckled then grimaced. "That reminds me, I've got to phone Rydel and check on Hellie."

"Hellie? What's wrong?"

"I was on my way to check on my new bull when your sister waved me down, covered with blood."

"What?"

"Someone ran over Hellie," Wolf said, calming the other man. "Sara stopped. She was trying to lift Hellie into her car, to get her to a vet." He smiled gently. "Soaked her sweater, probably would have ruined the inside of the car, and she didn't give a damn." His eyes had a faint, soft light in them. "Your sister is one hell of a woman."

Gabriel smiled sadly. "Yes. She loves animals. We had a dog, when we lived with my mother and her second husband." His face hardened with the memory.

"What happened?"

"He got mad at Sara and killed the dog," he said shortly. "He left it lying on the front porch, so she'd see it the minute she got home."

"Dear God," Wolf groaned.

"She never got over it," he continued. "She won't have a dog or a cat these days. She loves the horses, but she doesn't want an animal inside that she might get too attached to."

"And I thought I had a hard life."

"Did you tell Sara the full name of your dog?"

Wolf laughed out loud. "No. She thinks little enough of me as it is. I don't want any smart comments about a grown man playing kids' games on the PC."

Gabriel laughed, too, and tried not to sound relieved.

"A lot of grown men play them, including some of our colleagues."

"Yes." The smile faded. "Sometimes it helps to get away from the real world and into one where pain doesn't accompany every single damned minute."

Gabriel studied the older man's drawn face. "Try not to hurt Sara too much," he said gruffly.

Wolf's face was open for a few seconds, vulnerable. "She's the sort of woman who makes you feel…safe," he said, searching for the words. "Like you're standing out in the snow, and she's a warm, cozy fire in a small room."

Gabriel felt the shock down to his feet. Did Wolf even realize what he was admitting?

Apparently not, because he laughed shortly. "I don't trust women," he said. "She'd have to get close to me to be threatened, and that won't happen. She'll be safe with me. I'll watch out for her when you aren't around."

Gabriel hesitated, but only for a minute. "Thanks."

"No problem. Try not to get yourself killed."

"I have a big cape and a shirt with a letter *S* on it," Gabriel began wryly.

Wolf just laughed.

IT WAS A stupid idea. Wolf knew that before he parked his car at the end of the pasture where Sara was galloping on one of the new mares Gabriel had purchased. He'd done nothing but remember the feel of her soft lips under his mouth for several days, and he was aching. It was suicide to get involved with her. But he couldn't help himself.

He moved to the fence and put a big foot on the lower rung, just watching her. She was beautiful on a horse, elegant and poised and graceful.

She saw him and jumped gracefully down from the horse and up onto the high wooden fence. He was propped on the other side of it.

"You look pretty on a horse," he said, smiling.

She smiled back. "Are you all right?" she asked.

He shrugged. "A little better than before, maybe." He searched her eyes. "How about dinner in Houston and the opera after? They're performing Bizet's *Carmen*."

Her heart jumped, but she hesitated. She was remembering what Gabriel had said.

"Yes, we can hurt each other," he said, as if he'd read the thoughts in her mind. "It doesn't seem to matter. I want to take you out."

"I…would like to go," she confessed.

He smiled gently. "About six, Friday? We'll have supper before we go. I'll pick you up, where? Here?"

"Gabriel's leaving tonight. I'll be at the apartment in San Antonio until he gets back."

"Nice timing," he mused. "Did you offer him a quarter to go away?"

She laughed. Her black eyes lit up like candles, and her beautiful face radiated joy. "Not really."

He chuckled. "Okay. Wear something pretty. But not too sexy," he added with a raised eyebrow. "I don't fancy a trip to the emergency room if things get out of hand."

She colored, but then she laughed, too.

He shook his head. "Never thought about minor surgery?"

"There wasn't any reason to," she said after a minute. "I never wanted to…with anybody."

His pale eyes glittered. "I could make you want to. With me."

She bit her lower lip.

"I won't," he said gently, and traced patterns on the back of her hand. "I can't really afford to lose my only confidant."

She managed a smile. "That works both ways."

He searched her black eyes. "We know too much about each other, don't we?"

She nodded.

"Broken people."

She smiled. She wanted to mention that someone else had said that to her, but she didn't want to have to answer questions about her only real pleasure in life. "Yes," she said. "Broken people." She pursed her full, soft lips. "Maybe we could use duct tape."

He thought about that for a minute and suddenly erupted into genuine laughter.

"Yes, only two things in life you need, duct tape and WD-40." She grinned. "If it doesn't move and it should, use the WD-40. If it moves and it shouldn't, use the duct tape!"

"You're the sort of woman who would suggest using Saran Wrap for birth control," he muttered.

She did laugh, then, even though she colored a little with embarrassment. "How's Hellie?" she asked.

"Getting better by the day. She's clomping around the house on her cast pretty handily. I'll take you by to see her on the way home from the opera, if you like."

Dangerous. It would be very late when they came back from Houston. But she couldn't resist the danger. "I do like."

He was remembering what Gabriel had told him, that their stepfather had killed Sara's dog. He smiled sadly. "You love animals, don't you?"

"Yes," she replied with soft black eyes.

He glanced at the mare nudging her back impatiently. "I noticed." He let go of the fence. "Friday at six."

"I'll see you then."

He threw up a hand and drove away. Sara watched him go with faint misgivings. She hadn't really told him as much as he'd told her. She hoped she wasn't going to regret it.

SHE WENT THROUGH everything in her closet, and there were plenty of dresses, looking for just the right thing to wear. She settled on a sleek black cocktail dress with spaghetti straps that fell to just below her knees and flared out. The bodice was square, not too low, but not prudish, either. She left her hair long and accented the dress with her pearls and matching studs. She looked beautiful, but she didn't notice that. She didn't like looking in mirrors.

Wolf was wearing a dinner jacket with expensive slacks and a silk shirt and black tie. He looked elegant and so handsome that Sara caught her breath. Without his usual Stetson, his hair was thick and soft and black as a raven's head.

"Noticing the gray hairs, are you?" he mused.

"Gray hairs?"

He reached out and traced her cheek. His face was somber. "I'm thirty-seven years old, Sara."

"You don't look it."

He drew in a breath. "There's a lot of mileage on me," he murmured. "If I were a car, I'd be in a junkyard."

"You'd be in a showroom, as a classic collector's edition," she replied with twinkling black eyes.

He chuckled. His eyes were slow and appreciative on her face. "It's a shame I don't like brunettes," he teased. "You're really quite beautiful."

She flushed. "That's only what's outside."

He frowned slightly. "You don't like the way you look, do you?"

She clutched her purse. "I hate having men stare at me," she said a little unevenly.

"Why?"

She moved restlessly. "We should go, yes?"

"Yes."

She came out of the apartment and locked the door.

"I hope you like French cuisine," he said with a grin.
"I found a lovely little bistro just down the street."

Her breath caught. "It's my favorite place to eat."

He chuckled. "It's one of mine, too."

THEY HAD LAMB and herbed potatoes, with an exquisite
crème brûlée for dessert. Sara savored every bite. But
it had taken longer than they expected to get seated.
The ballet was at eight, and there was still the drive to
Houston. But Wolf didn't seem to be concerned with
the time at all.

"How can you eat like that and never gain an ounce?"
He chuckled.

"I run it all off," she replied, smiling. "Nervous en-
ergy, I suppose."

He reached across the small table and traced patterns
on the back of her small hand. "I'm the same," he told
her. "I can't sit still."

She studied his face quietly. "You seem different.
Less haunted."

He smoothed his fingers in between hers. "I'd never
talked about it. Not to anyone." He searched her black
eyes. "They sent me to a psychologist, too." He made a
face. "His idea was to drug me senseless and have me
tell him all about my childhood."

She drew in a breath. "Mine said that the whole thing
was my fault."

He didn't reply. He wondered that himself. A young
woman, beautiful, feeling her power, might have
grudges against her mother and take them out on her

by trying to steal her boyfriend. "I don't like being psychoanalyzed anyway," he said.

She nodded. She glanced up at him and away. "I never told anyone about, well, you know," she said, flushing. "It's so intimate a thing. I could never speak of it to my brother. I don't have close friends." She recalled her friend the ballerina, but that wasn't a close relationship. Lisette was more an acquaintance than a real friend. In fact, she'd never told Michelle about her physical issue, and Michelle was like her sister.

"I don't have close friends, either, except maybe your brother. And I could never tell another man what she did to me."

"It must have killed your pride," she said sadly.

He closed his fingers around hers. "I wasn't feeding you a line, you know," he said, his voice low and soft as he searched her eyes. "I haven't had a woman since Ysera. I could never trust anyone again."

"And I can't…have anyone," she replied. The skin on her high cheekbones colored. "Not in my present condition."

His fingers smoothed over hers seductively. "You do know that there are ways to pleasure a woman without penetration?" he asked outrageously.

Her hand jerked and almost upset her wineglass. She caught it just in time. "You beast!" she gasped, flushing.

He chuckled softly. "And out comes the broom," he teased, but not in a malicious way. His eyes fell to the bodice of her dress, to the hard tips poking against the soft fabric. "It excites you when I say intimate things to you. I like that."

She sipped wine, put the glass down and folded her

arms across her chest, glancing warily around to make sure he hadn't been overheard.

"We're alone in the world, Sara," he said softly. "Don't you know?"

She bit her lower lip. "Listen, I can't…"

His pale eyes glittered as his fingers slid intimately between her own. "You can. You're going to. With me," he whispered in a husky undertone. "Only with me."

She felt helpless. It wasn't really a bad feeling. Her whole body tingled as she looked at him, feeling the sudden hard clasp of his hand around hers. The look on her face made him want to stand up and howl. He wondered if she realized what she was giving away with that hungry, soft desire he could read in her eyes.

"We'd better go," he said stiffly, because he was fighting down the most powerful arousal he'd felt in years. There was still the drive to Houston and the opera to get through. But after, he promised himself as he helped her out of her chair, he was going to find out everything about her. He was going to know her, physically, as intimately as he could. Perhaps she was telling the truth about her innocence. But one way or another, he was going to find out.

SARA, BLISSFULLY UNAWARE of what he was plotting, smiled up at him with her heart in her eyes as he paid the tab and led her by the hand out of the restaurant and to the parking lot.

It was a cool night for May, and already dark. They were going to be very late for the ballet. She had on a soft cashmere coat that clung to her silky curves. He paused to unlock the Mercedes, but instead of putting her inside it, he drew her right up against his powerful body, so close that she could feel his sudden, instant arousal.

She caught her breath and tried to pull back, but he wouldn't let her. He wasn't brutal, but he was firm.

He stared down into her shocked eyes. "Do you feel how hard I am?" he whispered. "And I've barely touched you." One big lean hand held her against his hips while the other smoothed boldly right up her body and over her soft, hard-tipped breast. "I want to pull your dress down and put my mouth over your nipple and suckle you, hard."

She shivered. Her nails bit into the expensive fabric of his jacket and she actually gasped out loud.

"Yes, you want it, don't you?" he whispered at her lips. "I can strip you and put you in a bed under my naked body and have you, even without penetrating you." He shuddered at the thought. "You'll let me, won't you?" he breathed. "Breast to breast, thigh to thigh, in the darkness, moving against each other like the rapids in a river, driving for satisfaction, pleasuring each other almost to madness..."

She made a sound that ground into him like fire. He pushed her back against the car door and moved one powerful long leg between hers, lifting her as he bent to her mouth and kissed her with stark hunger.

His mouth insisted, demanded. It parted her lips, pushed them apart, while his tongue suddenly shot right into it. The rhythmic motion of his hips caused her to cry out.

The tiny, helpless cry brought him to his senses. With a groan, he stepped back, his tall body shuddering as he realized how close he'd come to having her, right there in public view. She looked every bit as shaken as he felt.

Tears stung her eyes. She hadn't realized how vulnerable she was, how seductive he could be. It was a mistake. She was going to get in over her head, and she wasn't ready. This was a man who wasn't ready, either, for a long-term relationship. He was a damaged man who was still bristling with revenge for what a heartless woman had done to his ego. She couldn't trust him, didn't dare trust him. But she wanted him!

Her eyes looked up into his, and he felt his whole body go rigid. She would let him. He knew it without a word being spoken.

He put her into the car and got in beside her. "Fasten your seat belt," he whispered huskily.

She swallowed. She could still taste him on her mouth. "What…is the ballet we're going to see in Houston?" she managed.

"The ballet starts in five minutes, and it's in Houston. We'd never make it before it was half over. We're going home," he returned roughly.

"Oh."

He caught her hand in his and held it tight. She could feel the tension in him like a living thing. She knew what he meant. He wasn't taking her to her apartment. He was taking her home with him. And it wasn't going to end well, but she couldn't find a single excuse not to agree.

For the first time, she wanted a man in ways that she had never thought possible. She threw caution to the wind.

HE PULLED UP in front of his house and cut off the engine. He opened her door and let her walk ahead of him onto the porch. He put the key in the lock, turned it, walked in with her and locked the door behind them. He turned off the porch light.

She felt the excitement like a living thing. She looked up at him. His face was like stone. His pale blue eyes were the only things alive in that inscrutable canvas.

He took her hand and led her into the living room, where a single lamp was burning. Looking straight into her eyes, he took off his dinner jacket and his tie, slipped out of his belt and dress shoes and unbuttoned his shirt all the way to his trousers.

He took the purse from her nerveless hands, tossing it into a chair. She stood helplessly in front of him while he unhooked the dress and slid it down her arms, leaving her in a low-cut black slip and a lacy bra.

His big hand slid under the hooks of the bra, and then the straps that were holding them up. Watching her face, he pushed the fabric away from her high, tip-tilted breasts and let it fall to the floor. His eyes, wise and soft, ate her like candy.

"I thought you'd be pink here," he whispered, tracing her hard nipples. "But you look like milk chocolate instead." He smiled tenderly and bent his head. "I thought I'd go mad before we got here. God, Sara, I'm so hungry…"

His mouth opened on her breast, taking the nipple inside, working it with his tongue.

She'd never felt the sensations he was teaching her. She arched her back to give him better access, her body shivering with new pleasures.

He lifted her and put her down on the sofa, smoothing his body over hers, while he fed on her soft, warm breasts.

"I think I dreamed you," he bit off. His free hand

went under her briefs and touched her. He felt her jerk, felt her hand go to his wrist. He lifted his head and looked into her wide, shocked eyes.

"You said it was imperforate," he whispered. "Let's see."

She colored fiercely. His pale eyes narrowed as he probed, felt the barrier, tested it. "I don't expect the truth from a woman," he said gruffly. "But this—" he pushed at the barrier gently "—is no lie."

"Ple...please?" she whispered, pushing at him. "Don't..."

"Don't?" His face grew mocking. His smile was full of sarcasm. "You tease and tempt me all night, and now you want to stop?"

"I'm not...her," she tried to remind him.

But he was blind with desire, reliving his nights with Ysera, hearing her laugh at him, ridicule him. Sara was like her, beautiful and eager, until he began to be intimate with her. Then she grew cold, just like Ysera. Then would come the laughter...

His hand was insistent. He watched the shocked pleasure that bloomed on her face as he touched her blatantly. "Yes, you like that, don't you?" he asked, and did it again. He laughed as she arched up, trembling, her mouth open, her eyes wide as saucers as her body responded to him.

"Please," she whimpered.

"So composed, so removed from passion," he said, hurting as he remembered how Ysera had baited him, teased him. "Cool and elegant, tempting men until they burn like torches and then laughing when they go up in flames. But you're not laughing now, are you?" he taunted, his eyes on her face while he brought her to ecstasy. "Yes, that's right," he whispered, his face flushing as he watched her go right over the edge. "Come for me, honey," he breathed. "Come for me. Yes. Just... like...that!"

She arched up, crying out endlessly, as she felt the first climax she'd ever known. And he was watching her, laughing, taunting.

"Now who's helpless?" he growled, his hand moving again, dragging sounds out of her throat that she'd never heard it make.

He stripped her, whispered what he was going to do, and how it was going to feel, laughing at her helpless response. He was years in the past, getting even, hating her for what Ysera had done to him.

She cried out, arching, her body shuddering over and over again as he forced her to climax.

He was dying to have her. He couldn't contain it. He threw off his clothes and went down on her, his mouth grinding into hers before he moved between her long, trembling legs. He didn't dare try to penetrate her, but he could find his own satisfaction without that. He whispered urgently, gathered her legs together and went between them, high on her silken thighs, and pushed down again and again, his body corded, his mind burning with need. He buried his hot face in her throat, and his hips drove against hers in the cool room. The lights were on, but she couldn't see him; he wouldn't let her see him.

He drove blindly for relief, her legs held in the vise of his own as he found, finally, the right pressure, the right rhythm, to drag those high-pitched little cries out of her throat. He felt her shudder even as he lifted and pushed down one last time, with the last bit of his strength, and

he shot off the edge of the world into such heated pleasure that he almost lost consciousness.

She was crying. He was vaguely aware of tears on
his cheek where it was pressed so hard into her throat.
His big body shuddered in the aftermath of the most
explosive climax he'd ever felt in his life. It was more
than that. It was orgasm. He'd never experienced it.

After a minute, he lifted his head and looked down
at her. Her face was almost white.

"Let...me...go," she whispered brokenly. "Oh,
please...!"

His face clenched. "Sara..."

She moved suddenly, struggling away from him,
grabbing her underthings. She ran for the back door.

He was still shaking with sated passion. He got up
and put on his slacks before he went after her, bare-
footed.

She made it into the stable, so hysterical that she
didn't even stop to wonder if someone might be in there.
She didn't care. She was sick. She dragged on her underthings and cowered against the corner wall, drawing
her knees up. She heard his voice, taunting her, laughing at her, getting even...

It was her own fault. She'd tempted him, and she
knew he wasn't ready. He was living in the past. Now
here she was, shivering like a whipped child, hiding in
the shadows, so ashamed that she couldn't even open
her eyes. Her stepfather had said vulgar things to her,
made her look at him, laughed as he tried to force her.

Afterward, her mother had called her names and said
she begged for it. The defense attorney had described
her as a teenaged seductress making playthings of men.
The tabloids had made her out to be a homewrecker.

Then the shooting, her stepfather's face as the bullets hit him, her mother's harsh curses afterward, the horror of trying to go to school, to live with the shame and disgrace…!

"Sara!"

She cried out as he stopped in front of her. He'd turned on the lights, and she hadn't even noticed. Her face was a study in terror. He moved a step closer, and she held both hands out, palms toward him, trembling.

"No, please, please, don't…!" she sobbed.

He'd been a policeman once, years in the past. He recognized the fear and the posture. He closed his eyes and shuddered. Dear God, why hadn't he realized…!

"Sara," he said softly, kneeling a few feet away from her, "how old were you when it happened? When your stepfather tried to force you?"

Her voice caught in her throat. "Thir…teen," she sobbed. "I was…thirteen."

His eyes closed. His hand clenched into a fist at his side. He'd assumed that she'd been a rival for the affection of her mother's boyfriend. He'd gotten the wrong end of the stick. God only knew how much damage he'd done tonight. He'd paid her back for what Ysera had done to him. Here was the result.

"Honey, it's freezing out here," he said in a choked tone. "Come on back into the house…"

"No." Her great black eyes were tragic. "No!"

He winced. He pulled out his cell phone and punched in a number. His hands were shaking. He had to put the numbers in twice before the phone rang on the other end. His face was like stone. "Madra, can you come down to the ranch? I've done something… There's a young woman. Please. I don't know how much damage I've done," he ground out. "Yes. Yes, I'll send a car. Hurry. Thanks."

He hung up and called a limousine company, gave them an address and an order. He hung up.

"Madra is coming down to take care of you," he said. "She's a physician. Sara, will you let me take you inside?"

She didn't even hear him. She was wrapped up in the past, in the terror, all alone.

CHAPTER SIX

WOLF HAD TAKEN a blanket from the tack room and dropped it around Sara's bare shoulders, careful not to touch her. She was still shaking. He couldn't even get her to answer him. He'd never felt so miserable, so cruel, in all his life. He hated what he'd done. He didn't know how he was ever going to make up for it.

Sara was aware of movement, of a car driving up. Wolf went away. A minute later he was back with a beautiful blonde woman.

She looked young until Sara saw her face up close. She had to be Wolf's age, or thereabouts. She spoke to Sara, very gently, and got out her stethoscope.

There was a cursory examination and then the prick of a needle in her arm. She was shivering. The blanket felt nice. After a minute, she began to relax.

"You need to bring her inside now," Madra said gently.

"Honey, I'm going to pick you up," Wolf said softly, a catch in his deep voice as he moved closer. "I won't hurt you. I swear."

She stiffened, but she didn't say anything. She closed her eyes and shuddered as he carried her into the house and into the guest room downstairs. He put her on the coverlet.

"Leave me alone with her," Madra said gently.

"Of course."

He went out, straight into his den, closed the door, opened a whiskey decanter and poured himself a glass.

"THAT WON'T HELP," Madra said from the doorway a few minutes later.

He finished the last bit of amber liquid from the glass. During her absence, he'd removed Sara's dress and shoes from the living room. He could put them in the guest bedroom later, when he had the opportunity. He didn't want to embarrass Sara even more by having them on open display in the living room.

He'd put his own things back on, minus the dinner jacket. It was embarrassing to have to catalog his sins for this old friend, but Sara had needed help. No way was he letting her leave here alone. Not after he'd seen the look on her face.

He turned, pale and somber. "Did she talk to you?"

She shook her head. "She's sleeping. All she could say was *please, don't.*" She stared at him.

He turned away from the accusation in her dark eyes. "I hadn't been with a woman in a long time. I just…lost it. I didn't force her," he added through his teeth. "That wouldn't even be possible. She's…a virgin," he said in a tortured tone. "Too much a virgin. It would require minor surgery." He drew in a long, harsh breath. "All the same, I scared her to death."

She drew in a breath and sat down on the leather sofa beside the desk. "Want to tell me about it?"

He laughed coldly. "No. But I'll have to. She was assaulted, almost raped, by her stepfather. All this time, I thought she'd tried to take him away from her mother, that it was a rivalry, he got hot, and she got scared." He ran a hand over his lean, hard face. "She was thirteen, Madra." His eyes closed, and he shuddered. "Thirteen years old."

"Dear God, what monsters men can be," she replied.

"Yes." He perched himself on the edge of the desk and crossed his arms over his chest. "I could talk to her," he confessed. "About Ysera. She listened. She wasn't judgmental. I thought the coy act was just that, an act. Some women think it's a way to get a man's attention, pretending innocence. I didn't really even believe her about the…physical issue." He stared at the floor. "I was a fool. I've damaged her, when she was already damaged enough. Her brother said we could hurt each other badly, because neither of us had faced the past. He was right. Oh, God, I wish I'd listened!"

She shook her head. "She should have had therapy. So should you," she added, "as I've been saying for years."

"I can't talk to a total stranger about Ysera," he said through his teeth. "And she—" he nodded toward the hall "—couldn't even talk to her own brother about her stepfather. He went to prison on her testimony. I knew that, and I didn't trust her. I didn't realize how young she was when it happened…" He closed his eyes. "God, Madra, what am I going to do? I can't let her go home alone. Her brother's overseas. She has no family. But making her stay here…she'll hate me even more."

"Bring another woman here to stay with her, until she's able to go home," Madra suggested.

He glanced at her. After a minute, he nodded. "I'll call Barbara Ferguson. She runs a café in town. Her son is a police lieutenant. She'd do it for me." He grimaced. "Everyone will find out. That will hurt her more…"

"I know Barbara," she said. "She isn't a gossip. She won't tell anyone the real reason. But you have to get a grip on yourself, Wofford," she added gently. "This is no way to live."

He lifted his head and ran a hand through his thick hair. "Her brother will mop the floor with me," he mused. He laughed coldly. "I'll let him. It might help us both."

"Therapy is what will help."

He hesitated, but only for a moment. "I know a female psychologist in D.C., a therapist," he said after a minute. "She was Colby Lane's therapist. She keeps snakes," he added on a laugh. "Maybe Sara would talk to her, if I agreed to talk to her, as well. If she doesn't load one of my guns and shoot me with it in the meantime."

"Take it one day at a time," Madra said gently.

He got up and hugged her warmly. "Thank you for coming down here."

"Mark would never forgive me if I hadn't," she said with a smile. "The three of us have been friends since grammar school."

"He cut me out or I'd have married you first," he teased.

She just laughed. They'd been like brother and sister all those years. "Sure you would." She glanced toward the whiskey bottle. "That is a very bad idea," she reminded him.

He shrugged. "A pistol is a worse one."

She grimaced. "We all make mistakes."

"This one is the worst of my life, and I'm not the one paying for it," he said sadly. "Will you stay until I call Barbara and see if she'll come?"

"Of course," she replied.

"I'll make coffee," he said, and smiled.

BARBARA CAME WITH an overnight bag. She winced when she saw Wolf's face. The big man with the Arctic-blue eyes had spent a lot of time at her place of business. She'd grown fond of him. He'd been reticent on the phone, but when she arrived and got a look at him, she began to understand what had probably happened. Sara was so innocent, so unworldly. And she'd heard things about Wolf from her son, San Antonio police lieutenant Rick Marquez, who was friends with Rourke, a mercenary who spent time in Jacobsville on covert ops. Rourke knew Wolf.

"I've done something unforgiveable," he told Barbara quietly. "Thank you for coming. I can't let her go home. She'd be alone, and I've…rekindled some terrible memories for her."

Barbara nodded. "It's okay. I have people who can take care of the café while I'm here," she said softly.

"Okay."

"I have to go home. Thank you for sending the car," Madra told Wolf. "You call that psychologist. I'm going to hound you until you do."

He nodded. He hugged her. "Tell Mark I appreciate him letting you come."

"You know he'd do anything for you," she said. "Besides, you're godfather to our sons. How would it look if I'd refused?"

"She'll be all right?" he added worriedly.

"She's traumatized," Madra said. "But it's mental, not physical. You haven't hurt her."

"That's what you think," he said miserably.

She patted his shoulder. "Get some sleep. In the morning, you can apologize."

"In the morning, she'll be looking for the key to the gun cabinet," he said heavily.

Madra said goodbye to Barbara and went to the limo waiting to take her home.

BARBARA WENT INTO the guest bedroom and looked at the pale, quiet young woman asleep under the covers of the big bed. He glanced at the chair where he'd draped her dress and shoes while Barbara checked on Sara.

"She'll never forgive me," Wolf said through his teeth. "And Gabe's going to beat the ever-loving hell out of me when he finds out."

"How will he find out?" she asked.

"Because I'm going to tell him," he said shortly. "I deserve every damned thing I get." His face drew up in a pained expression. "She listened to me. I poured out my heart, and she listened. Then I repaid her with… this." He turned away.

"Madra's right. You can apologize tomorrow. Sara isn't vindictive," she added gently. "Give it time."

He shook his head. "It won't help."

"Try to get some sleep. I'll turn in, too."

"Thanks for coming," he said.

She smiled. "I like Sara."

THE NEXT MORNING, Sara woke with a faint hangover and memories of the night before. She was still in her slip, and she almost gasped when she saw a head on the pillow beside her.

But it was Barbara, who rolled over and gave her a sleepy smile.

"Good morning," the older woman said softly. "How do you feel?"

"Terrible." Sara colored. She looked around. "I don't remember…"

"Madra Collins came down to examine you," Barbara said. "She gave you an injection and put you to bed. Wolf asked me to come and stay while you were here. He said he couldn't let you go home alone, in the condition you were in." She hesitated. "He's in pretty bad shape. He says your brother's going to beat the hell out of him, and he's going to let him do it."

Sara lowered her eyes. Her memories of the night before were vivid and embarrassing. She was ashamed that she'd let things go so far. But what she remembered most was Wolf's expression when he knelt beside her and pleaded with her to let him take her back inside. He'd been sickened when she told him the truth about what had been done to her. Sickened and ashamed and guilt-ridden.

It wasn't really all his fault. She'd wanted what had happened, until she realized that he was paying Ysera back with Sara's body. She wondered if he remembered that. Of course he remembered. She felt bitter. Sick.

She sat up and pushed her legs off the side of the bed. She realized suddenly that her dress and shoes were still in the living room, where he'd stripped them off her…

"I don't have any clothes," she whispered. "My dress…"

"Isn't that it?" Barbara asked curiously, nodding toward the chair against the wall. Her dress was draped over it, her shoes on the floor beside it.

"Oh. Yes. Can you drive me up to my apartment?" Sara asked in a ghostly whisper.

"You can't go home yet."

"But I…"

"I'm going to stay here with you," Barbara said. "But none of us are willing to leave you alone. You've been traumatized, Sara."

She colored and her great black eyes were tragic. "He…told you?"

"He just said that things got out of hand, that's all. Honest."

That made it a little easier. She brushed back her tangled hair. "One of his women came to look after me," she said with a bitter laugh.

"She's married to his best friend," Barbara returned. "And he's godfather to their sons."

"Oh."

"Our Mr. Patterson doesn't have women," Barbara mused, and her blue eyes twinkled when Sara flushed. "Gossip gets around. Apparently, he takes gorgeous blonde women to the theater and the opera and the ballet, and then deposits them at their front doors and goes home. Some of them are frustrated enough to talk about it."

For some odd reason, that made last night more bearable. But Sara still felt the stress of what had happened. "Where is he?" she asked uneasily, glancing at the door as if she was afraid he might come through it.

"I'll go and see. I'll make breakfast for all of us, then I'll go up to San Antonio and get you some things from your apartment if you'll trust me with the key."

"I want to go home," Sara said with a stifled sob.

Barbara put her arms around her and hugged her tight. "You just need a little time," she said gently. "You haven't let a man touch you since it happened, have you?"

She pulled back. "He told you...?"

"No. I've seen the symptoms before," Barbara replied gently. "Rick brought me a young woman once who'd been raped. She stayed with me until he had her assailant in custody. I went with her to the trial and sat with her."

She felt hot tears rolling down her cheeks.

"You don't have to tell me anything you don't want to," Barbara added.

Sara drew in a breath. "My stepfather tried to rape me when I was thirteen," she confessed. "My brother got to him just in time. He was arrested. There was a trial." Her eyes closed. "I had to testify. He went to prison, and my mother threw me out of the house, along with Gabriel. We were brought up by a relative of one of the public defenders, at the second trial."

She didn't mention what the second trial involved. She smiled sadly. "She was the family we never had."

"At least you had someone to love you," Barbara said.

"Yes."

"The trial was the worst part, I imagine."

Sara shuddered.

"Defense attorneys can be brutal," Barbara recalled. "I didn't believe it, until I saw it with my own eyes."

"He said I tempted my stepfather until he went crazy, that it was all my fault."

"Bull excrement," Barbara said.

Sara let a tiny laugh escape her. She wiped at the tears. "Sorry. I'm a watering pot this morning."

"Could you eat something?"

"I'd love coffee, at least. If he's...not in there," she

added, shivering as she thought about facing Wolf again with the memories of the night before between them.

"I'll go and see."

Barbara got her clothes on and walked into the kitchen. It was deserted. She recalled that Wolf didn't have a housekeeper. It was a joke locally that he wouldn't let any woman into his house, much less his kitchen. He was an immaculate housekeeper and, gossip also said, a gourmet chef.

She couldn't find him anywhere. Then, noticing a cracked door down the hall, she pushed it open. And there he was. Wolf Patterson. Sprawled across his desk with an overturned glass and half a bottle of whiskey at his elbow.

So he wasn't as cold as Sara thought, after all.

Barbara went to the desk and shook him gently.

"My fault," he said, half asleep. "My fault. She'll hate me forever. Oh, God, I hate myself!"

A sound broke from his throat, and his broad shoulders shook.

Barbara winced. "Mr. Patterson, you need to go to bed."

"No. No, I need a gun…"

"You stop that!" She half dragged him to his feet. But he was heavy. She could only get him as far as the sofa. She grimaced as she eased him down onto it.

"Damn me," he groaned. "Damn me, for what I did to that poor, tormented little soul!"

He put his arm across his eyes.

Barbara got an afghan that was draped over an easy chair. She covered him with it and pushed back his black hair, as if he'd been her adopted son, Rick, when he was hurting.

"It will be all right," she said softly. "Try to sleep."

"She was afraid of me," he said in a tortured voice. "She was shaking all over…!"

She smoothed his hair. "Go to sleep."

"Damn…me," he breathed. Seconds later, he was snoring.

Barbara went out and closed the door gently behind her. As she started back toward the guest room, she saw a cowboy standing at the front door.

She opened it. She had to be very discreet. She smiled. "Hi. Are you looking for the boss?"

"Uh, yes," he began. "The boys are ready to go, our foreman just needs to know if he's got anything else planned for today besides rounding up strays."

"He's pretty sick," Barbara said, thinking up nice lies. "He went out with Miss Brandon last night. She brought him home. Miss Brandon couldn't leave him, but she didn't want to stay here alone. Gossip, you know, so she called me." She smiled. "We're just going to be here until he's better."

The cowboy relaxed. "I hope he's better soon. If you need something, you just tell us, okay?"

"I will. I'm sure he'll appreciate it."

"You're Mrs. Ferguson. You run that café in town," the man said suddenly. "Gosh, ma'am, the boss is going to be one lucky guy to have you doing the cooking." He chuckled. "Your steak and potatoes is just the best on earth."

"I hear your boss cooks even better than I do," she mused.

"Yes, ma'am, but he likes all those fancy sauces and spices," he said, shrugging. "Me and the boys don't mind it once in a while, but a man gets hungry for biscuits. Sure was a happy day for us when we got that new cook for the bunkhouse." He grinned.

She laughed.

He tipped his hat. "Tell the boss we'll be working hard, and we hope he gets better soon."

"I'll tell him."

She closed the door back. She'd have to remember to prompt not only Sara, but the boss, as well, once he woke up. He was going to have a king of a hangover when he did.

BARBARA MADE BISCUITS and country ham with gravy and an omelet with the window tray of herbs that Wolf grew in the kitchen.

"Where is he?" Sara asked, because her friend hadn't said.

Barbara buttered biscuits with a sigh. "Passed out on his desk."

"Passed...out?"

Barbara nodded. She scooped eggs onto a platter. "With half a bottle of whiskey beside him."

"But he doesn't drink," she stammered. "My brother said he wouldn't even touch hard liquor."

"I think he probably felt the need for it last night," came the quiet reply. "I got him onto the sofa, and he went out like a light."

"Did he say anything?" Sara probed.

"Just that he wished he had a gun..."

Sara moaned out loud. "I should have told him the truth," she said huskily. "I should have made him understand. It's my fault!"

"You're both carrying scars," Barbara replied. She put the food on the table and poured coffee into two cups.

"Yes, and even more of them because of last night."
She put her face in her hands. "I didn't know, didn't
dream, that it would be so hard to stop…" She flushed.

"I was married, you know," Barbara said with a kind
smile. "I know all about passion, believe it or not."

"I don't know anything," Sara confessed. "Or, I
didn't." She bit her lip. "I never even dated after it happened. Well, I did once," she confessed. "He was a nice
boy. I was in my senior year. He was too impatient and
I just…lost it and started crying. He thought I was nuts.
So word got around, and nobody else asked me out. I
wouldn't have gone anyway, after that," she said heavily, sipping coffee. "I thought I'd never be able to feel
anything with a man."

"But that isn't quite true, is it?"

She shook her head. "He's…a very masculine sort
of man," she said, keeping her eyes down. "He's handsome and sensuous, and…" She looked up. "I thought,
maybe, just maybe…" She looked down at her coffee
cup. "So I tried, and now both of us are paying for it."
She sipped more coffee. "He'll never forgive me."

"It's himself he's having trouble forgiving, I think,"
Barbara replied. "It just needs a little time," she added.
"Things will get better. For now, don't let those eggs get
cold. They turn to rubber when you have to heat them
up again." She laughed.

Sara managed a smile as she lifted a forkful to her
mouth.

WOLF STILL HADN'T shown up when Barbara drove up to
San Antonio to fetch Sara's clothes. Sara had tried to go
with her, but Barbara was firm. The younger woman
couldn't see the anguish in her own face, but the older

one did, and was afraid that once she got into her apartment, she wouldn't leave. Barbara didn't want to let her be alone.

She didn't add that she knew things Sara didn't about Wolf's past and the woman whom Rick said was now hunting him. Sara would be in danger anywhere except here until her brother was home again. Barbara prevaricated and said that someone was targeting Gabriel, that Rick knew and had told her, and that it would be dangerous for Sara to be alone.

Which meant that Sara couldn't even confide in Michelle or ask her to leave her college dorm to stay in Sara's apartment. That wouldn't have been fair, anyway. The young woman was doing very well in her journalism class, but she was having some problems with one of her core courses. Sara didn't want to be the cause of having her fail it.

She'd borrowed a pair of slacks from Barbara, along with a button-up blue plaid shirt and some flats—luckily the two women were of a similar size, even in shoes. She looked very different from the poised, elegant person who'd come home with Wolf the night before.

SHE KNEW THAT he kept horses. She glanced at the stable with unpleasant memories in her black eyes and turned her attention to the corral. One of the mares was prancing there, with a colt beside her. They were Appaloosas. It had been a long time since Sara had even seen one, although a neighbor in Wyoming ran them. They were beautiful with their striped hooves and spots. She smiled as she watched the mare nuzzle the colt. It whinnied with delight.

"She's four years old," a deep, quiet voice came from

behind her. "She was a rescue. Her previous owner beat her almost to death with a tire iron. It took a lot of work to gain her trust."

She swallowed hard. She couldn't look at him. She knew her face was scarlet.

She felt him behind her. Not too close, but she could almost feel the warmth of his body.

"I thought about blowing my brains out last night," he said in an almost conversational tone. "But I decided it would be better to wait and let your brother do it for me."

She turned, very slowly, and looked up at him with wide, uncertain black eyes.

He winced at her expression. His hands were deep in the pockets of his jeans, and he looked like a man with a raging hangover. His pale eyes were bloodshot. His face was like stone.

"I hope you can understand why I wouldn't let you go back to your apartment, why I asked Barbara to come over here," he said in a subdued tone. "I did a lot of damage. I'm no more enthused than any other man about having to see the results of my own stupidity, but you're fragile right now. I won't leave you by yourself."

She swallowed and averted her eyes. She wrapped her arms around her body. She was trembling. "Okay," she said.

"Barbara will be here, all the time," he promised. "I won't…try to get you by yourself. I won't touch you again."

She just nodded. She couldn't manage words.

He moved away a little, his eyes on the corral. "You were honest with me about almost everything. Except the age you were when it happened."

"I know."

His chest rose and fell. "I thought she was out of my life. She never left. I'm still trying to make other people pay for what she did to me. You can't possibly imagine how ashamed I am for what I did to you."

"I couldn't talk about it," she said after a minute. "He did…vulgar things to me. Said vulgar things. I didn't even understand some of them, until the trial. That was bad enough, being painted as some teenage harlot. But what came after…"

He put one booted foot on the fence and looked toward the horses, not at her. "Tell me, Sara."

She smoothed her cold hands over the wood of the fence. "My mother got another lawyer for him. He found a loophole that would allow a retrial. But when he got out, all he wanted to do was make me pay for putting him in jail. He came after me, with a gun. I was just coming out the door, on my way to school, when he was suddenly there. He called me names, and he laughed. He said I'd never live to testify against him a second time." Her eyes closed. She wasn't aware of the man beside her, standing like a statue with eyes that were terrible to look into. "Our next-door neighbor was a police officer. He was on his way to work, too, when he saw what was going on. He pulled his service revolver and ordered my stepfather to put down his weapon. He had it aimed at me when the policeman shot him, right through the head." She shivered all over. She couldn't say anything else.

She felt arms enfolding her, a strong, warm body holding her tenderly, without passion. She felt hands at the back of her head, tangling in her long hair. A mouth pressed to her temple. She heard words, tender, soothing words, while she shivered and relived the trauma.

"There were charges against the police officer. I testified, because I didn't want him to have to pay for saving me. It led to something...truly wonderful. The public defender had a maiden aunt who took Gabe and me in, made a home for us, treated us like the children she never had."

"The policeman?"

"My testimony exonerated him," she said. She closed her eyes and shivered again. "But the shooting was just one more terror, one more thing, to keep me awake at night. I hated him. I really hated him. But I watched him die. I felt...responsible. My mother screamed at me at the trial. She said I was a murderess, that she hated me." Sara drew in a shaky breath. "My life...has been such a hell," she sobbed.

He kissed her wet eyelids, his tongue smoothing over the long, elegant lashes, his hands gentle and slow in her hair. "My poor baby," he whispered. "God, I'm so sorry!"

Her clenched fists rested on top of the denim shirt he was wearing. He smelled of coffee and smoke and some pleasant cologne. She let her forehead rest against his mouth, let him hold her.

He shuddered at that trust, when he'd done everything in the world to betray it.

"I would never have touched you if I'd known," he said in a rough undertone.

She drew in a shivery breath. "I know."

He was too unsettled to realize what she was admitting. He smoothed her black hair and lifted his head, letting the cool breeze move the dark strands of his own hair, which were drenched in sweat.

She stood in the circle of his arms, her eyes closed. Amazingly, it was the first peace she'd ever known.

The sound of a car coming up the driveway caught their attention. She moved back from him, a little inhibited, as a dark limousine drew up at the front door.

"That isn't Barbara. She took her own car," she said.

"No. It's definitely not Barbara," he said heavily. "I just hope she didn't bring her pets with her."

"She?" She looked up at him, worried.

"I can almost see what you're thinking," he replied quietly. "It's not one of my women. I don't have women, since Ysera. I told you that, and it was the truth."

She just looked at him.

"I hope you'll be able to forgive me for this," he added, nodding toward the house. "I can't let you go home until I'm sure you won't look for some drastic way to forget what I did to you," he added.

"I don't understand."

He put his hands in his pockets as a woman got out of the limo. It drove away, and there she stood on the porch, beside a rolling suitcase.

"You will," he said.

He led the way to the porch.

A young woman was standing there. She had black, spiky hair with purple highlights. She was wearing a black dress that came to her ankles, with a lot of silver jewelry. Her nail polish was black. So was her lipstick. She had a stud through her nose.

She turned with silver eyes trained on the two people who were just joining her on the porch.

"I'm Emma Cain," she introduced herself. Her sil-

ver eyes twinkled. "I'm guessing one of you is Wofford Patterson."

Shocked, a tiny laugh escaped Sara's tight throat.

"She's too short," Wolf said, nodding at Sara, "so it's
probably me. Nice to meet you." He shook hands. "This
is Sara Brandon," he added, indicating his companion.

"I can only spare two days," she said. "So we'd better get things going. I need a quiet room and a pot of
black coffee. And we'll have to do this one at a time. I
don't like joint sessions."

Sara was having the most horrible, unspeakable
thought. "Joint…?" She looked up at Wolf with an expression of such shock that he burst out laughing.

"Not joint sex," Emma said with one corner of her
mouth drawn down. "Didn't he tell you? I'm a psychologist." She gave Sara a wicked grin. "You're both broken, and I'm going to fix you!"

CHAPTER SEVEN

EMMA CAIN WAS not what Sara had expected a therapist to look like. The young woman was outrageously dressed, and she looked more like a goth than a psychologist, but her intelligence was apparent from the outset.

She seated Sara in an easy chair in Wolf's study and brought out an iPod. She looked at her notes, pursed her lips and then leaned back on the sofa.

"First question," she said, and she smiled. "How do you feel about Wolf Patterson this morning?"

Sara bit her lower lip.

"None of that. Don't search for an answer. Just tell me."

"I don't know how I feel," Sara replied. "Things went too far. He was… He…" She tried to find words.

"He used you as payback for a woman who humiliated him," came the reply.

Sara nodded miserably.

"And you were hoping for something entirely different."

There was a hesitation. Then Sara nodded again. "I was never able to feel anything, with other men," she confessed. "But from the first time I saw him, I just fell apart when he looked at me. I was antagonistic, because I was afraid of what I felt."

Emma smiled. "He doesn't know that."

"No."

"You wanted him."

Sara flushed red.

"It's not a sin to want someone," Emma told her gently. "It's a natural, human reaction. It's why we get babies."

"Well, yes, but…"

"But?"

Sara's great black eyes were bright with unshed tears. "It was my fault that things went so far," she whispered, as if it was shameful to even say it. It shocked her to hear it. Until that moment, she hadn't realized it herself. "I thought he felt something for me."

"Which made what happened all the worse, yes?"

"Yes. Because it didn't mean anything to him," she said dully. "He was very badly treated by a woman. She ridiculed him when he made love, humiliated him. She looked like me," she added with a sad smile.

Emma nodded. She made notes.

"How much do you know about him?" Emma asked after a minute.

"I know that he has terrible memories," she replied. "Like mine, only worse. Nobody knows exactly what he does, or did, for a living. He said he worked for the FBI, but he and my brother are friends. And my brother is a professional soldier, an independent contractor."

"Believe me, I know about mercs," Emma said. "People think they're hard as nails, that they'll do anything for money." She shook her head. "If I had fewer ethics, I could tell you stories."

"Mr. Patterson…Wolf…told me some."

Emma cocked her head and smiled. "Mr. Patterson?"

"It's what I always called him, before," she said.

Emma made more notes. "Do you know anything about his childhood?"

"Yes." She bit her lip. "But that's something he needs to tell you. I don't talk about people," she added apologetically. "I had to tell you about the woman who humiliated him, because it was why he did…what he did to me."

"Admirable," Emma mused.

"I don't think he'll tell you much about me, either," Sara added.

Emma chuckled. "Nothing at all, in fact," she said, lifting silver eyes to Sara's surprised face. "He was pretty vocal about himself, and how badly he'd hurt you." She studied Sara. "Actually, I was expecting bruises…"

"No!" Sara exclaimed, leaning forward intently. "Oh, no, he never hurt me like that! He would never hurt me physically!"

Emma cocked her head, like a bright little bird, and waited.

"He…he's very tender," she whispered. She flushed.

Emma didn't say anything. She just made more notes.

AN HOUR LATER, Emma and Sara went into the kitchen. Barbara was sitting there with a subdued Wolf Patterson.

"Your turn," Emma said, grinning at him.

He got up, glanced at Sara and winced and followed Emma into the study.

"SHE'S NOT AT ALL what I expected," Sara told Barbara as they sipped coffee. "My goodness, I could tell her anything!"

"She has a rather unique outlook," the older woman said and chuckled.

"Oh, yes."

"I brought your clothes," Barbara said. "And I stopped by the café to make sure things were running smoothly."

"I'm so sorry…"

"You're one of the nicest people I know, Sara," Barbara interrupted. "This is no problem, believe me."

"Thank you so much."

Barbara smiled. "I'm thinking of it as a vacation," she mused. "I haven't had one in years."

"Yes, but you're cooking here."

"Not because I have to," came the amused reply. "See the difference?"

Sara had to agree that she did.

SHE CHANGED INTO slacks and a black turtleneck sweater, slipping into a knee-length sweater vest to help camouflage the tight fit of the sweater. She didn't want to look seductive. She pulled her long hair back into a ponytail and secured it with a pink ribbon.

When she got back to the kitchen, Wolf was sitting there with Barbara.

"Where is Miss Cain?" Sara asked.

"Gone to her hotel," Wolf said. "She'll be back in the morning."

"She isn't staying here?" she wondered aloud.

Wolf sipped coffee. "If you're willing to share a room with her and Willie, I'll ask her to come over."

"Who's Willie?" she asked.

"Her eight-foot python."

Sara remembered then what she'd heard him say

about the unorthodox psychologist when she first arrived. "She keeps snakes."

"Oh, yes," he agreed. "And Willie's just a baby."

"The mind boggles." Barbara chuckled.

"She's very good," Sara said as she sat down beside Barbara at the kitchen table.

"She is," Wolf replied.

"I need to see what you've got in the freezer," Barbara began.

"Just sit down," he replied. "I'm doing quiche and crepes for supper."

"You cook?" Sara asked, surprised.

"Yes."

"This will be a treat." Barbara chuckled. "Every cook gets tired of her own stuff once in a while," she added when they stared at her. "Need some help?"

"Yes." He glanced at Sara. "Can you chop the herbs for me?" he asked her quietly.

She didn't look at him. But she nodded.

"Then while you two are doing that, I'd like to catch the news. Do you mind?"

"Go right ahead," Wolf said. "I have satellite and all the channels. Knock yourself out."

"Okay." She picked up her coffee cup and hesitated.

"I spill things all the time," he told her, and smiled. "Take your coffee with you. Carpet's clean."

She laughed. "I'm not planning to spill it, but some people don't like beverages in the best room."

He shrugged. "I'm a bear with furniture."

Sara burst out laughing. "What?"

"There's a female comedienne," he said. "I loved to watch her act, a few years ago. She said men were just bears with furniture. It made an impression."

She averted her gaze when he tried to hold her eyes. He smiled sadly. It was early days yet.

SHE CHOPPED HERBS with an excellent knife from his exotic wood block full of them.

"You do that very well," he remarked while he heated oil in a sautéing pan.

"I love to cook."

"I noticed. You have almost as many cookbooks as I do."

"Yes, but I can't do crepes," she confessed. "I burn them."

"It takes a lot of practice. That's all."

They worked well together, sharing space, not talking. She liked the way it felt. Companionship was something they'd never really tried.

"How do you like Emma?" he asked.

She nodded. "She's not at all what I expected a psychologist to be."

"That's why I like her. She doesn't try to make square pegs fit in round holes."

She scraped the herbs into a bowl. "If you're wondering, I didn't tell her anything about you. Well, except for…" She flushed.

"I told her the rest," he said a little stiffly. "She said she thought I'd hit you…"

"She did not!" she exclaimed. "I told her you'd never hurt me. That you never would hurt me physically!"

He was surprised at her spirited defense of him. He searched her black eyes slowly. "She said that. After she put my back up." He smiled slowly. "It amused her that you defended me." He lowered his eyes to the pan. "It shames me that you would, after what I did to you."

She drew in a long breath. "You must have noticed that I wasn't fighting very hard."

He stopped what he was doing and turned to her.

She bit her lower lip. "You're acting as if I were a victim. I'm not. You didn't hurt me."

"I didn't hurt you physically," he said curtly. "What I did to your pride is something else."

She moved one thin shoulder. "Pride is what you have before life makes you ashamed of being a woman. You see, I couldn't even let a man touch me, for years after the trial. It was worse when he was shot, and people in my circle of friends in Wyoming knew about it. That's one reason that Gabriel got us the apartment in San Antonio, and the house in Comanche Wells, because nobody knew us here. It was someplace I could live and not have people gossip about me."

He leaned against the counter, his pale eyes narrow, watching, waiting.

"I tried to go out with a man just once, when I was a senior in high school. He knew all about what happened." She stared at her hands, bare of rings. "I liked him. I thought, maybe... But when he took me home, Aunt Maude wasn't home and Gabriel was in the service. He pushed in past me and started kissing me. I just...panicked. I fought him and screamed. He looked at me as if I were a crazy person. He walked out and left me there. He told his friends, I guess, because it was all over the school that I got hysterical if a boy kissed me." She shrugged. "So I stopped even trying. Men were pretty repulsive to me, anyway."

He was watching her. "Not me," he said, his voice deep and slow.

She looked up, flushing. "Not you," she confessed in almost a whisper. "I...I'd never felt anything like that."

His heart dropped into his boots. He turned away. "It was too soon," he said, combining ingredients to make the quiche.

"Yes. I thought I could..."

"Not you. Me. It was too soon, after Ysera." He whipped milk and eggs into the herbs she'd chopped. "You get your ego ground into the dirt for two years, it takes time for the scars to heal."

"Someone should have hung her from a light post," she muttered.

He drew in a long breath. "We tried," he said. "The local militia combed the hills looking for her. But she sold everything she owned and bought her way out of the country."

"You never saw her again?"

"No. But one of the units attached to ours did, just recently, in Buenos Aires," he replied. "Word is that she has a millionaire lover who's going to fund her return to Africa."

"She's going back? Why?"

"She was involved in illegal drug trafficking," he said. "She's a high-level dealer, with contacts all over the world. That's why we were after her. We worked with Interpol, until I got stupid enough to trust her as an informant." He glanced at Sara wryly. "Rule number one in espionage—never get involved with a source."

"Espionage?"

He nodded. "I worked with a number of federal agencies in this country, and at one time I did jobs for Interpol." He put down the whisk and turned to her. "But my last job was as an independent contractor. I worked with your brother, in fact, in an incursion in Africa. That's how he knows me. It's why he tried to keep us separated, because he knew what Ysera did to me."

"I see."

"It gets worse, Sara," he said quietly. "Drug trafficking isn't the only business she's involved in now. She's also bent on revenge. I helped put her out of business, and she lost a lot of money. While she was in hiding, it didn't matter. Now it does. She's got a grubstake, and she wants my head in a sack. She put out a contract on me."

Her heart seemed to stop beating. She looked up at him with fear in her eyes, her pale face, her stillness.

"So you might not need to worry about whether or not I'll be paid back for what I did to you last night," he said calmly. "Ysera will do it for you."

"You're safe here, though, yes?" she asked, worried and unable to hide it. "You have friends like Eb Scott and Cy Parks. And my brother."

He studied her soft mouth. "Your brother will likely save Ysera the trouble when he knows what I did."

"He won't hear it from me," she said stubbornly. "Or from you," she added, just as stubbornly. "It's our business. Not his."

He cocked his head. "Shouldn't you hate me?"

She smoothed the countertop. "Probably."

"But you don't."

She shook her head.

"Why?"

She didn't answer him.

He put his big hand over her small one. "Why?"

She turned and looked up at him with liquid black

eyes, full of pain and sadness. "I wanted what happened," she said, wincing. "I thought…"

He moved a step closer. "You thought what, honey?" he asked tenderly.

"I thought, maybe, with you…"

He caught a strand of her black hair and toyed with it. "You were never in any real danger of that," he said. "We both knew it couldn't go that far."

She flushed.

"But it went far enough," he continued grimly. He searched her eyes. "How much do you know about basic anatomy?"

"What do you mean?"

"Do you know that sperm are mobile, and that they can crawl?"

Her face went white. She recalled vividly what had happened between them.

"I didn't penetrate you. But I didn't have to. I was right against you when I came," he whispered.

"That couldn't happen," she began.

"It did happen, in fact, to a friend of mine in basic training. He and his girl were religious. No sex before marriage. But they played around, the way we did last night. She became pregnant while she was still, technically, a virgin. Fortunately for her, he did know some basic anatomy. They got married. They have four kids now."

Her mind was spinning. She could get pregnant. Her hand went to her stomach. She didn't know whether to laugh or cry. He'd hate her even more if that happened. She winced.

"We'll handle it," he said firmly. "Whatever happens. But you listen to me." He tilted her face up to his piercing blue eyes. "It takes two people to make a baby. So just one shouldn't make a decision that affects both parents. Do you understand?"

She swallowed. "Yes."

"You tell me, one way or the other," he said. "I won't forget, and I won't forgive."

She drew in a shaky breath. "Okay."

He touched her flushed cheek. "When was your last period?"

She bit her lip.

"When, Sara?"

"Two weeks ago."

"Damn!"

He turned back to the quiche and didn't say another word. He was in agony. He'd done something incredibly stupid out of uncontrollable passion and abstinence and she'd have to pay for it. Whatever they decided to do about it, if she got pregnant, it should never have happened. But he hadn't been playing around. He'd wanted her to the point of madness. Even without the ultimate act of love, it had been more satisfying than any physical pleasure he'd ever had in his life. He'd had an orgasm with her, from what was basically heavy petting. And she'd had nothing, except insults and humiliation.

"I really should let your brother shoot me," he muttered.

She didn't know what to say. He looked shattered. She didn't know what to do, either. She would have wanted his child, if he'd shown the least interest in having it. But he only wanted to know if she got pregnant. She was certain that he didn't want to be tied to her for the next eighteen years. He'd want a termination.

It was just one more horrible complication from a

situation that she could have prevented by just saying she didn't want to go home with him.

"I didn't even try to say no," she said aloud, in a haunted tone.

"We're both human," he said quietly. "I wanted you to the point of madness. I think you wanted me just as much."

"At first," she agreed.

He whisked the eggs and set them aside while he made a crust. "You were a virgin," he said heavily. "I did things to you..." He ground his teeth together. "It should have been with some kind young man, someone with a loving family. A man who'd cherish you, give you children, grow old with you." His eyes glittered. "I'm thirty-seven years old. You're barely twenty-four," he bit off. "Almost another generation from me."

She looked up at him, not seeing his age, only how handsome, how virile, he was. "I could never let any other man touch me like that," she confessed, and lowered her eyes before she saw the utter shock in his. "So what does age really matter?"

He turned toward her, his hands caked in flour. "No other man? Ever?"

She shook her head. "Only you. That way."

His high cheekbones flushed. "That just makes it worse."

She looked up into tormented Arctic-blue eyes. "It was my fault, too."

He actually winced.

She had to look away. Her whole body felt tight when he looked at her that way. She folded her arms over her breasts.

He didn't say another word.

THEY ATE QUICHE and the delicate crepes and ate a perfect crème brûlée for dessert.

"You should open a restaurant," Barbara enthused when they were stacking dishes in the dishwasher. "I've never had better food."

He laughed softly. "I love to cook. One thing foster homes all have in common is that mostly the food is inedible. I got tired of it, so I found a woman who could cook and had her teach me."

"Foster homes?" Barbara asked.

He nodded. But he didn't volunteer any more information. Neither did Sara, who knew a lot more about his past than anyone else did.

AFTER SUPPER, BARBARA found a movie she wanted to watch. Wolf went outside with Sara to watch a meteor shower that had been advertised earlier on the news. She was wearing one of Wolf's leather jackets. He'd insisted, because she hadn't asked Barbara to bring her a coat. The weather was unseasonably cold.

"The radiant is in the northeast, there," he indicated, pointing up.

"You know a lot about this."

"I have a Schmidt-Cassegrain telescope," he confessed. "With a ten-inch aperture. It's up in the attic. I never take it out because it's a lonely business, watching for celestial events by yourself."

"I have a reflector telescope," she confessed. "I don't use it for the same reason."

"You should come over here once in a while and we'll watch meteor showers together."

"That would be nice."

"I'd do anything in the world to make it up to you,

you know," he said after a minute. "You're the only confidant I've ever had. I don't trust people. It's hard to share things, especially unpleasant things, from the past."

"I know."

"Do you think you can forgive it?" he asked.

She felt the tautness of his body beside her. He was almost vibrating while he waited for her to reply.

"I can forgive it," she said.

His posture seemed to relax. "In your place, I don't know that I could."

"You didn't know," she said. "I couldn't tell you all of it." She snuggled down into the jacket. It smelled of him. It was warm and pleasant. "I overreacted."

"I came on like a runaway train," he confessed. "I got drunk on you. It hurt that I went in headfirst, after what I'd been through, that I couldn't control what I felt. I took it out on you."

"But isn't that what happens to men?" she faltered.

"Until Ysera came along, there had never been a woman who could make me lose control."

She wondered about that. It seemed strange.

He shifted and turned toward her. There was just enough light from the windows to let him see her face. "One of my foster mothers tried to seduce me. I was twelve. She liked young boys." He bit his lip. "I couldn't control it. I was so ashamed. She tried to tell me that it was natural, but then her husband came in and…" He turned away.

"I hope you told Emma all that," she said.

"I can't tell Emma the things I can tell you," he said heavily.

Her small hand slid into his big one. She felt the

shock of it as he tensed. But his fingers curled around hers hungrily.

"So I spent the next twenty years trying not to lose control with women."

"On top of that, it must have been devastating, what happened with her."

"Devastating." His fingers entwined with hers. "Want to hear something funny?"

"What?"

His hand contracted. "I had the first orgasm of my life last night."

She was glad that it was dark.

He turned and looked down. "Are you flaming red?"

"Yes. Don't look."

He laughed very softly. "We have such intimate memories for two enemies, don't we?" he mused. "I shouldn't tease you." His hand contracted. "But it's the truth. I didn't know it was possible, pleasure like that."

She swallowed. "Neither did I," she confessed in a whisper.

He bent down and laid his forehead against hers. "I made you come, too," he whispered. "Over and over again. I watched you."

"You mustn't…!"

"Your face was the most beautiful sight I'd ever seen when you went over the edge. When I gave you pleasure, and watched it take you. I wanted nothing more than to tell you that. But I let the past ruin it for both of us."

She stood very still. She didn't speak.

"I wanted to go inside you," he whispered at her forehead. "Deep and hard and slow. I wanted to…" He bit off the rest of it. He'd wanted to make her pregnant. He couldn't admit that. He was thinking now that it might have happened, just the same. She could have his baby in her belly right now.

"Wolf..." she protested.

"Can you imagine how it would feel?" he asked huskily. "You and me, like that, so close that even air couldn't get between us?"

"You shouldn't..."

His mouth moved down to hover just over hers. "I can't...do it...with other women," he whispered roughly.

"Wh...what?" she gasped.

"You heard me," he bit off. "I can't get aroused with anyone except you."

She was shocked speechless. "All those beautiful blonde women..."

"Beautiful. Experienced. Willing." He sighed. "I took them home and left."

"Why?" she asked, stunned.

"I don't know why, honey," he said. His fingers smoothed through her ponytail, pulling the ribbon away so that her hair fell like a smooth black curtain down her back, around her shoulders. "Your hair is so beautiful, Sara. Beautiful, like you."

"I don't understand," she said.

"Neither do I. But all I have to do is touch you," he murmured wryly. He pulled her to him and gasped as his body became capable the instant his hips brushed against hers. "See?"

She stood very still.

"God, I'm sorry!" He started to pull away.

Her arms slid under his and around him. She was trembling, but she wouldn't let go.

"Sara," he ground out.

"It's all right," she said softly. "I'm not afraid of you."

His big hands spread between her shoulder blades, resting lightly, then pulling. He swallowed her up whole against him, shivering with desire, and held her. But he didn't touch her intimately, or even try to move her closer. He just stood there, in the darkness, holding her.

"Sara," he whispered. "What if we made a baby?"

"I...don't know."

"They can do a blood test and find out. It doesn't take long."

"Yes."

He tilted her face up. "You'll tell me."

"Yes." She sighed and laid her cheek against his chest. "I'll tell you."

She closed her eyes. It was heaven, standing so close to him, feeling safe, protected, wanted. The only thing that would have made it more perfect would be if he loved her. But that would be wishing for the moon.

CHAPTER EIGHT

SARA HAD ASKED Barbara to bring her laptop computer down. Late that night, after Barbara had gone to sleep, she got up and pulled up her game, careful to keep the sound down so that it wouldn't disturb anyone.

She logged into the game on her character and smiled as Rednacht whispered her.

How's it going? he asked. You haven't been on in a couple of days.

Had some problems, she replied.

Yes. Me, too, he said. I let somebody down.

So did I.

I feel like a heel, he typed. She trusted me and I hurt her.

I did the same thing to someone. I made him feel guilty for something he couldn't help.

There was a lol on the screen. Real life can be a pain.

Tell me about it, she said.

Want to run a battleground?

I wish. It's very late, and I have to get up early.

Right. The haircutting job, he replied.

She'd given that fiction as fact, and now she was stuck with it. I guess you have to strap on a gun and go chase lawbreakers, huh? she teased.

Something like that. I have an enemy. Very dangerous.

Her heart jumped. You be careful. I don't have anybody else in the world to play with.

There was a hesitation. Neither do I. You take care of yourself.

She felt warm inside. He was such a caring person. She wondered what sort of law-enforcement work he did.

Well, I'll see you on in a few days, she said. I'll be putting in some overtime.

So will I, he replied. Keep well.

You, too.

Good night, my friend, he typed.

She almost wept. Good night, my friend, she typed back.

After a minute, she logged off and closed down the computer. There were tears in her eyes.

EMMA CAIN WAS back the next day. She and Sara were making good progress. It was the first time Sara had ever been able to talk to anyone about her childhood, about her mother's betrayal, about the trial and its aftermath. It came much easier because she'd told Wolf.

She mentioned that to Emma. "He's the oddest sort

of confidant," she confessed. "I can tell him anything. I can't even talk to my own brother about these things."

"Apparently, he can talk to you in the same way," came the amused reply. "It's a good thing, too. A man's soft spot is his prowess in bed. It would be difficult for him to tell another man how he was treated and demeaned by that woman."

"He's such a kind person," she muttered. "I'd like to shoot that woman."

Emma laughed.

"What's funny?"

"He was saying the same thing to me about your stepfather," Emma confided. "He said it was too bad the man was dead, and he couldn't take the past out of his hide for you."

She smiled. Then the smile faded. "Do you know much about anatomy?"

"I'm a doctor," Emma said. "We specialize."

"You're a psychologist..."

"I'm a forensic psychologist," Emma said, chuckling at Sara's fascinated expression. "I do counseling on the side. My specialty is the mechanics of violence."

"My goodness!"

"So, yes, I have had training in anatomy."

Sara swallowed. "Can a woman really get pregnant even if there's no penetration?"

Emma cocked her head. "Was there intimate contact?"

"Yes."

"Was he excited during it?"

"Yes."

Emma sighed. "Then, yes, a woman can get pregnant from it." She made notes. "Have you told him?"

"He told me."

"I see."

Sara sighed. "I would love to have his child," she confessed. "But he wasn't enthusiastic about it. In fact, he was insistent that I tell him the minute I know something." She wrapped her arms around herself. "I can't have a termination. I just can't!"

"Wait until you have to face a situation before you dwell on it," Emma advised. "Until you know something definite, it's nothing. It's air."

"I suppose so."

"Why do you think he wouldn't want it?"

"He thinks I'm too young," she replied.

"You're twenty-four, I believe?"

"Yes, but he's thirty-seven," she replied.

Emma chuckled. "My best friend has a husband who's seventeen years older than she is," she said. "They have three children, and she'd die for him. He didn't think she knew the difference between infatuation and love. Was he in for a shock!"

Sara laughed, surprised.

"So ignore him. He's talking through his hat. Now, about the pregnancy. How do you feel about it?"

"I'd give anything to be pregnant by him," Sara said softly. "Anything!"

Emma pursed her lips. She made more notes.

WOLF WAS LESS forthcoming when Emma spoke to him.

"She's too young," he said, when she'd asked him how he felt about a child. "Too naive. She never really grew up. She was lost in the past, in bad memories. She's never really dated, gone out with men, learned about relationships. It wouldn't be fair to her."

"What if she wanted it?"

"She wouldn't," he said firmly. "I pushed her into an intimate relationship that she didn't really even want. If I hadn't insisted…"

"She said that she insisted."

"Well, she's lying," he bit off. "I pushed her off balance, kept her off balance, used tricks I should be ashamed of to make her give in." He closed his eyes. "If she didn't have an imperforate hymen, I'd have taken her. That would have been the ultimate betrayal. She should have the right to choose her first lover. At least I didn't take that away from her."

She wondered how men could cope with anything. They certainly had odd ideas about what women wanted. But it wasn't her place to tell him how to feel. It was her job to listen and then advise. Which she did.

EMMA HAD TO go back home. She left reluctantly, because these two were going to need ongoing therapy.

"I wish I could take you both on as patients," she told them at the front door. "I have serious doubts that you'll even talk to another psychologist," she said, frowning.

Sara bit her lower lip. Wolf grimaced and jammed his hands deep into his slacks pockets.

Emma sighed. "Listen, do you both have Skype?"

"Yes," they said in unison, and then laughed at each other.

"We can do sessions that way, if you like," Emma told them. "We'll set up regular appointments. It will be almost the same as being in my office."

"That would be lovely," Sara exclaimed, relieved.

"I can manage that," Wolf agreed.

Emma smiled. "Okay, then. I'll be in touch." She

glanced toward the limousine waiting for her. The driver, in a becoming black suit and tie, was standing outside looking very uncomfortable.

"He looks impatient," Sara remarked.

Emma chuckled. "He's scared to death. I've got my baby in a carrier in the backseat with me."

"The python," Wolf said, nodding.

"Odd, isn't it, how some people are afraid of snakes?" She sighed then shrugged. "It's kept me single and dateless for years."

"You need to find a nice man who loves reptiles," Sara advised.

"Or at least one who doesn't look hunted in the presence of one," Wolf agreed.

Emma just shook her head. "One day," she mused. "I'll be in touch."

The driver met her halfway, standing well back as he opened the back door for her and quickly shut it.

"What do you want to bet he double-checks that sliding window between the driver's compartment and the backseat is closed tightly?" Sara asked gleefully.

He laughed out loud. "I'll bet he wishes he had locks on it."

They both waved, although they couldn't see Emma through the tinted windows.

They went back inside.

"I need to go home," Sara told him quietly.

He drew in a long breath. He didn't want her to leave. The house was going to be empty. He'd be alone. Again.

"Tomorrow," he suggested.

She hesitated. She didn't really want to go. "Tomorrow," she agreed.

HE TOOK HER with him to the henhouse to gather eggs.

"Watch where you put your feet," he advised. "Chickens function all over the place around here."

She laughed softly. "I grew up with chickens. We had them in Canada, on the ranch where we lived when my father was still alive."

"Your father was paramilitary, you said."

"Yes," she replied sadly. "He was the sort of man who couldn't live without danger."

"I know how that feels."

She glanced at him with wide, soft eyes and then lowered them when his eyes cut around, so that he couldn't see the vulnerability. "I suppose you'd find it hard to settle down, too."

"Probably," he had to agree. "I've lived here going on four years, but I haven't been home all the time. I still do jobs as an independent contractor."

Her heart went cold. She hadn't realized that. She should have. He'd said he met Ysera in Africa, and it hadn't been that long ago.

"You take chances," she said.

"Not many. I'm careful. Usually." He glanced down at her and winced. "Not careful enough, with you." He paused, looking down at her bent head. "You may forgive me someday, but I'll never forgive myself. Never!"

She looked up into turbulent, pale blue eyes, in a face contorted with regret.

"It isn't your fault that I behaved like a two-year-old, at the last," she said, although she flushed. "You never hurt me."

His jaw clenched. "I hurt your pride, just as she hurt mine."

She cocked her head, studying him. "Don't men…

say things like that to women, when they make love?" she asked in a hushed, slightly embarrassed tone. "I watched this racy movie once. He said things to her that shocked me." She lowered her eyes. "Sort of like the things you said. But he wasn't mad at her, or trying to hurt her..."

His body reacted to the words in an uncomfortable way. He averted his eyes, and turned just a little, so that his condition wouldn't be as noticeable. "Men say all sorts of things," he agreed roughly. "But I meant to hurt you. That's why it shames me."

"I substituted for Ysera, you mean," she said heavily.

He drew in a breath. He lifted his head and looked out over the expanse of acres of land to the horizon. "Only...at the last," he said roughly. "Up until then, until the memories started lancing into me, I'd never had so much pleasure from a woman's body. Even sex, real sex, was never so good."

That took the sting out of the memory. She didn't say anything. She just looked at him, fascinated.

"I...I don't know anything," she stammered.

He turned then and looked down at her, with quiet, soft eyes. "Maybe that's why it was so good. I've never been the first, with anyone, in my life."

"Oh."

His chin lifted. He felt impossibly arrogant. "I was your first," he said.

She grimaced, and her eyes burned with tears.

"Sara!" He put the egg basket on the ground and framed her face in his hands, lifting it so that he could look into drenched black eyes. "Being forced doesn't qualify as experience," he said softly. "Baby, he wanted to hurt you. He didn't want to love you."

She swallowed.

He bent and kissed the tears away, tenderly. "I gave you your first taste of pleasure," he whispered roughly. "I'm sorry I made it an experience you won't want to remember. I'm so sorry!"

She bawled. He kissed the tears away. Then he kissed her soft mouth, there in the warm sun, his arms enveloping her tenderly, holding her just close enough, but not too close.

"It was like...shooting headfirst into the sun," she whispered into his mouth. "Like bursting inside..."

His body clenched. "Yes."

Her eyes opened into his. "Is it like that, when you go all the way?"

His face hardened. His arms around her were tense.

"I shouldn't have asked," she said, trying to move back.

"Stand still," he said roughly.

She didn't understand.

With a grim smile, he drew her just close enough to let her feel what had happened to him and then moved her back.

"From...just talking?" she faltered.

He drew in a heavy breath, and nodded.

"I'm sorry. I didn't realize."

He closed his eyes and shivered. But after a minute, he began to relax. "It's been too long," he said in a husky tone. "And you arouse me, quite frankly, more than any woman's ever been able to." He smiled at her transfixed stare. "I like it," he said. "At my age, it's more a blessing than a curse."

"Your age?"

"You don't understand."

She managed a faint smile. "No. I'm not very worldly."

He smoothed her hand against his shirtfront and examined the pretty nails with their clear varnish. "As a man ages, it's harder to get aroused."

"Not for you," she said and then flushed and lowered her eyes.

He chuckled wickedly. "Not with you. That doesn't happen with anybody else."

Her eyes shot back up to his, fascinated. "Those beautiful blondes..."

"Don't do a thing for me," he replied. He shrugged.

"Wow."

He cocked an eyebrow. "Wow?"

She smiled hesitantly. "I feel almost dangerous."

"So do I. So it's a good thing you're leaving tomorrow, before I put any more scars on your emotions."

"You want to sleep with me."

"I do not," he returned. His face was hard, his eyes glittered. "I want to make love to you. All night, all day, for a week."

She went scarlet.

He laughed and moved away from her. "And that would put both of us in the emergency room," he added with a wry glance. "That being the case, let's gather eggs and talk about something less stimulating."

She moved beside him. She felt lighter than air. As if she was almost new and young and full of adventure and hope. "I hear they're developing an acoustic weapon for the defense department," she commented.

He burst out laughing. "Not that unstimulating."

"Okay. They have a new bra that makes you look twice the size you actually are," she said wickedly.

He paused and looked down at her. "Why are you self-conscious?" he asked gently. "Your breasts are beautiful. I ache just looking at them through fabric."

"I'm small…"

He put a soft kiss on her forehead. "Size doesn't matter. Well, maybe it does, in one sense," he added, frowning. He looked down at her. "If you ever have that surgery, we may have some issues."

"Why?"

"I'm a little better endowed than most men, Sara," he said quietly. "I'd have to be very careful."

She recalled at the very last that night, when he'd lifted himself up and shown himself to her, and she'd been almost hysterical at the sight.

"Sorry," he said shortly. "I shouldn't have brought back that memory."

"I was too upset to notice very much, at the time." She looked up at him, her eyes wide and curious.

"And men are more potent sometimes than others," he whispered roughly.

"They are?"

He groaned.

She looked down below his belt and back up again, flushing. "They've sent a robot up to the International Space Station to keep the astronauts company," she blurted out. "And there's a rumor that that government secret agency is implanting cameras in the latest crop of cantaloupes."

The absolute absurdity of her last comment almost doubled him over with laughter and took away his heated reaction to her innocent comments.

She grinned. "Did that help?"

"Yes, you little witch, it helped." He bent and kissed her fiercely, for a few seconds. "Stop doing that to me."

She grinned bigger.

He shook his head. "Going home tomorrow may save you." His eyes cut around to meet hers. "For now."

She felt so exhilarated that she could have walked on air. She followed him into the henhouse, feeling all the bad memories drifting away, like wisps of smoke.

LATER, THEY HAD coffee in the kitchen after a wonderful supper that Barbara had prepared for them.

"You're a good cook," Wolf told her with a smile. "I'm going to miss having somebody else do the hard work in the kitchen."

"You cook better than both of us do," Sara commented.

"Yes. But it's a big house. Nice to have company," he said, and averted his eyes from the women.

"We can come back anytime you like." Barbara chuckled. "I like getting out of town."

"Me, too," Sara confessed. "I don't get out of San Antonio unless Gabriel's home at the Comanche Wells ranch. And he's away more than he's home lately."

Wolf didn't reply. Gabriel was involved in some tricky diplomacy in one of the African states. He didn't dare tell her that. She worried enough about her brother. The thought led to another, to something he'd been told about Ysera targeting him. She had the money and means. He glanced at Sara. What if she put Sara in the crosshairs?

His heart went wild. He couldn't bear the thought of Sara being in danger because of him. His jaw tautened. There was only one thing to do. He had to avoid her for a while, throw Ysera off the track by putting his bachelor status on overdrive, taking out as many women as he could. That would confuse the issue. People might know that Sara had been staying with him, but so had Barbara.

He could concoct a story and put it out. Barbara was in danger, and her son had asked Wolf to keep her at the ranch, but he couldn't do that without making gossip so he asked his best friend's sister to play chaperone. He nodded to himself. That might work.

"I want you both to do something for me," he said out of the blue. "Barbara, I want you to put it around that you were in danger because of an arrest Rick made and you came here for security while Rick was out of town. Sara, my best friend's sister, came to play chaperone. Got that?"

They both stared at him.

"I told your men that you were sick when Sara brought you home, and I came to chaperone you," Barbara said.

He smiled. "Not bad. But I'm obviously well now, and you're both still here." He put down his coffee cup. "I have an enemy. A deadly one. I don't want either of you in the crosshairs because she thinks I've got something going with you."

"Oh," Barbara said. She grinned. "I'm flattered. I think I'm at least five or six years older than you are," she added, pursing her lips. "Maybe ten."

He laughed out loud. "Women don't start being spinsters these days until they hit fifty, honey," he teased. "You're still pretty. And you can cook. You need to have Rick take his captain down to see you. The man has a few issues, but he's pretty cool-looking. To women, I mean."

Barbara cleared her throat. She had her eye on someone else, but she wasn't telling anyone. Not yet. "Well!"

Sara felt uneasy. "Okay," she said. She worried about Wolf. What if Ysera had someone after him? She was far less concerned for herself and Barbara. "You've got plenty of people here who can look after you, right?"

That concern made him feel odd. "Yes. At least two former feds and one who used to work for the mob. Or at least that's what they say about him."

"Fred Baldwin," Barbara said, with an odd little smile. "He was on the police force, just after he turned state's evidence and saved Carlie Blair's life."

"He'd still be there, but he didn't like carrying a gun all the time," Wolf remarked. "I'm still amazed at how well he fits in here as a foreman. He does the job with real competence."

"He's a sweet man," Barbara said. "Loves kids." She smiled sadly. "It's a shame that he's all alone."

Wolf's eyes met Sara's. He saw the same surprise in them.

"He's lost a lot of weight," Wolf said. "But it's hard to get him to eat healthy things."

"I'll speak to him, the next time he comes to the café," Barbara said thoughtfully. "He's there several days a week."

Sara's eyes were sparkling with unholy delight, but she hid her reaction.

"Yes," Wolf replied, clearing his throat. "He doesn't really like the bunkhouse chow. Todd, who cooks for us, can make steak taste like burned coyote."

"Your cowboy who came to the door said he cooked great."

"That would be Orin." Wolf shook his head. "Honest to God, the man doesn't have taste buds. I made beef Wellington, and he thought I'd ruined a good cut of meat."

Barbara laughed. "I'll talk to Fred about his diet," she promised. Her face lit up.

Sara and Wolf exchanged amused glances, but they didn't say anything.

THAT NIGHT, SARA was back in the past again. She was with her stepfather, backing away, her clothing half torn off her, the big man threatening and vulgar and explicit as he groped her. Then the dream changed into something astonishing. She let out a cry and sat straight up in bed, the shock still in her eyes.

She glanced beside her. Barbara wouldn't wake if a freight train came through the bedroom, she mused, and that was just as well. She hoped nobody else had heard her. The scream must have carried.

She got up and went to the bathroom, bathing her face. Then she opened the door to go toward the kitchen.

The hall was blocked by a very tall man wearing nothing but black silk pajama bottoms.

She looked at him with pure lust. He was the most beautiful thing she'd ever seen, broad-shouldered, his body muscular without overt muscles, his chest covered with thick hair, arrowing down his narrow waist into the low-slung pajama bottoms. Her breath caught at just the sight of him.

She was wearing silky pajamas, royal blue, pants that fell to her ankles and a button-up shirt with a collar and long sleeves. She looked prim, but her nipples were standing up like little flags under the fabric.

He groaned and picked her up in his arms, crushing her to his chest as his lips moved in her hair.

She clung to him. Tears stung her eyes.

"Nightmares?" he whispered.

"Yes."

"Me, too."

He carried her into the kitchen and held her very close for another minute, until he could regain the control he'd almost lost.

"Want coffee?" he asked softly.

She looked past him at the wall. "It's 3:00 a.m."

He shrugged. "I usually watch YouTube in bed while I drink coffee and eat dinner rolls or croissants when I can't sleep. But I heard you. God knows how, the walls are pretty thick."

She buried her hot face in his throat. "You have nightmares about Ysera, don't you?"

"Yes. And yours are...pretty evident." He lifted his head. "Did I say something, do something, this afternoon to cause them?" he asked worriedly.

"No. It doesn't take a trigger," she confided. "They just happen."

He nodded. "Mine, too." He levered her over a chair, but hesitated to put her down.

"What is it?" she asked.

"I want you to know that I don't mean to be a threat to you," he said gently. "Will you keep that in mind when I put you down?"

She nodded, although she didn't understand what he meant until he let her go and stepped back.

He was already capable, and he'd barely touched her. He was much more aroused than he'd been, even the night they were intimate. Her eyes were like saucers. The silk pajamas did nothing to camouflage him.

He laughed hoarsely. "Sara, could you stop staring, please?" he asked as he turned away, uncomfortable, and started to make coffee.

"You really are...magnificent," she said huskily. "Sorry!"

He lifted an eyebrow and chuckled as he glanced at her. "You're a virgin. You aren't supposed to notice things like this, or understand them if you do."

"Some movies are very explicit," she said primly. "And we won't even mention romance novels."

"You read those, do you?"

"Well, yes. It was the only substitute I had for a physical relationship. Until you came along, anyway."

He glanced at her with darkening eyes. "We don't have a physical relationship," he pointed out. He turned back to the coffee. "I made a dead set at you and destroyed your life."

"You brought Emma down here to fix me. To fix you, too." She smiled. "It's the first real peace I've known in years."

"But you had a nightmare."

"Well, yes, but it was sort of odd."

He started the coffee and sat down at the table, leaning his elbows on it. "Odd, how?"

"This time, when he started toward me, I picked up a chair and knocked him out," she said. She laughed. "I screamed, like always, but this time it wasn't out of fear. It was out of, well, triumph."

His eyes softened. "Progress."

She smiled. "Real progress." She searched his eyes. "How about you?"

He shrugged. "Same damned dream. Same agony."

"I'm sorry," she said softly. "I hoped Emma could help you, too."

"I think she will, eventually." He studied her. "It's just that I can't open up with her, the way I can with you." He grimaced. "It's difficult to talk about it with a woman."

She understood. "I can't tell Gabriel," she agreed. "And he's my brother."

"So it looks like if I need counseling in that department, you're going to be it," he said flatly. "You can tell Emma what I tell you and ask for advice," he added. "But I'm not telling her exactly what Ysera did to me."

She was immensely flattered. "Okay," she said softly.

His high cheekbones flushed. He studied her closely. "I have to stay away from you for a little while," he said. "I don't like the idea. But I won't put you in danger, you understand? She'll target anyone close to me."

"So I can't be close."

He nodded.

She drew in a long sigh. "Okay."

"I didn't say I like the idea. Or that it's what I want."

She smiled.

The coffeepot shut off. He got up and poured them cups. "You like opera, don't you?"

"I love it."

"Come with me."

"You're taking me to a concert in my pajamas?" she asked, with the first flash of humor she'd felt in days.

"I can't let you get dressed. You might let the flying monkeys out to get me," he teased.

She laughed and hit his arm. "Stop that."

He felt the change in her with delight as he led her into the living room.

CHAPTER NINE

WOLF TURNED ON the television, but not to a channel or even to the Blu-ray player he had on the big entertainment platform. He turned on his Xbox 360 and moved to YouTube. He sat down beside her and pulled up a 2012 YouTube video of a young man and woman and started playing it.

"They're kids," she said.

"He's seventeen in this. She's sixteen. Listen."

There was an interview. The boy told of being picked on by other children, of his loss of confidence. Then he told how his partner, a beautiful young woman, had given him back that confidence and led him to go on the stage to audition for *Britain's Got Talent*.

He walked out onto the stage with his partner. One of the judges asked the name of the duo and was told "Charlotte and Jonathan." There were a few questions. The boy was shy and said little. The judges, and the audience, seemed less than impressed.

Then the music started. And the boy opened his mouth and began to sing "The Prayer" with his partner. By the end of the first stanza, the entire audience was on its feet applauding.

Sara watched with tears rolling down her cheeks as the last tremulous notes faded away.

Wolf cut off the video and looked down at her. "Triumph after tragedy," he said softly. "Can you imagine how he feels, to have the audience on its feet applauding him, after being put down again and again for his appearance? Like his partner says, you really can't judge a book by what you see on the outside."

"He's amazing," she said. "Absolutely amazing."

He nodded. "One day we may see him at the Met."

"We?" she asked softly.

His pale eyes narrowed. "We."

She wasn't sure what to say. She searched his eyes with faint hope.

He averted them and turned off the television and the game box.

"You game," she said, surprised.

He shrugged. "It's the only real hobby I have." He glanced at her. "Do you game?" he asked and laughed as if he thought it was a ridiculous question.

She thought of Rednacht and the warm friendship she had with him. She was reluctant to put that on display, even to Wolf. She just smiled. "I'm not much of a gamer," she lied.

He shook his head. "To each his own, I guess. Come on. I've got croissants in the fridge. I'll heat us up a couple."

THEY WERE DELICIOUS with strawberry preserves. She savored every bite and sipped coffee with them. "You make good coffee," she said.

"I like it strong. In most cafés you get hot brown water. Not at Barbara's Café," he added, chuckling. "She likes good coffee, too."

"She's been very kind, to stay out here with me. She likes Fred, did you notice?"

He laughed softly. "He must like her, too. He spends as much time in the café as he does here. Funny, I didn't notice until she mentioned it."

"Neither did I."

He smoothed his long fingers down the side of the coffee mug. "Think you can sleep now?"

She started to speak, hesitated.

"Can you sleep?"

She winced.

He put the empty dishes and the cups in the sink. "I may have a solution," he said.

Before she could ask what it was, he bent and lifted her in his arms and carried her into the living room. He grimaced as he put her down on the sofa where he'd been so ardent days before.

"I know, bad memories," he said gently. "Maybe we can erase them, a little." He lay down beside her and pulled an afghan over them. He reached up and turned off the table lamp, leaving the room in darkness except for the glow of lights on the entertainment center.

"Ground rules," he said softly as he drew one soft little hand onto his chest. "No intimate touching, no moving closer than you are right now. And most important of all," he said, turning his head toward her, "no snoring. Got that?"

"I do not snore," she said with mock indignation.

"I'm going to find that out." He smiled in the darkness. A deep sigh moved his chest under her fingers. He moved restlessly, because the feel of them was intoxicating.

"You stop that," she said. "No moving closer than you are right now," she quoted him.

He laughed. "I'm trying. I like your hands on me."

Her heart jumped.

He felt that. His teeth clenched. "Maybe this wasn't such a good idea," he bit off.

She rolled over toward him and pillowed her cheek on his bare chest. Her heart was absolutely throbbing. But she was still. Her small hand reached up and smoothed his thick black hair.

"Go to sleep," she whispered. "We'll keep each other safe."

He had to fight a mist in his eyes. He'd never had a woman be tender with him. Passionate, yes. Even demanding. But never, never, tender. He drew in a shaken breath and closed his eyes. He loved the feel of her soft body against his, the calming stroke of her fingers in his hair. He was sure that he was too aroused to sleep...

HE CAME AWAKE QUICKLY, with the reflexes of a man who'd spent his adult life in dangerous places.

He looked toward the doorway into the hall and found Barbara standing there, trying not to laugh at the picture they made. Wolf, with Sara asleep in his arms, covered with a soft afghan.

"She had a nightmare," he said softly.

"I'm sorry," she said at once. "I sleep so soundly."

"It's all right. I woke up, too." He didn't want to admit to her that he had nightmares, as well. He looked down at Sara and smiled softly. "She slept soundly."

"I imagine you did, too," she replied. "I didn't mean to wake you."

"I'm a light sleeper," he said. "I've had to be."

She nodded. "I'll go make breakfast. Anything special?"

"I've got croissants in the freezer. She likes those

with strawberry preserves. But I'd like eggs and sausage. Fridge is loaded with raw mats."

She lifted both eyebrows. "Mats?"

"Sorry." He grimaced. "Materials. It's a gaming term."

"You guys and your video games." She chuckled. "They're even turning our police chief into an addict. And he's taught Tris how to play! Tippy has to sit and monitor her now, so she doesn't get in trouble online."

He grinned. The thought of Cash Grier with a wife and a young daughter still blew his mind. He knew Grier from times past.

"I'll get started," Barbara said, casting a last smile at Sara's prone body.

Wolf nuzzled Sara's face with his nose. "Wake up, sleepyhead," he whispered. "Barbara's making breakfast."

"Breakfast. Mmm." She sighed and rolled over. And there he was, bigger than life, so handsome that he made her heart jump, looking down at her with an expression she didn't quite understand.

"Beautiful Sara," he said in a low, tender tone. "Like the sky at dawn. Breathtaking."

Her eyes opened wide. "Have you been drinking?" she asked abruptly.

He threw back his head and roared with laughter. "Serves me right, for getting poetic before breakfast," he mused. He got to his feet, stretching hugely.

Sara sat up. She was barely awake, but she remembered going to sleep in Wolf's strong arms. She smiled at the picture he made, with those hard muscles taut as he stretched his powerful body.

He glanced down at her and turned, amused. "And I was worried."

"About what?" she asked.

He slid his arms under her and lifted her, afghan and all. "Men are dangerous early in the morning. Didn't you know?"

She searched his pale eyes. She shook her head.

He drew in a long, deep sigh and smiled at her. "The house is going to be empty," he said, and his smile faded. "All the color will leave with you."

She bit her lip and fought tears. "Don't you go after that horrible woman," she said abruptly. "Let somebody else go."

He brushed his mouth over her nose. "Afraid for me?"

"Of course."

"Even after what I did?" he asked, and winced.

She snuggled close, burying her face in his warm throat. "I was remembering that I slept in your arms," she whispered.

Those arms contracted suddenly, bruising her soft breasts against him in an agony of grief and regret.

"Wolf!"

He drew back at once. "I'm sorry. Did I hurt them?" he asked softly. He looked down at taut little breasts with very hard tips. His face changed.

She saw the intent in his eyes. "You wouldn't dare," she said. "Barbara's right in the kitchen…"

He turned, marched her into the guest bedroom, closed the door and brought his mouth down right over the tip of one hard breast and suckled her, hard.

She arched, shuddering.

"Yes." He put her onto the bed and went down with

her, flipping buttons out of buttonholes with amazing dexterity. His mouth was on her bare breasts then, making a banquet of them while she shivered and arched closer and made not even the slightest appearance of protest.

After a minute, he lifted his head and looked into her wide, soft eyes. "You'd let me," he said through his teeth.

"Yes," she whispered, shivering.

His hand cupped one soft little breast. His eyes were blazing, like blue flames. "This is hopeless," he ground out. "Absolutely hopeless!"

"Why?"

He lowered his mouth to the hard tip and brought it inside his warm mouth. He drew on it, harder and harder, until he felt her body stiffen, heard her soft little cry. He increased the pressure and felt her go off a cliff. His own body was racked with need, but he wouldn't listen to it. This was for her, only for her.

When he felt her relax, he lifted his head and looked at the red marks he'd left. Love bites, he thought with possession. She was his. She belonged to him. He looked into her wide, shocked eyes.

"I know," he said heavily. "I'm a rake."

She shivered. "It embarrasses me when that happens."

"It shouldn't. Your breasts are very, very sensitive. I like sending you off the edge," he whispered. He smiled, but it wasn't a taunting smile. He searched her eyes. "And I didn't watch."

She colored.

He drew in a breath. "I've got issues. You've got issues. I've hurt you badly, when I never meant to." He

smoothed his hand over her soft little breast. "Maybe
a few weeks apart will be a good thing. Because if we
keep this up, Sara, surgery or no surgery, we're going
to have each other."

"I know." Her face was sad as she looked up at him,
her black hair rayed around her beautiful face on the
comforter. "You don't want it to go that far."

"No, I don't," he said seriously. "I'm thirty-seven.
I hate to keep harping on that, but you're very young,
even for your age. You haven't known physical pleasure
with any man except me. These days, that's not really
a… Why do you look like that?"

"Do you think I could ever, ever, let another man
touch me the way you do?" she asked, absolutely aghast.

His face went very hard, without expression.

"What does that have to do with age?" she asked,
miserable and unable to hide it. "I get sick when I think
of other men touching me. I always have."

"Dear God," he whispered, and there was reverence
in the way he said it.

She sat up, pulling her pajama top together. "Yes,
I have issues," she confessed heavily. "Lots of them."

He sat beside her, staring at the carpet. "Me, too."
His face was unreadable.

"I guess it's different with men," she faltered. "You
said you don't, well, do things with other women. But
after you've talked to Emma for a few weeks, that might
change. You might not have problems…"

He wasn't listening. His mind was on what she'd just
said. He thought about it with subdued joy. She wanted
him. Even after he'd made a total fool of himself, hurt
her, damaged her pride, she still wanted him. He could
have burst into song.

"What?" he asked, suddenly coming back to the present.

"I need to start packing," she said.

He got up. "If you see anything suspicious, you call me," he said firmly. "Watch who you're around, watch what you do. I'll have men watching you, but you won't see them. If you do," he added darkly, "I'll fire them on the spot."

She searched his face. "You think I'm in danger?"

"I don't know, Sara," he said. "If she has someone watching, if she thinks I might be involved with you, perhaps. That's one other reason I'm staying away. But if you need me, I'll be there."

She managed a smile. "Thanks."

He sighed. "I can't let anything happen to my confidant," he mused.

She smiled back. "Okay."

"You don't snore, by the way," he said as he opened the door. He grinned at her. "You looked like a dark angel, asleep in my arms."

She pushed back her long hair. She didn't reply. The words were like a fire burning in her heart.

"I'll see you at breakfast."

He went out and closed the door. Sara took off the pajama top and looked at herself in the mirror. It was the first time in so many years that she'd wanted to see herself. She was amazed. The beautiful woman in the mirror was sensual and happy. Her eyes were like black stars, gleaming with pleasure.

The door suddenly opened. "I meant to tell you..."

He stopped dead as she turned, his face clenched. He actually shuddered.

She didn't try to cover herself. She let him look.

"Were you seeing how much damage I did?" he asked softly.

She shook her head.

"Then what?"

"I was seeing how hungry you were for me," she whispered, "and thinking how sweet it was to let you touch me."

He closed his eyes. His tall body shuddered again as he fought his instincts, which were to throw her on the bed and do something, anything, to stop the ache.

She retrieved the pajama top and put it on, buttoning it up. "Sorry," she whispered. "I never seem to say the right thing."

"I want you so much that I'm almost bent over double with it," he confessed roughly. "It wasn't anything you said."

She studied him quietly. He was violently aroused. "Just from…looking?"

"Yes," he bit off.

His very vulnerability made all her fear vanish. She relaxed.

"You aren't afraid of me," he remarked as he fought for control.

"No," she said quietly. "I'm…" She searched for a word. "Proud," she concluded finally. "Proud that you can want me, after what that awful woman did to you."

"Oh, baby," he breathed.

"I like it when you call me that."

He lifted his chin. "That's because you remember the last time I called you that," he said with helpless arrogance. "When you were crying out with passion."

She wasn't embarrassed. Well, not so much. She nodded slowly.

Weeks. Weeks. He wouldn't be able to see her, contact her, for weeks. *I'll die*, he thought to himself.

"What did you come back to tell me?" she wondered aloud.

"That Barbara's going to drive you up to San Antonio," he said with a harsh sigh. "I wanted to do it, but I don't want us seen together, just in case."

"That's all right."

He studied her, sketched her with hungry eyes and then turned away. "Come have breakfast before it gets cold."

"Okay."

He went out. He hesitated outside the door. There was still that small possibility, however faint, that he'd made her pregnant during the heavy petting session. But it was a long shot. She didn't have any symptoms yet. Probably she wouldn't, though. Not just yet.

He thought about Sara growing big with his child, pregnant and her black eyes shining like lamps while she nursed the baby. She'd make a wonderful mother.

He closed his eyes. No. It was too soon for that. She was just coming out of the darkness. She needed time, to explore, to see other men, to be certain that he was what she wanted. He didn't want to push her away. For the time being, for her own safety, he had to. He was going to be seen with a bevy of beautiful blondes to throw Ysera off the track. If she knew, with her vindictive nature, that Sara was his heart, she'd find a way to hurt her, perhaps to kill her. The only thing on earth that Wofford Patterson couldn't live without was Sara Brandon. He had to keep Ysera from realizing that.

HE WAS GENTLE with Sara when he said goodbye at the door while Barbara waited discreetly in the car.

"It won't be for long," he said hesitantly. "Just until we can find her."

"We?" she asked, her eyes widening with fear.

He framed her face in his big hands. "They. I meant they."

"Don't die," she whispered, fighting tears.

"Oh, God," he groaned against her mouth as he kissed her, and kissed her, and kissed her, there in the shadows of the porch, out of sight of Barbara and the few cowboys moving around the corrals.

He had to force himself to let her go. He kissed her tears away.

"You remember what I said," he told her, his voice deep and firm. "Watch your surroundings. Never go out at night alone, for any reason." He hesitated. "If anyone calls you and tells you that I'm hurt, or that I want to see you, don't listen. You call me directly. The same for Gabe," he added. "They might try to use your brother to draw you out. They got Carlie Blair by pretending that her father was hurt."

"I remember." She searched his eyes. "Just be careful."

"I'm always careful. Usually." He shrugged. "Not with you," he added sardonically.

She smiled. "I'll see you, then."

"Yes. You will." The way he looked at her was almost a statement of intent.

SHE CLIMBED INTO the car with Barbara and waved. But she didn't look back. If she did, and saw him standing there, so alone, she couldn't have left.

"Are you sure you're going to be all right in that apartment?" Barbara worried. "You could stay with me in Jacobsville."

"And put you in danger, too?" she asked.

Barbara frowned. "All I got were bits and pieces. What's going on? Can you tell me?"

"Not really," Sara said. "Except that Wolf has enemies, and one of them might come after me. It's not so far-fetched. One of Gabriel's did come after me, but Gabe was home when he broke in the house. It was over very quickly."

"I didn't know. I'm sorry."

"Michelle doesn't know, either," she added, referring to the ward she shared with her brother. "I haven't told her anything about what's going on, and I'm not going to. She's doing very well in college. I don't want to upset her."

"Michelle is very nice."

"Yes. My brother's crazy about her." She laughed. "But don't you dare let that get out. He's playing a waiting game, until she's through school."

"She graduates very soon, doesn't she?"

"She does, in fact. She already has a job lined up, too. She'll make a good reporter. I'm very proud of her. So is Gabriel."

"She's had a hard life. Losing both her parents and then being landed with her idiot stepmother, having her stepmother die of a drug overdose in front of her." She shook her head. "It was a good thing Gabriel took her in."

"And called me down to chaperone," Sara said. "She and Gabriel have been my life for the past few years."

"I think you may have someone else in that circle

pretty soon." She glanced at Sara's flushed face. "He's very much a man."

"Oh, yes," Sara said. "But he's not a marrying man," she added sadly.

"Sweetheart, every man is a marrying man with the right incentive. You wait and see."

Sara was going to do that. But despite Wolf's passion for her, she wondered if there was anything behind it. He wasn't a man who trusted emotion. He felt guilty about the way he'd treated her, and she knew intimate things about him that nobody else did. They were confidants. But whether he could love her was another matter. She couldn't settle for a loose relationship based on intimacy, not with her past. But considering what he'd gone through, she wasn't certain he could ever trust a woman enough to marry her. Ysera had put paid to that.

She would have to wait and see, she supposed. She just hoped she could get through the next few weeks unscathed. She was already feeling the effects of leaving him behind. The weeks that she was apart from him were going to be excruciating. She didn't really know how she was going to cope. She'd never loved a man before.

Her heart jumped up into her throat. Love. She... loved. She closed her eyes. How incredible that she hadn't realized it. How else could she have been so intimate with a man, except if she loved him? What a time to realize it. And what would she do now?

WOLF WENT BACK inside the house after the women drove away, morose and quiet. He looked around the empty rooms and thought that they were like his life. Empty. Some rooms open, many closed. He was alone.

He'd liked that, before. Being alone. But now it was a cold existence. He could picture Sara in every room, especially in the living room, where he'd taught her pleasure and then destroyed her pride. He closed his eyes, hating himself for that. But then he looked at the same sofa where he'd had her innocence, in a sense, and recalled her lying in his arms asleep, so trusting that it broke his heart.

"Sara," he groaned to himself.

He went into the kitchen and took the cup she'd held to her lips and put his own lips against it, where pale lipstick remained. He shivered.

He forced himself to put the cup in the sink along with the breakfast dishes. He stared at it with eyes that didn't see it. She was gone. He'd let her go.

Then he remembered why he'd let her go.

He put the dishes in the dishwasher and turned it on, mopping up the sink. Then he went into a locked room and turned on a scrambler unit and called Eb Scott.

"WHAT'S UP?" EB asked at once.

"Any news?"

"Yes. Bad news. I was going to call you later. Ysera got through the security we'd put in place, and she's back in Africa. She bought her old hotel and moved in with her millionaire lover. I have a contact who knows him. The word is that she paid half a million to someone we don't know, to take you out."

Wolf grimaced. "Vindictive."

"Yes." He hesitated. "You've had Sara Brandon out there this week…"

"I've had Barbara Ferguson out here this week," he lied. "Rick Marquez put a man in jail who threatened vengeance. Sara came over to chaperone. Her brother, Gabe, is probably the only friend I've got."

"Oh, I see." He laughed. "Sorry. I was thinking other things."

"She's too young for me," Wolf said quietly.

"Beautiful, though, isn't she?" Eb asked.

"What else did you find out?"

Eb saw the change of subject in a light that Wolf didn't guess, but he managed to keep the smile out of his voice. "The men she hired got on a plane to Heathrow, and we lost them. We figure they'll be in the States pretty soon."

"I'll make sure my own security is beefed up. Got a couple of extra men you can loan me? How about Rourke?"

There was a hesitation. "Something's going on with him. He was in Africa, then he was in Manaus, now nobody knows where he is."

"Something classified, I imagine."

"Exactly. But I have two good men with solid backgrounds. I'll send them over. Make sure one of them stays on your tail, all the time."

"I'll do that."

"And, Wolf, it wouldn't be a bad idea to have a few dates with several women," he said quietly. "So Ysera doesn't get the idea that you're set on any one of them. She'd be an immediate target—perhaps the primary one."

"I'm two steps ahead of you there."

There was a hesitation. "Gabriel's in some trouble, too."

His heart jumped. "What sort?"

"It's nothing big, yet. He's helping guard the oil fields

in one small Middle Eastern village, but there are insurgents who don't want them safe. I'm afraid there may be a big blowup one day soon."

"I trained Gabriel," he reminded Eb. "He's one of the best professional soldiers I've ever known."

"Almost your equal," Eb agreed. "Almost. I've never known a man who could pull off the strategies you did."

He chuckled. "I had a great tutor."

"Yes. I remember. Keep yourself safe."

"I'll do that."

"And stay clear of women you…care about," he added.

"No worries there. I hate women."

Eb almost bit his tongue through. "Okay. See you."

"See you. And thanks."

"That's what friends are for."

The connection went still. Wolf leaned back in the chair. Sara. He couldn't afford to see Sara, speak to her, touch her. He'd put a target on her forehead if he did. Ysera would kill her. He shivered gently as he recalled how vindictive Ysera was. The woman was psychotic. Emma had told him that, from the crumbs she dragged out of him. Sara had told her everything as he'd asked her to. Wolf couldn't open up to Emma. Perhaps he could manage that, later. He had to come to grips with the past so that he had a future with…

He bit down hard on the thought. His life was still full of danger. He did odd jobs for the government, black ops. He hadn't told Sara about them, but he thought she knew anyway, or suspected. He couldn't live without the adrenaline rushes.

If he got involved, he'd have to give it up. He was almost thirty-eight. He was slowing down just a little. He was physically fit, but he was slower. That made him a liability in a forward unit. So he was usually the tactical officer now, the planner.

He thought about Sara's beautiful breasts with a tiny head pressed against them, nursing. He thought of them with real hunger.

That was when he remembered what he'd done with Sara, and what the result could be. But he put it out of his mind. It wasn't likely. Besides, he couldn't think about a shared future until he dealt with the present, and he couldn't afford distractions. He was going to have to lay some false trails, to convince Ysera that he was really playing the field.

He picked up the phone and called the first number on his contacts list.

CHAPTER TEN

WOLF HAD SAID that he was going to break all contact with Sara for several weeks, while he made sure that she wasn't targeted by Ysera. Despite the pain of not seeing him, that would have been all right. Except that the third week after she left the ranch, she started losing her breakfast.

She hadn't really believed what Wolf, and then Emma, had told her, that pregnancy could result from intimacy that didn't include going all the way. She didn't know what to do. So for several days, she did nothing.

She noticed that she was followed everywhere she went. She tried to limit her trips to the store, to shop for groceries, to once a week. She had restaurants send food to the apartment, without knowing that every delivery boy was stopped and gently questioned by her unseen bodyguards. But she was nervous about what to do.

It would be impossible for her bodyguards not to notice that she went to a doctor, but she coughed loudly on the way there, hoping they'd hear and think she had a cough.

Dr. Medlin was young and sweet, blonde and pretty. She had the nurse draw blood and left Sara long enough to see another patient. But in minutes she was back with the results, and she wasn't smiling.

"You have decisions to make," she told the younger woman.

Sara closed her eyes. "I'm pregnant."

"Yes, you are. About three weeks, from what I can tell. Now, this might be a false positive. That can happen. But the other symptoms make it a fairly safe diagnosis. Do you want the baby?"

"With all my heart," Sara managed, averting her eyes.

"What about the father?"

She fought down fear. "He said he wanted to know, if it happened. He didn't…mean it to," she confessed. "It was a heavy petting session. You know I can't have, well, I've got that issue…"

The doctor put a hand over hers. "I know."

"So it didn't go all the way, but…"

"It doesn't have to."

Sara drew in a long breath. "I don't know what to do. I'll have to tell him. But if he wants me to go to a clinic…I don't know if I can." Her face was tragic. "I just don't think I can do that. But he said a decision that concerns both people shouldn't be made arbitrarily by one of them."

"I agree." She went on about prescriptions she was giving Sara and what they were for, but Sara rather blanked out during the conversation. She was thinking about her baby and how Wolf would react to the news that he was going to be a father. He'd never spoken of marriage. He was thirty-seven, and he'd only been seriously involved, as far as she knew, with one woman, with Ysera. If he'd stayed single all those years, it had to be from choice.

"Sara, did you hear me?" the doctor asked gently.

Sara smiled. "Yes. Of course." Sara stared at her hands. "Could you do something for me while I'm here?"

"Certainly. What?"

Sara flushed, but she told her.

The doctor only smiled. "Let me call the nurse in."

SHE BROODED FOR three days. But then she picked up her cell phone and sent a brief text to Wolf. She was afraid that it would make him angry. He'd warned her to have no contact with him. But he'd also said he wanted to know. She couldn't tell him over the phone. So she just asked, Will you be at the symphony Friday night?

He texted back one word, Yes.

He typed nothing else. Neither did she.

FRIDAY NIGHT, SHE put on a new black evening gown, one that had a little extra fullness in the belly, because there was new tautness there, a slight rise in the flesh. She looked radiant. Her eyes were wide and soft, her face more beautiful than ever. Her skin was extraordinarily clear and bright.

She smiled at her reflection. The drape of the gown left just the slopes of her breasts bare. It fell to her ankles, cut low in back, with wide straps and no sleeves. She paired it with diamond-and-emerald drop earrings, an emerald necklace that matched and an emerald-and-diamond dinner ring. She looked expensive, beautiful and happy.

She thought of the evening ahead. When Wolf saw her, his resolution to keep her at arm's length might go into eclipse. He might offer to take her home. She flushed, thinking about what could happen then. She could tell him much more easily if he was kissing her. She recalled the feel of his mouth, and she flushed even more.

It was going to be, she decided, the happiest night of her life. Wolf would want the baby. She was certain of it.

SHE HIRED A limousine for the evening. The driver, known to her, eased her into the backseat and drove her to the symphony. The orchestra would be playing Beethoven, not one of her favorite composers. But then, she wasn't really going to hear it. She was going to see Wolf, for the first time in weeks. Even Michelle's college graduation hadn't made her this happy.

She was nervous, but it didn't show. She spoke to people she knew on the way down the aisle. But her eyes ached for one particular sight, for a tall, handsome man in an evening jacket, a man with black hair and Arctic-blue eyes.

She went to her reserved seat and slid into it. She heard the orchestra already tuning up. She grimaced. She'd hoped to have time for a word with him, but it was going to be too late if he didn't hurry. He'd told her he'd be here. But what if he didn't show up?

Just then she saw a movement to her side. She turned, and there he was, so handsome that her heart twisted in her chest. He had a beautiful blonde woman in a white satin gown by his side. He was kissing her, laughing. She was holding on to him as if he held the keys to paradise.

Sara, so confident minutes before, felt her body go rigid with the beginnings of grief.

Wolf saw her and schooled his face to show nothing. Eb had phoned earlier. Ysera had someone working backstage. The man would be watching. Wolf had to put on a good act, to protect Sara. It was going to hurt her. He knew that, and it hurt him. But her life might depend on his ability to act. He'd taken a procession of gorgeous women to events like this over the past few weeks, to throw Ysera's spies off the track. He had to keep it up. He couldn't put Sara in danger, even if it meant snubbing her.

"Miss Brandon," he said with involuntary carelessness, as if she were only an acquaintance. "Cherry, this is Sara Brandon. Her brother is my best friend."

"So happy to meet you," Cherry gushed. "What a lovely gown!"

"Not as lovely as yours," Sara said, hiding her grief.

"I love clothes." The other woman laughed. "Especially I love wearing them for him." She looked up at Wolf with her heart in her eyes.

"He loves it, too." He chuckled, and bent to kiss her.

They sat down beside Sara, who was twisting her theater program into a rope. She averted her eyes to the stage and thanked God that the curtain was going up.

SHE NEVER KNEW, later, how she managed to get through the evening. Wolf was very polite, but it was as if they'd never talked, never kissed, never been intimate. She had his baby under her heart, and she could never tell him. Not now.

The concert concluded. Sara didn't even remember which of Beethoven's symphonies it was. She felt as if this was a dream, as if she wasn't even really here.

"Wasn't it lovely?" Cherry enthused. "Such gorgeous music!"

"Yes," Sara choked out. "Lovely."

"I hope I'll see you again sometime, Miss Brandon."

"Me, too."

"Good evening, Miss Brandon," Wolf said without meeting her eyes, and just a faint smile on his hard lips. "Let's go home," he told Cherry. "It's late."

"Oh, yes, isn't it?" Cherry replied and giggled as she pressed close to Wolf's side.

Behind him Sara stood like an elegant statue, her heart breaking inside her, a smile plastered to her face.

At the doorway, Wolf looked back at her. He had to drag his eyes away and harden his heart. If he did what he felt like, gathered her up in his arms and kissed her until the hurt left her beautiful face, he'd put her in the bull's-eye that he was already wearing. He left the theater smiling, with his heart breaking in his chest. He'd hurt her so much already. This was almost unbearable!

Sara went back to her apartment and cried herself to sleep. Wolf was involved with another woman. He was very involved. He didn't want Sara. He couldn't possibly have made that more evident.

She got up in the wee hours of the morning and turned on her computer. The minute she logged on, Rednacht whispered her.

Bad night? he asked.

The worst of my entire life, she confided.

Join the club, he typed.

She wanted to spill her heart out, to tell him what had happened, to cry on his shoulder. But he was a stranger and she was too shy, even with him, to talk about what had happened.

Love, she typed, is the most terrible emotion man ever discovered.

You can take that to the bank, he typed back. There was a hesitation. Someone hurt you.

Yes.

I hurt someone, he typed back slowly. Someone I care about. Because I had to. Because I cared.
That didn't make sense. Why?

I put her in danger, just by being seen with her.

She recalled that he was in law enforcement. He'd even said that he had enemies. Because of your job, she guessed.

Yes.

Does she know?

I can't tell her, he replied. He hesitated. Battleground or dungeon? he added. I feel like killing something.
She laughed to herself. So do I, she confessed. Battleground, she said. Higher body count, she added, and a lol.
He laughed back. Group with me. I'll queue us.
She did, thinking how grand it was to have at least one friend in the world whom she could talk to, in a sense. He had a woman in his life. That made her feel better, because she didn't really want to get involved with a stranger online. Sadly, the man she wanted didn't want her. It was a particularly bad time to discover it, too.

SHE WALKED TO a clinic that was two blocks from her apartment. She went in and out of stores, even took a taxicab for a block, to throw her escorts off the track. She didn't want this to get back to Wolf. It would hurt him, because he knew her so well. Even if he didn't want the baby, and how could he with his beautiful blonde companion, he would feel bad that Sara had been forced to go to such lengths. But she would do what she had to do. She was strong. She could manage it.

At least, she thought she could, until she was inside, filling out the paperwork. And right in the middle of it, she burst into tears.

The clerk patted her hand. "Honey, you're not ready for this," she said gently. "You go home and think about it for another day or two, okay? Then if you really want to do it, you come back."

Sara looked into the sympathetic black eyes. "Thanks."

The woman smiled. "You're welcome."

Sara got up and walked out, tears still rolling down her cheeks. She didn't realize that she was being seen. Her escorts weren't so easy to lose.

SARA ADVERTISED ONLINE, at a trusted source, for someone to stay with her. Gabriel had suggested it, because he worried about her being by herself, now that Michelle had an apartment of her own. She was alone, and Michelle was so involved in her new job as a reporter for a San Antonio newspaper that she wasn't really available. Besides, Sara didn't want her to know about the baby. It wouldn't be long before she started showing.

She had plans, though. She was going to go to the ranch in Catelow, Wyoming. It would be remote, but she had help there, good help. One of her head wranglers was ex-FBI. Another was a former policeman from

Billings, Montana. Nobody would threaten her; she'd be safe. And there would be little chance that she'd ever run into Wofford Patterson, which was the real draw. Of course Wolf did have a ranch himself in Wyoming, and it was very near the Brandons'. But in recent months, he hadn't visited it. She knew that from Gabriel. Besides, with his beautiful blonde girlfriend, he wasn't likely to stray so far.

She couldn't give up her child. She wasn't going to. For the first time in her life, she'd have someone to love her. She'd have a baby of her very own. The thought made her warm inside. If Wolf found out someday, she'd deal with it. Right now she had other things to organize.

Dr. Medlin had a friend in Sheridan who was an obstetrician. She gave Sara his office number and spoke to the doctor for her, to make sure she could fit into his schedule as a patient. He was fine with that.

Someone had answered the ad Sara placed for a companion online minutes after she placed it. The woman had agreed to come this morning. So when the doorbell rang, Sara went to answer it with vague misgivings. It was a big step, to share her life with a total stranger. She hoped the woman wouldn't be a kook.

She opened the door, her thoughts full of the baby, and met a pair of dark brown eyes in a frame of pale blond hair gathered into a tight bun. The woman was in her twenties, probably mid-twenties from the look of her. She didn't smile. Her mouth was pretty, but it made a straight line. Her posture was absolutely rigid.

"Miss…" She looked at the card in her hand. "Miss Brandon? I'm Amelia Grayson."

"I'm happy to meet you, Miss Grayson. Please come in."

The woman marched into the living room and took a straight chair. She sat very straight, staring at Sara. "What exactly do you require?"

"A companion," Sara said heavily.

"For what?" came the slow, suspicious reply.

Sara saw what she was thinking and burst out laughing. "No, not that. I'm sorry. I need someone to keep me company on a ranch in Wyoming," she said. "It's mostly men, you see." She grimaced. "I, sort of, have a hard time with men."

The other woman relaxed. Well, a little. "So do I," she said stiffly. "What sort of chores would be expected?"

"I'll do the cooking," Sara said. "I'm a gourmet chef. But I'll need help with housework. I have a dishwasher, all the usual appliances. You'd have Saturday evenings and Sundays off. And I pay quite well." She named a figure that had the other woman's jaw dropping.

"Miss Grayson?" Sara prompted.

The jaw closed. "The last place I worked," she said slowly, "I was expected to do cooking and cleaning and babysit four children, wash the car, walk four dogs and I got Sunday night off. They paid me about one-fifth of the figure you just quoted." She colored.

"Good Lord!" Sara exploded.

Miss Grayson was less stiff. "Shall we call it a probationary period, for a month, to see if we suit each other?"

Sara smiled. "Done. You can move in today if you like."

"I'll live here? I had a separate apartment where I came from…"

"Miss Grayson, you've been very badly treated by

someone," Sara said shortly. "But you're going to be my treasure. Of course you'll live here. You'll have insurance and benefits, as well...Miss Grayson!"

The other woman was crying. She pulled a tissue from her purse and dabbed at her eyes. "Sorry," she said abruptly. "Something in my eye." She looked at Sara and dared her to comment.

Sara smiled. "We're going to work well together. Quite well. Now let me show you to your room!"

GRAYSON WASN'T ONLY a treasure, she was a tireless worker. She could do the books, she knew how to sew and knit and crochet, and she was an ongoing handbook for the military, of all things. But when Sara asked if she'd ever been in the military, the other woman just laughed and denied it.

She'd worked for several families in the past four years since graduating from college, with a degree in, of all things, chemistry. She had an incredible brain. Sara was surprised that a woman of such intelligence would be willing to confine herself to menial tasks working as a domestic. But she didn't pry. It was early days yet. Sara was already delighted with her. She didn't want to risk losing her by digging into her private life.

THE WYOMING RANCH was huge. It covered hundreds of acres of land, adjoining a national forest. The ranch ran purebred Black Angus cattle and a small stock of horses, mostly a remuda from which the cowboys chose their working mounts. Sara had a horse of her own, a beautiful Appaloosa mare, snow-white with brown hailstone-patterned markings on her flanks. She was called

"Snow," and Sara loved her dearly. Her greatest sadness was that she was afraid to go riding, in her condition.

Grayson, fortunately, didn't know about the baby. She kept her secret. She'd noticed that Grayson had a Bible and read it at night while Sara watched movies on the Blu-ray player. A religious person might find her condition, out of wedlock, distasteful. She was reluctant to offend a woman who was quickly becoming indispensable.

THE NIGHTMARES HAD receded for a time. But back in Wyoming, they returned with a vengeance. She sat up in bed, having screamed herself awake, drenched with sweat and crying.

Grayson came running, in a long gown and an equally long robe, both of serviceable cotton.

"Miss Brandon, what is it?" she exclaimed. Her long hair was escaping from its bun. She looked very unlike the prim, sedate young woman Sara had come to know.

"Night…mare," Sara choked out. She leaned her head on her raised knees. "Sorry. I should have told you that I have them." Tears fell harder.

"I'll be right back," Grayson said.

She returned a minute later with a wet washcloth, sat down beside Sara and proceeded to mop up her face. "I put on some chamomile tea," she said gently. "Come into the kitchen."

Sara slid into a robe that matched her cotton jersey pajamas and went almost stumbling behind Grayson into the kitchen. She sat down at the table. For some reason, this time Wolf had been in the dream. He'd been in some dark, dangerous place. She didn't remember much of it, but there had been blood. So much blood…!

"Here." Grayson put a cup of tea in front of her. "You drink that. It will help calm you."

"Thanks, Miss Grayson," Sara said huskily. She bit her lip. "I'm sorry…"

"Everybody has nightmares," the other woman said gently.

Sara smiled sadly. "Not like mine, I'm afraid."

"Something bad happened to you," was the surprising reply.

Sara's eyes came up, shocked.

Grayson nodded. "When you were a child?"

Sara bit her lower lip.

"You don't have to talk to me about it. But you should talk to someone."

Sara laughed softly. "I have a psychologist. We have sessions on Skype." Her black eyes gleamed with faint humor. "She keeps snakes."

Grayson frowned. "Emma Cain?"

Sara gasped. "How in the world…?"

"Don't ask. I won't tell you."

Sara opened her mouth and then closed it.

"That's right, fight those impulses," Grayson said with a hint of humor. "I don't talk about my past, either."

Sara was intrigued. Her eyebrows arched.

"Shame, shame on you for thinking things like that!" the other woman said tartly. "You should have your brain washed out with soap!"

Sara burst out laughing.

Grayson actually grinned. "That's all better."

Sara sighed and shook her head. "Grayson, you're the best idea I ever had in my life. And if you ever try to quit, I'll have Marsden track you down and bring you right back."

"Marsden?"

"He's a former FBI agent. Our foreman here."

"Oh, that tall man. He's nice."

"Very." Sara sipped her tea. She was feeling a little queasy, but the liquid really was calming. "This is good."

"I like herbal teas. You drink too much coffee," she said gently.

"It's decaf," Sara said. "I just make it strong. I can't give it up entirely."

"I had to," Grayson said sadly. "I miss it."

"You could have decaf."

"It would be like eating steak through a straw."

Sara laughed again. "Okay, I give up."

"Good thing. I almost never lose a battle." She leaned back in her chair and sighed. "I'm so glad you wanted to move up here instead of down to Comanche Wells," she said conversationally.

"But the ranch there is just like this one," she began, puzzled.

"He lives in Comanche Wells," she said through her teeth.

"He?"

"A man I...know," she faltered. "I'm never going back there."

Sara felt sympathy pains. She thought of Wolf's huge ranch, and the joy she'd felt at being with him, despite the troubling intimate memories she shared with him. He hadn't called after the opera. She'd hoped that he might call, or text, or tell her it was a mistake, he didn't care about his gorgeous companion. But that was stupid. It was painfully obvious that he didn't want Sara. She had to learn to accept it.

"Don't worry," Sara said gently. "I don't ever want to go back to Comanche Wells, either."

Grayson looked at her evenly.

"For the same reason you have," she said stiffly.

"Oh." Grayson sipped her own tea. She looked thoughtful. But after a minute, her face became placid again. "Think you can sleep now?"

Sara smiled drowsily. "I think so. Thanks, Grayson. Thanks very much."

"It was no trouble at all," she replied.

"YOU CAN'T DO THIS," Eb Scott raged. "You'll be walking headfirst into a trap if you go near her, don't you know that?"

The tall man with blue eyes wasn't listening. He was assembling his gear, putting on clothes that would alert any intelligent viewer that he was highly involved in black ops. Black clothing, Velcro holster that strapped around one powerful thigh, automatic weapons, leather gloves, combat boots. He looked professional. Which he was.

He turned to Eb Scott. "I have nothing left to live for," he said bluntly. "She's destroyed my life, any chance I might have had for happiness. She's out there, right now, plotting to take other lives. I'm going to give her a chance at me, to bring her out into the open. I've called in markers from three nations. I'll have all the backup I can get, including a couple of covert federal agencies that I won't even tell you about. If she kills me, so what?" he added shortly. "It will just stop the pain."

Eb grimaced. "Listen, I know you didn't want to put Sara on the firing line. You can tell her when we've got Ysera in custody…"

"She will never speak to me again as long as I live," he said in a haunted tone. His eyes were so full of pain that Eb couldn't even meet them.

"You don't know that."

"I do."

"How? You haven't had any contact with her..."

"Your men kept a written record of her movements until she went to Wyoming, the week after I saw her at the symphony concert," he said quietly. "I read it."

"So?"

Wolf looked down at his unzipped kit with eyes that didn't see. "She went to a clinic, Eb," he said in a voice as cold as death. "I was making up to the woman I was with. Sara didn't know why, and I couldn't tell her. She thought I didn't want her anymore, that a baby would complicate everything. So she went to a...clinic." He had to stop. His voice broke. He dashed at a wetness in his eyes that he hadn't felt in years.

"Oh, God, I'm sorry!" Eb groaned.

"It will hurt her even more, to have done that. And she was carrying enough scars already, from her past."

"The baby was yours?" Eb asked slowly.

Wolf's eyes went dangerous. He moved closer to the other man. "What the hell kind of woman do you think Sara is? Of course it was mine!"

He was sorry about the baby. From what he knew about Sara, she couldn't even swat a fly. What it would do to her emotions was unthinkable.

"Sorry," Eb said gently.

Wolf backed down. "Same," Wolf replied tersely. "This, all of this, from the way I've been for years to Sara's termination, was Ysera's fault." His eyes grew cold. Ice-cold. He turned to Eb. "She's going to pay for what she did. I'm going to make sure of it."

He turned and zipped up the bag.

"WHAT THE HELL is going on?" Gabriel asked, aghast at Wolf's unexpected presence in his camp. "You're retired!"

"Not anymore," Wolf said. He looked different. He was different. The rancher who teased his sister unmercifully, made her mad and laughed, was gone. In his place was this cold-eyed mercenary, the man Wolf had been when Gabriel first met him.

"Sara won't tell me anything," Gabriel persisted. "She's gone to live on the ranch in Wyoming, for God's sake. Sara talked to me, but under it there was a terrible sadness..."

"Don't," Wolf said huskily, and averted his eyes.

"All right. Let's have it!" Gabriel got right in his face. "Now!"

The other man didn't even react. "You're the best friend I have in the world. This is going to hurt you."

"Tell me!"

Wolf looked down at his combat boots. "I don't know how."

"You've hurt her."

Wolf nodded. He drew in a breath. "Yes," he said, lowering his eyes. He closed his eyes and shuddered. "She asked me if I was going to the Beethoven concert, in a text, and I told her I was. She looked...like an angel, so beautiful that she almost blinded me. I was there with a companion, a blonde woman I'd dated. I was making up to her, pretending I cared about her..."

"You what?" Gabriel exploded.

"Ysera had someone in the theater," he continued, blind to the other man's sudden stillness. "I couldn't put Sara in danger. I didn't dare pay her any attention, show in the least way that I… So I ignored her, treated her like an acquaintance." He closed his eyes and shivered. "I hurt her so badly. I couldn't even tell her why. I couldn't talk to her, contact her, without giving Ysera a second target." He couldn't look at Gabriel. "Sara thought I'd turned my back on her. So the next morning…" He had to stop before he could finish it. "She went to a…clinic."

Gabriel stared at him. "A clinic?" He suddenly realized what Wolf was saying. His mind almost exploded with the realization that his sister, who couldn't tolerate a man's lightest touch, had become pregnant by his best friend. "A clinic?"

Wolf nodded. His eyes had a fine mist. He turned his head. His face was pale, tormented. "She can't hurt anything," he said dully. "Not anything. To do that, to have it on her conscience…" He turned back to his friend. "Shoot me," he said. "It would be a mercy."

"Dear God." Gabriel saw it all, saw what the other man felt, saw what Sara felt. "Dear God," he repeated, almost reverently. "She loves you," he said slowly.

"I know," the other man said in a strangled tone. He averted his eyes. His high cheekbones were flushed. "I had plans. All sorts of plans. And then Ysera decided to get even. I told Sara that I wouldn't be able to contact her for a few weeks. She knew about Ysera. But she didn't know what I was going to have to do to protect her. That I was going to have to be seen with a parade of women, so that Ysera didn't realize there was one that I couldn't…live without." His eyes closed. "Sara had my baby under her heart, and she thought I was involved with someone else, that I didn't want her. She thought… the baby would be in my way. I can't…live with it!"

"God, I'm sorry," Gabriel said heavily.

Wolf straightened, his eyes terrible to look into. "No. I'm sorry, for the mess I made of her life." He took a minute to get his emotions back under control. "To my credit, I did get her into therapy."

"Therapy? Sara? You did? How?" Gabriel asked, aghast. He'd tried for years to accomplish that.

"You remember Emma Cain?"

Gabriel shuddered. "She keeps snakes."

Wolf nodded. "But she's good at her job. As to how I got Sara to do it, I…talked to Cain, too."

Gabriel was stunned. "You never…"

"I never would agree to it," he said, nodding. "But Sara and I, well…" He paused. He couldn't talk about it to his best friend, not when it was about Gabriel's sister. He colored. "We sort of had an encounter. Sort of. There shouldn't have been a baby. But there was."

Gabriel read between the lines. "Sara had to love you, for that to happen…"

"Yes." He lowered his head with an unsteady intake of breath. "She must be in hell now, because of me. I hate having her alone…!"

"She isn't," Gabriel said. "She advertised for a companion when she went up to the ranch, so I had made sure that the woman she hired was someone I trust to take care of her. She'll be all right."

"Someone you know?"

"Never mind who. I would call Sara," Gabriel said, miserable, "but we've got orders to maintain radio silence. I can't even tell her where I am or what's going on."

Wolf's face was like stone. "Ysera is the reason Sara went to the clinic. She made me hurt Sara, in order to protect her. She cost me our child. And I'm going to make her pay for it, if it's the last thing I ever do in this life!"

"You care about Sara," Gabriel said slowly.

"Care!" He laughed hollowly. "My God!" His face was a study in anguish. He drew in another breath. "I need a few things," he said after a minute, trying to erase the pain from his hard features.

But Gabriel saw. He understood. He put a big hand on the other man's shoulder. "Whatever you need. I'll get it."

"Thanks."

"She'll get over it," Gabriel said haltingly. "When she knows the truth, she'll get over it."

Wolf looked him right in the eye. "No," he said. "She won't."

YSERA HAD BOUGHT a nightclub, right in the marketplace. Called El Maroc, it featured authentic Moroccan dishes and it had belly dancers imported from Spain, because no decent Arab woman would dream of showing her body to men. But the real purpose of the establishment was a cover for what went on inside. It was a den for thieves who dealt in kidnapping, prostitution, drugs and worse.

Wolf looked around with cold, pale eyes. He had a .45 automatic hidden in a holster under the black jacket he was wearing. He had a Ka-Bar in a sheath on his belt, a hide gun in a big boot. He was ready for anything she could throw at him.

In the shadows he recognized a contact, a fed who

worked in black ops in the region. He pretended not to see the man, who returned the favor.

He walked slowly down the aisle and seated himself at a table near the open area where the belly dancers were doing their thing to the rhythm of an imported Moroccan band. He ordered a whiskey and settled back to watch the dancers. He knew without being told that he was also being watched, by the not-so-concealed surveillance cameras mounted near the ceiling.

Sure enough, he'd had just one sip of the drink when he caught a whiff of a very familiar perfume.

He turned his head, just barely, and a tall brunette wearing a slinky black dress, dripping with diamonds, came toward him. Her long black hair was flowing down her back. Her black eyes were amused, as they'd always been amused every time she looked at him. Under the amusement was utter contempt.

"Hello, Ysera," he said in a conversational tone.

CHAPTER ELEVEN

SARA DROVE HERSELF to the obstetrician's office, having lied to Grayson about needing a few things from town and just wanting to get some fresh air. It was spring, and everything was blooming and beautiful.

Dr. Hansen was tall and lanky, with an easy smile and a good personality. He examined her while the nurse stood by. He poked and prodded, frowned and then ordered lab work. When he came back, he was frowning.

"Oh, please, there can't be anything wrong with my baby," she cried.

"No, no, the baby is fine!" he said at once.

"Thank God!"

"There's a slight problem. It's nothing major." His eyes narrowed. "You have a heart condition."

She bit her lower lip. "It's not a bad one. It's a birth defect…"

"Wolff-Parkinson-White Syndrome," he said, nodding. "It shouldn't cause problems, but it can. You have to be monitored. I want to send you to a local cardiologist, just to make sure there aren't any complications when you deliver."

"Okay," she said.

"He can talk to you about the hypertension, as well."

"All right." She was puzzled. Dr. Medlin had mentioned that term. "It's something to do with stress, yes?"

"It can be. Just keep taking the tablets," he said, grinning, assuming that Dr. Medlin would have told her all about the hypertension. "Nothing to worry about there. Honest."

She was relieved. She held a soft hand over her belly. She didn't even show yet. That hard little lump, however, was beloved to her.

"You really want this child," he said, fascinated.

"More than anything in the world."

He hesitated. "Does the father know?"

She paused. She shook her head. "He doesn't want me. I...can't tell him. I will," she promised. "I'll have to. But not right now. Okay?"

"I don't pry," he said. "But a man has a right to know."

She nodded. "I agree."

He smiled. "Okay, then. Joan will make the appointment for you and call to tell you when it is. I'll want to see you again in about a month."

"Thanks," she said.

"All in a day's work." He chuckled.

WOLF GLARED INTO Ysera's eyes as she slid a long-fingered hand across the table and teasingly drew it over the back of his hand.

He didn't move it, as he once might have done because she aroused him that way in the past. He just looked at her.

She was startled. But she hid it quickly. "I'm surprised to see you here," she said. Her smile turned to pure sarcasm. "Wasn't destroying my business revenge enough for you? Have you come to pay me back? I don't see why. All I did was teach you pleasure," she purred.

"No. You taught me subjugation and humiliation," he returned blandly. "I was a good student."

"You wanted me more than any other." She laughed. "Once we did it on the floor of the bar, behind the counter, with people all around because you couldn't wait."

The humiliation of that encounter made him sick. But he didn't react. This was another way she'd controlled him, with embarrassing memories. He just stared at her.

"You're...different," she said slowly. Her dark eyes narrowed, and she smiled with vengeance. "I knew there had to be a woman, somewhere. I've got men digging. They'll find out who she is. When they do—" she leaned forward, almost purring "—I'll kill her, lover. I'll have them rape her..."

"You aren't killing anyone. Ever again." He cocked the pistol under the table. His smile was so cold that she shivered.

She hadn't seen that coming. She would never have expected it of her old lover. She looked around.

"Your men are being rounded up as we speak," he said, still smiling. "Your records have been confiscated by the appropriate agency, your business associates are being questioned. And you are headed for a very long prison sentence, if not capital murder charges."

"You'll go down with me!" she said furiously. "You killed that man and his family...!"

"Sent by you, on a tip," he said. "The incident was investigated, and my men and I were cleared. But you weren't. It's why you ran. But your number's up, honey," he added. "You aren't running. Never again."

"Let them arrest me," she said angrily, reaching

into her pocket unobtrusively. She pushed a button and prayed that it would work, that the man who held the receiver wasn't yet in custody. "I can work from prison," she said. She smiled. "I can find your woman and have her killed, from the deepest, darkest jail cell they can put me in! You'll never be safe! She'll never be safe!"

While she was raging at him, a man ducked out from behind a curtain and took aim.

Wolf saw the intent, the triumph in her eyes, a split second too late to save himself. But even as the bullet sang through his chest from behind, his finger on the trigger, the safety off, he sent another bullet under the table, right into Ysera's body. As he lost consciousness, he saw the utter shock in her eyes and the tiniest trail of blood running out of her perfect red lips…

SARA DROVE BACK toward the house, but she was unsettled by Dr. Hansen wanting to send her to a cardiologist. Surely he didn't think her little heart defect would be dangerous to the baby? And what had he said about hypertension? She knew she'd been under a lot of stress lately, so maybe that was the reason for the capsules he'd prescribed. Stress could cause a lot of problems.

She touched her belly, smiling to herself as she drove. The baby would be fine. It only hurt that she couldn't tell Wolf. But he didn't want her. He'd made that perfectly clear. A baby would only complicate his life, so it was better to say nothing.

She was so busy with her thoughts that she missed her turn. Instead of going to her ranch, she was on the road to Rancho Real. It belonged to the Kirk brothers, Mallory and Dalton and Cane. But Mallory's wife was her friend. She and Morie Brannt Kirk had been friends

for many years, having met at a society function in San
Antonio when Morie was still living in Branntville with
her father, mother and brother.

Sara smiled, remembering that Morie had been a
tireless worker when it came to the huge ranch sales
that King Brannt was famous for. He ran purebred Santa
Gertrudis cattle, and his young bull crop was sold out
every single year. In fact, the Kirks had purchased a
new seed bull from him over a year ago.

It had been a rocky road to the altar for Morie and
her husband, Mallory Kirk. Morie, sick of men wanting her for her father's money, had run away to Wyoming and signed on at the Rancho Real as a cowgirl.
King had never allowed her to become involved in any
way with ranch work, so she'd learned it with the help
of Darby Hanes, the Kirks' foreman.

She'd been doing quite well at it, too, until Mallory's
evil girlfriend had planted evidence and accused her of
stealing a priceless objet d'art from a curio cabinet in
the Kirk home.

Morie had gone home heartbroken that Mallory
hadn't believed her protestations of innocence.

Then Mallory had gone to the production sale at
Skylance, King Brannt's ranch in Texas, and come
face-to-face with a beautiful young debutante dripping
diamonds—Morie.

King had almost had Mallory for supper.

Morie still laughed when she told the story. Mallory's ex-girlfriend, who'd accused Morie of the theft, had
been speechless and terrified when she'd discovered her
victim wasn't some poor cowgirl, after all.

Then Mallory was kidnapped by an escaped criminal. Morie had gone to save him, despite protests from

her father, because she knew the man who'd threatened him. She'd managed to get the criminal to tell her where Mallory was. It had been a very brave thing to do, but Morie had loved Mallory too much to sit by and let him die.

Remembering how King and Mallory had made peace afterward, Sara smiled. From enemies to good friends. King had even been at the ranch just after Morie's son was born to go trout fishing with Mallory.

Sara pulled up at the front door and got out. Morie must have seen her drive up, because she came to the door with the baby in her arms, her eyes wide with surprise when she saw her old friend.

"Come in and have coffee!" Morie said, hugging her. "I was going to come over to see you in a day or two. I only just heard that you were back on the ranch." The last comment was almost an accusation.

"Sorry, I didn't let anyone know I was coming," Sara said softly. "I've had…a few problems."

Morie led her into the living room. Mavie, the housekeeper, was hovering.

"I haven't gotten to hold him all day," Mavie complained. "How about I get you and Sara something to eat, and then I'll take the baby."

"That's a deal." Morie laughed.

Mavie brought coffee and cake on an antique silver service, then took the little boy in her arms and left for the child's room.

"She's such a treasure," Morie told her friend. "I don't know what we'd do without her."

"She seems very nice." Sara sipped coffee and frowned. Her eyebrows arched. "Latte?" she asked.

"Where did you get a latte? Is there a Starbucks nearby?"

Morie grinned. "It's a European coffee pod. I get them from Germany. Isn't it delicious?"

"It really is. Just like going into a coffee shop." She sighed and savored the taste.

"If you're here, then Gabriel must be overseas," Morie remarked.

"Yes. Another dangerous place, I assume," she agreed. "He can't live without the adrenaline rushes. I do worry, though."

"I know you do." She put her cup down and studied her friend closely. "Something's wrong."

Sara made a face. "You could always tell, couldn't you?"

"We've been friends for a long time." Morie leaned forward. "Come on. Give."

Sara bit her lower lip. "I'm…pregnant."

Morie, who knew Sara's whole history, sat with her jaw dropped and her eyes like black saucers. "You're…"

"Pregnant," Sara repeated helpfully.

Morie fanned herself. "Well, he must be one special man, considering your background."

"Yes. He was…very special." Sara lowered her eyes. "But he didn't want me. Not for keeps. I saw him in San Antonio. I'd asked if he was going to be at the symphony concert that night. He said yes. I was going to tell him about the baby." She closed her eyes and shivered. "He was there—with a gorgeous blonde. He was very cool with me, indifferent. He was playing up to his companion for all he was worth. I knew then that it was all over."

"I'm so sorry, Sara," Morie said gently, placing her hand over the other woman's.

"I thought… Well, you know, a baby needs two parents, and he didn't want me. I thought it would be for the best…" She swallowed. "I went to a clinic. Well, I tried to go to a clinic. I just broke down completely. The lady was so sweet. She said I needed to go home and think about it some more. So I did." She smiled ruefully. "I couldn't do it. Maybe he doesn't want a child, but I do," she said with breathless tenderness as she smoothed her hand over her stomach with a tiny smile. "I want him more than anything in the world."

"That man should be keelhauled," Morie bit out.

"It's not his fault, really," she said. "You have no idea what he's been through in his life. It was much worse than anything I've had to endure. He doesn't trust people. In his place, I wouldn't, either. I wanted to love him, but he wouldn't let me."

Morie's dark eyes narrowed. "You still love him."

Sara smiled ruefully. "With all my heart," she confessed. "You can't kill love. I've tried, believe me."

"He may find out," she said.

"It's not likely. He and my brother are friends, but Gabriel doesn't know. And I can swear him to secrecy. He'll be angry, though."

"No doubt about that."

She drew in a breath and sipped more coffee. "So I don't have to worry about being discovered for a while, anyway. Meanwhile, I'm going to enjoy the peace and quiet up here. I have an obstetrician. I also have a companion," she added with a grin.

"A companion?"

She nodded. "Her name is Amelia Grayson. She's a

sweetheart. She takes care of the house and me. She's been badly treated by people she's worked for, but I'm spoiling her. She's already indispensable. And besides that, she can cook." She laughed.

"Truly indispensable," Morie agreed.

"Your little boy is precious. I can't decide if he looks more like you or Mal."

"Both of us," she said, her smile dreamy. "I never imagined I could be so happy." She shook her head. "I thought my father was going to kill Mal before I'd ever have the chance to marry him."

"Nobody who knew you would ever think you'd steal something."

"Yes, well, Gelly Bruner was very convincing. She never wanted Mal, but he was wealthy and she wanted to be." She laughed. "If you could have seen her face when she and Mal showed up at the production sale! She looked as if she'd tried to swallow a watermelon whole!"

"I imagine Mal looked pretty much the same," Sara said drily.

"Yes, he did. I didn't know that Dad had invited Mal to the sale. Not until he walked in with Gelly and my father made a beeline for Uncle Danny when he greeted them. Then Uncle Danny motioned me over with Darryl— You remember Darryl?"

"I do, indeed. He's a very nice-looking man."

"Very sweet, too, but I didn't really want to marry him. I was hurting from Mal's rejection, feeling sorry for myself, or I'd never have agreed to be engaged to him."

"He'll find someone one day."

"Someone who deserves him, I hope."

"How's your brother?"

She rolled her eyes. "Who knows? He's having chicken problems."

Sara blinked. "Excuse me?"

"His next-door neighbor has a rooster. The rooster hates Cort. It actually comes onto the ranch to attack him. The last I heard, it had run through several cowboys, one of whom landed in a very unmentionably smelly substance. And then it chased Cort clean up onto the porch. He tried to shoot it and missed…"

Sara was laughing uproariously. "A rooster?"

"A rooster. He's complained to the owner, but she loves the stupid animal, and she won't get rid of it."

"Who is the owner?"

"A sweet young woman who's trying to run a small ranch all by herself, with a little help from her great-aunt. I think she's sweet on Cort, but that rooster is making an enemy of him. Besides," she said sadly, "there's Odalie Everett."

"Heather's daughter," Sara said as she nodded, recalling the beautiful young woman with the voice of an angel.

"She wants to sing grand opera. Cort wants to marry her, but she's full of herself and thirsting for a career in music. He just mourns constantly. Right now she's in Italy training with a voice teacher."

"Poor Cort."

"He was sweet on you once," Morie said, tongue in cheek.

She laughed. "Only for one day, until he realized that I don't date."

"At the time, I thought you'd never have a normal life," Morie told her gently. She smiled quizzically.

"You look...I don't know...different. You don't have that haunted look I remember."

"It's the baby," Sara replied. "I've never been so happy. Or so miserable." She looked down into her cup. "If he could have loved me, I'd never have wanted anything more from life."

Morie sighed. "Men. You really can't live without them, but they can be one big headache."

"I noticed." She glanced at her watch. "Goodness, I have to go. Amelia's making crepes for supper."

"She can make crepes?"

"She's a marvelous cook," Sara said.

"Coming from you, that's high praise," Morie replied, because she knew that her friend was a gourmet chef.

"I'm hungry. I never have much appetite when I have to go to the doctor."

"What did the doctor say?"

Sara smiled. "That I'm doing well, the baby's doing well and I have to go and see a cardiologist," she added heavily.

"A cardiologist?"

"I have a heart defect," Sara said, smiling. "It's just a small one, and he says it won't impact delivery, but he wants to keep an eye on it just the same. He said it's nothing to worry about."

"Thank goodness!"

Sara hugged her. "You're a nice woman. I'm sorry I haven't visited until now, but things have been pretty hectic. I've been living in San Antonio for the longest time. It takes some getting used to, being up here again."

"You'll love it when you get acclimated. Spring here is unbelievable!"

"Better than Texas?" Sara teased.

"Different," her friend replied, smiling. "But beautiful."

Morie walked her out to the car, looking around at the towering lodgepole pines swaying in the breeze.

"Aren't they magnificent?" she asked. "We don't have trees like this in Texas."

"No, we don't. And they are magnificent."

"Come back when you can stay longer," Morie coaxed. "I'll let you play with the baby."

"That's an incentive!" Sara laughed. "I'll need lessons. I don't even know how to do diapers or make formula…"

"You might consider breast-feeding," Morie replied. "It gives the baby a head start. And it's much better than formula."

"I'll research that," Sara said.

"You and the internet," Morie said, shaking her head. "Still playing that video game every night?"

"Almost every night," Sara agreed. She smiled. "I have a friend. He's in the same faction I am. We sort of hold each other together. He's damaged, too," she said with a sad smile. "I don't know who he is, but he says he's in law enforcement. He's very kind. I don't really have anybody to talk to."

"You do. Right here," Morie said, indicating herself.

"Thanks."

"You're welcome. I'll call you in a week or two and we'll go out to eat."

"I'd like that." She opened the door and climbed in under the steering wheel. "Thanks for being a good listener."

"That's what friends are for. You call me if you need me. I don't care what time it is."

"I will. Thanks again."

"Drive safely," Morie said.

Sara smiled, turned on the ignition and pulled away.

Grayson was waiting at the front door when she got home.

"Finally!" she said. "I was getting worried."

"You could have called me." Sara laughed.

"On what?" Grayson held up a cell phone. It was Sara's. She'd forgotten to take it with her.

"Ah, well, how nice that I wasn't kidnapped by marauding terrorists on the way home," she said with a grin.

Grayson grinned back. "It's nice to see you smile for a change," she remarked.

Sara drew in a breath as she put up her jacket and purse. "I haven't had a lot to smile about," she confessed. "But I'm getting better."

She turned. Grayson did look worried.

"I'm really getting better," Sara emphasized.

"Okay, then. I've got crepes almost ready. I made meringues for dessert, too."

"My favorite!"

Grayson laughed. "I noticed."

Sara followed her into the kitchen. She was still a little queasy, but she didn't dare let on. Grayson didn't know that she was pregnant. The other woman was deeply religious, and she might find Sara's condition offensive. She might quit. Better to let explanations ride for a time, Sara decided. Grayson was a treasure.

They'd just finished supper when someone knocked at the front door.

Grayson immediately got between Sara and the door. She looked out the peephole and drew back as if she'd seen a snake.

"Who is it?" Sara asked.

Grayson opened the door without speaking.

A tall man with pale gray eyes moved into view. He smiled at Sara.

"Ty!" she exclaimed. She knew him because he'd helped the defense attorney gather information to clear the police officer who'd shot her stepfather. She'd liked him. He and Gabe had become friends. Later, Morie had told her about Ty helping to track an escaped criminal who had taken Mallory prisoner, when Morie had searched for him. "What are you doing up here?"

"I'm on a case," he said. "Amazing how much business we're doing in Wyoming lately, and I work out of Houston."

"Come in! Have you eaten? Amelia made crepes. I think there are two left..."

Ty spotted the blonde woman standing beside Sara as the door opened all the way. His smile vanished. He gave Amelia a long, quiet look.

"Hello, Grayson," he said.

She nodded slowly. "Harding."

Sara frowned. "You two know each other?"

"Slightly," Grayson said tautly. "Very slightly."

Ty took longer to adjust to the unexpected encounter. He lifted his chin. "It's been a long time."

Sara was puzzled at the tension. "He lives in Houston, and you're from San Antonio, aren't you?" she asked Grayson.

"I grew up in Comanche Wells," Grayson said in

a dull tone. "He spent summers there with his grand-parents."

"We were in high school at the time," Ty agreed. He studied Grayson quietly. "It was a long time ago."

Grayson nodded. She didn't meet his eyes.

"Have you seen Currier?" he asked.

She went very stiff. "No. He's in Africa."

Ty grimaced. "He wouldn't let it go, would he? It wasn't your fault."

"It was my fault," she returned, moving away.

"Come have coffee at least," Sara coaxed, fascinated with what she was learning about her new companion without a word being spoken.

Ty hesitated. Amelia looked tortured. "I'd better go. I just wanted to say hello and see how Gabriel was. I haven't heard from him."

"He's doing very well," Sara said, "as far as I know. They're involved in some sort of secret project, probably classified, in a country near Saudi Arabia."

"When you hear from him, ask him to call me, would you?" Ty said. "I've had an offer. I think he might be interested, too."

"Aren't you still working for Dane Lassiter's private detective agency in Houston?" Sara asked.

"Yes, but I'm looking at a change," he said.

Sara smiled. "And that's all I'm getting out of you, yes?"

He chuckled. "That's it."

"Well, it was good to see you just the same."

He smiled. "Good to see you, too, Sara."

"I'll have Gabe call you," she promised.

"Thanks." He glanced past her at Amelia's straight back. "I'll see you, Grayson."

She didn't reply. She just nodded.

Sara closed the door and went to her. "You know him," she said.

Amelia nodded, eyes downcast. "We were friends once," she said.

"Just friends?"

Amelia closed up like a sensitive plant. Her smile looked forced. "Only archaeologists should dig up the past," she said. "How about a meringue?"

Sara gave up. "Okay. I'd love one."

Amelia led the way back into the kitchen. Sara was having a hard time getting her breath. Amelia turned, frowning. "You're huffing like a steam engine."

Sara laughed. "I guess I am." She hesitated, remembering. "I went by to see Morie Kirk on the way home. We were friends when she lived in Texas. We had lattes," she added. "I don't drink caffeine much anymore. I guess that's what did it."

"No more coffee," Amelia fussed.

Sara laughed. "Okay. No more coffee. I have a slight heart defect," she confessed. "I'm not supposed to drink anything caffeinated. But the coffee was so good!" she added with a sigh.

"I like lattes, too," Amelia confessed with a laugh. "But you should probably leave it alone."

"I do agree."

That night, before she tried to sleep, Sara's mind again went over the encounter with Wolf at the symphony concert, at his indifference to Sara, his intense interest in his blonde companion. It was like a knife straight through her. They'd been so close, just for a brief time at his ranch, after the trauma that had opened the floodgates of the past for each of them.

She'd loved him. She'd thought they had a real future together.

Then she'd seen him with his companion. She'd planned to tell him that night about the baby. She'd planned more than just that. But fate had thrown a spanner into the works. What had begun in breathless anticipation had ended in heartache.

Now here she was, pregnant with a child he'd never know. He was going around with other women and apparently no regrets whatsoever about Sara. It hurt more than anything else had in her whole life, even more than her tragic past.

The worst of it was that she still loved him. How she could love a two-timing, heartless rat like him was one terrible puzzle. She should hate him. She'd tried to hate him. But he haunted her, even in memory.

She gave a thought to Grayson's odd behavior with their visitor, Ty Harding. There was something there. She knew there was. She wondered what. Maybe someday, if she ever got her own life straightened out, she could do something to help poor Grayson. She had a feeling that Amelia had her own tragedy to deal with.

She turned out the light and tried to sleep. But it was almost daylight before she finally did.

SARA WAS FIXING a salad when the phone rang. She reached for it, certain that it would be the nurse giving her news of the cardiologist or Michelle with news about her job. It was neither.

"Sara?" Eb Scott said solemnly. "Is that you?"

She sat down hard, shaking. She remembered the nightmare she'd had, almost as if her mind had been connected to Wofford Patterson's in some strange manner. "It's Wolf. Something's happened to Wolf!"

He could hear the terror in her voice. "Slow down, it's okay. He's been shot, yes. We've airlifted him back to a hospital in Houston. He's very bad, but he's calling for you…"

"I'll be on the next plane out of here!"

"Get a limo to the airport," he said firmly. "I'll have a plane waiting for you, to take you straight to Houston. Someone will meet you in the lobby at Sheridan with a sign. Go with him."

"Yes. Yes." She was sobbing. "He has to live. He must live!"

"The doctors are doing everything they can. It's just…"

"What?"

"Contact the limo company. Then call me back. I'll tell you everything."

She phoned the service, begged for a car for an emergency and got one on the way. She called Eb back while she directed Grayson to start packing for her.

"I'll explain in a minute," she told the other woman.

"Scott," came the reply when she'd punched in the number.

"It's me. Tell me!"

"He knows you went to the clinic," he said heavily. "He went crazy. You see, he didn't dare talk to you that night. Ysera had a man in the theater. Wolf was scared to death that if she knew he had any feelings for you at all, she'd have you killed. She had the money and the means, and people in place to do it. He took out a lot of women for a few weeks to throw her off the track."

"Dear God." She shivered. Tears ran down her cheeks.

"So he didn't care what happened after that," he said, hating to tell her. "He went after Ysera himself."

"Oh, no," she groaned. She clenched her teeth. "She shot him!"

"No. She called in one of her hired guns to do it. But she made a fatal error. Wolf had a .45 aimed at her. When the henchman fired, so did he. I'm not sure he meant to. He really wanted her in custody to stand trial. It was reflex, when the bullet hit him."

She was sobbing now. "He must live," she whispered. "Or I can't. I can't. I won't! I won't live without him!"

"Sara," he said urgently, "Sara, he's still alive. You have to come up here. Tell him. It might be enough…"

She heard a car drive up. She looked out the window through tears. "The limo's here."

"The plane's landing at the airport now. It's a big DC-3. Ex-military, and no creature comforts, but you'll get here safely. Okay?"

"Okay. Eb…thank you!"

"Thank you. He's my friend, too."

"Have you spoken to Gabriel?"

"I can't," he said miserably. "There are things going on, classified things. I can't contact him and neither can you. I'm sorry. He'd come, if he knew. Wolf is his best friend."

"I'm on my way."

"I'll see you in Houston."

She hung up. Grayson had everything packed for a couple of nights. Sara kissed her cheek. "Thanks. I'm sorry. I must go." Her eyes were red. "He may die," she said with trembling lips.

"He'll be all right," Grayson said gently. "He will. You believe me. A man that tough isn't going to go down without a fight."

Sara didn't question the strange remark. She was too upset. She just smiled and ran out to the car, Grayson two steps behind with two rolling suitcases.

"I only need one," Sara said, looking at them.

"I've locked up and phoned Marsden to look after everything in the house. I'm going with you," she said firmly. "No way am I letting you go alone."

Sara started crying again.

"Come on," Grayson said gently. "Get inside. We need to leave."

Sara nodded through her tears and climbed into the backseat.

THE HOSPITAL WAS new and modern. It had long, wide corridors and modern lighting, with green plants everywhere. Sara would have been impressed if she hadn't been so frightened. Eb Scott was waiting for her. She ran into his arms and let him comfort her while she sobbed.

"He's holding his own," Eb said. "The hospital chaplain service has been of great help."

She drew back, dabbing at tears with an embroidered lace handkerchief. "Does he have any family left?" she asked. "I know he was a foster child, but maybe cousins?"

He shook his head and smiled. "Just you and me. Figuratively speaking."

Sara put her hand on her belly and drew in a shaky breath.

Eb's face was a study in delighted shock as he met her eyes.

She flushed. "You can't know," she faltered.

"I have two of my own," he said with laughing green eyes. "I remember the symptoms very well indeed." He pursed his lips. "So, you walked in the front door and out the back door of the clinic without stopping?"

She laughed self-consciously. "Something like that."

"When he's better," he told her, "he's going to take that out of my poor associate's hide, that he didn't record the length of time you were actually in the clinic."

"He wasn't supposed to know," she said sadly. "I was trying to protect him."

"And he was trying to protect you."

She nodded. Tears stung her eyes, hot and salty. "When?"

"When will we know? Soon, I hope," he said.

They sat down in the waiting area. There was a family nearby. An older woman was crying. Beside her, a somber teenage boy was trying not to. She looked at them and managed a watery smile. They gave her one back. Then they all waited.

Minutes passed. A doctor came out and spoke to the family nearby. The woman burst out with an expression of such joy that Sara felt good for her. She laughed. The teenager beside her grinned from ear to ear. They gave Sara a smile and a look of great sympathy as they followed the doctor down the hall.

"At least someone has good news," Sara said heavily. "Oh, I wish we did!"

"You didn't come alone?" Eb asked, concerned.

He was thinking what might happen if Wolf didn't make it. She knew that, but she didn't say it out loud.

"Grayson came with me. She's my personal assistant." She managed a smile. "She wouldn't let me come alone. She's lining up hotels and cars."

"Grayson?" he asked slowly, and there was an odd look in his eyes. "Amelia Grayson?"

She lifted both eyebrows. "You know her?"

He smiled. "Never mind."

She started to ask what he meant when a man in surgical greens came out a door, pulling his mask down on the way. He approached Eb.

Sara slid her hand into Eb's, terrified, praying, begging, as the man stopped just in front of them.

"The bullet did some damage," he told Eb. "Punctured a lung, broke part of a rib, ricocheted and took a chunk out of his liver and nicked an intestine. But I'm a great surgeon," he said with twinkling eyes. "I excised the damaged tissue, removed the bone splinters, sewed up the intestine and removed the bullet—something I wouldn't have done if it had meant causing more trauma," he added. He grimaced. "He's carrying enough lead as it is." His dark eyes narrowed. "You people keep my job challenging."

Sara was almost glowing with relief. Tears rolled down from her tragic black eyes, staining her cheeks as she stood still, listening, hoping.

Eb shrugged. "Think of it as practice. Look how much we give you."

He chuckled. "If you want to take him home, Micah Steele can take over. He's probably treated more of these cases than even I have. Not to mention your guy Carson, who's back in training as a physician in Jacobsville."

"All true." Eb shook hands. "Thanks."

"What are friends for?" He glanced down at Sara. "Are you a friend of my patient?"

"You might say that," Eb drawled. "She's carrying his child."

"She's…"

All the excitement, all the fear, caught up with her. Sara slid to the floor before either man could catch her.

SHE CAME TO on a hospital bed. She tried to sit up, but a nurse who obviously had Mafia ties pushed her gently back down and glared at her.

"Oh, no, you don't," she said. "I've never let a patient get away yet!"

"But he's out of surgery," she pleaded. "You have to let me go to him. I have to see him…! You don't understand. He doesn't want to live!"

"Yes, he does," the nurse mused with pursed lips. "Eb Scott told him you were here. He's awake and aware and cursing doctors because he can't get to you."

Her face flushed with pleasure. She lay back down. "He knows I'm here?"

"Yes."

She took deep breaths, joy shining out of eyes that had been tragic with grief and fear until now. "When?"

"When can you see him? As soon as your blood pressure goes down."

"But I don't have high blood pressure."

"You do, my dear," the nurse said gently. "Your physician in San Antonio prescribed a blood pressure medication. Didn't you realize that's what you've been taking?"

"She said something about hypertension. I thought she meant I was tense…" Sara flushed. "I used to be intelligent. I think pregnancy makes people susceptible to periods of stupidity," she added, blushing. "Nobody told him, about the baby...?"

"Not yet. We all think that should be your job," she added softly.

Sara sighed. "He'll be angry, that I kept it from him."

"That man isn't going to be angry about anything," the nurse replied. "Except being kept away from you." She paused. "Listen."

There was a loud voice, a very loud and deep voice, using words that might get him arrested if he didn't stop.

"Please?" Sara asked, because she knew the voice.

"Let me get a wheelchair."

THEY WHEELED HER into the recovery room. He was awake and demanding access to Sara. When he saw her, his whole face changed.

She got up out of the wheelchair and went to him. He was hooked up to half a dozen machines. A tube was feeding him oxygen. He smelled of antiseptic and blood, and something else that she couldn't quite identify—gunpowder, perhaps. He had blood everywhere, even on his face.

But he looked beautiful to Sara, who'd been terrified since Eb Scott's phone call. She went close and brushed back his black hair. She bent with tears in her eyes to kiss his forehead, his nose, his dry mouth.

"Sara," he choked out.

"It's all right," she whispered. "I'm here. I'm right here. I'm not going anywhere."

"I killed her," he whispered back. "Didn't I?"

She looked at Eb Scott, standing nearby. He nodded grimly.

"Yes," she said. She winced. "I'm so sorry...!"

"I knew from the way she looked that she had something planned, but I was too slow." His eyes closed. "I had the .45 under the table, because I didn't trust her. It was cocked, safety off. I was going to arrest her and put her in custody. When the shot came, it was just reflex. The gun went off. I never meant to kill her."

"The authorities know that," Eb said, coming closer. "No charges are being filed. Her whole organization is against the ropes. Many arrests were made. Some of them are going to be surprising, because they're here in the States." He nodded. "Her influence was international." His face hardened. "We also have the man who was in the theater, the night you and Sara went to the symphony."

Wolf's eyes flashed murder. "Hold on to him. When I can get up again, I'm going to kill him."

"I had him sent home to Africa, to stand trial," Eb returned. "You're not landing yourself in prison, however noble the motive."

Wolf was still glaring. Sara went close, and the ferocity went out of him, just like that. His pale eyes searched over her face. "You've been crying, honey," he said softly. "I'm okay. It's a lot better than it looks."

"No, it's not," she choked out. Her lower lip trembled. "I thought you didn't want me..."

His big hand drew her wet face to his chest and he shuddered. "You little fool!"

She laid her cheek against him and let go of her tears. She could barely manage to stop, to lift her head. "I'm sorry," she whispered. "I didn't mean to do that."

His thumb brushed against her lower lip. He looked

as anguished as she did. "Eb said you fainted," he said grimly. "I'm so sorry that you were frightened."

It was her pregnancy, not fear, that had caused the faint. But she wasn't going to tell him that, not just yet. She knew he felt something for her. But she didn't want knowledge of the child to push him into a relationship he didn't really want. She was going to take her time, see what he really wanted, when he wasn't traumatized, before she decided whether or not to tell him.

"I just needed to see that you were all right," she said.

He smiled. "I wasn't. I am now," he added, searching her wet eyes. "Don't cry anymore. It hurts me."

She dabbed at tears. "Okay."

His eyes were on the frilly handkerchief, and he smiled. "You never wear lace."

She shrugged. "My one little vice. Frilly handkerchiefs."

He chuckled, lay back, winced and closed his eyes. He drew in a long breath. "They drugged me," he complained. "It wasn't working, because I was scared to death about you when I knew you passed out." He opened his eyes. "You're sure it's nothing?"

"I'm sure," she lied convincingly.

"All right. I may sleep, for a bit…" He dropped off, the trauma and the drugs finally catching up with him.

Sara was drained, completely drained, of emotion when she and Eb went out into the hall. Grayson was standing there, waiting.

Eb took Sara to her. "I had them call your physician," he told her, "just to make sure you had what you needed. The fainting spell worried me."

"Thanks, Eb," she said gently. "I'm so tired…"

"Take her to a hotel, Grayson, put her to bed," Eb said quietly. "She's been through hell."

"So has he, I imagine," Grayson said gently. She smiled at Eb. "Good to see you."

"Nice to see you, too, Grayson. She'll be in good hands," he added, and a silent message passed between the two of them.

"I think I could sleep now." Sara turned to Eb. "You're sure he'll be all right? You'll call me, if…"

"I'll call you. I promise."

"All right." She followed Grayson down the long corridor.

SHE SLEPT LIKE a log, for the first time in years. Grayson woke her up, finally, with the news that they were transferring Wolf into a room, out of intensive care, where he'd spent the night. Sara hadn't known about that, or she'd have been out of her mind.

"Nobody told me," she muttered.

"Nobody dared," Grayson replied with a smile. "You'd had enough. But he bounced back so quickly that even his surgeon was surprised. They think he can be transferred in a couple of days, if he's still improving."

"I'm going with him," Sara said. "I'm sorry. You can go back to the ranch in Wyoming and stay there…"

"I'll manage," Grayson said shortly. "I'm not leaving you alone."

Sara bit her lip. "Grayson, you're the nicest person I know."

"No. You're the nicest person I know." She put a platter of eggs and bacon on the table and retrieved croissants from the basket. She'd had room service deliver food before she woke Sara. "Now eat."

"Croissants," Sara said, brightening.

"You mentioned how much you liked them," came the amused reply. "The restaurant had them on the menu."

"And strawberry preserves." She prepared a croissant, creamed her coffee and actually enjoyed breakfast for a change.

As soon as they ate, they took a cab to the hospital. Sara had phoned Eb, who was waiting for her in the lobby. He smiled.

"He's not happy. He wants to go home. But I think if he can see you, he'll shut up for a few minutes anyway, before the nurses shove a washcloth in his mouth and tie him to the bed."

She laughed. "Is he that bad?"

"Worse, actually."

He led her toward a closed door and pushed it open. Wolf was sitting up in bed, a hospital gown barely covering the broad expanse of his chest. He looked up when he saw Sara, and the glower turned into a beaming smile.

"Hello," he said gently.

"Hello." She smiled back.

"I have some things to do. I'll be back," Eb said discreetly, and went out to join Grayson in the hall.

"How has she been?" Eb asked the woman, and he wasn't smiling.

"Bad," she replied. "I'm watching her like a hawk. I don't think there's any danger, but you never know. Ysera had paid someone to do Wolf. I'm not sure about who or where, if you know what I mean."

He nodded. "We'll take him to the ranch as soon as he's mobile, and I'll send over the best men I have." He studied her drawn face. "Not him," he added gently. "He's in Africa."

She relaxed. "Okay. Sorry."

"So am I," he said.

Her face closed up. "She has high blood pressure," she said. "The doctor was treating her for it, and she didn't realize," she added. "She doesn't know that it might impact her pregnancy. The obstetrician wasn't forthcoming, but he sent her to a cardiologist. She won't make it to the appointment. It's two days from now." She laughed softly. "She doesn't know that I'm aware of her pregnancy. I haven't let on."

"Good. I'll get Micah to refer her to a doctor in Ja-cobsville. Tell her the cardiologist phoned you, that you gave him your number and told him what was going on. Say he referred you to Micah. Okay?"

"I can do that," she agreed.

His eyes narrowed. "Still packing that .45?"

"You'd better believe it," she returned. She pulled back her jacket, just enough to let him see the butt of the pistol resting under her arm. "Nobody's getting to her, or him, unless they go through me."

He smiled. "I believe it. You're good, Grayson. Get-ting her to hire you without giving yourself away was an act of absolute genius."

"I had a good teacher," she replied, and smiled back.

"What did you tell her, so that I can pretend I don't know anything?"

She gave him the whole spiel about her former em-ployers, the works. She laughed. "She was so sympa-thetic that I felt like a dog for lying to her."

"It was for a good cause. We can't take the chance that Ysera didn't know about Sara. There's still the threat to Wolf."

"Not with me around," Amelia said with a grin. "I'm a dead shot, I am."

"Yes, you are, and I ought to know. I trained you myself," he said, grinning.

WOLF WAS GLARING at the meal they'd brought him. "I don't like hospital food," he muttered.

She went close, opened the tray, picked up a fork and proceeded to ladle food into him.

"Don't fuss," she said softly, smiling.

He watched her while he ate, his eyes soft and warm. Almost loving, she thought. Then she remembered the night at the theater, the beautiful blonde woman. He'd told Eb it was to throw Ysera off the track. Was it?

His big hand caught her wrist. He winced, because it was painful to use his hand. The bullet had impacted the muscles in his chest. "I couldn't tell you," he said, his face drawn with guilt. "Ysera had a man in the theater that night…"

"Eb told me," she said.

"It was the truth," he said. "You have to believe that, if you believe nothing else. I couldn't make you a target. I couldn't let her hurt you!"

She saw the emotion. He wasn't even trying to hide it. His expression calmed all her fears. "She was quite beautiful," she said slowly.

"She wasn't you," he whispered huskily. The way he said it made her toes curl up in her shoes. "And there isn't, anywhere on earth, a woman as beautiful as you are. There isn't a woman I want more."

She flushed with pleasure.

"When I get out of here," he said huskily, "and back on my feet, I'd love to prove that to you."

Her whole body tingled. She lowered her eyes to his mouth. "Would you?" she whispered.

"You could have a little minor surgery in the meantime," he said with a wicked smile.

"Wolf!"

"Watch out, you're spilling that coffee."

"Sorry." She held it to his lips and watched him sip it. Her hands were unsteady.

"It won't be like last time, Sara," he said huskily. "I swear it!"

She drew back the cup. "I know that."

He reached up and touched her face, wincing with the movement. "And if you'll let me," he whispered softly, "I'll do my absolute damndest to make you pregnant."

CHAPTER TWELVE

COFFEE WENT EVERYWHERE. She flushed, dropping the cup on the tray, as she grabbed a washcloth from the table and used it to mop him up. "Sorry," she said tautly.

He groaned inwardly. He hadn't meant to say that, to remind her of the child they'd lost. "It doesn't matter. I can use something," he said quietly. "It's too soon to discuss it, anyway. I've got a lot of healing to do. Are you going to come back to the ranch with me, when they let me out?"

She searched his face. He'd sounded as if he wanted a child, just for a few seconds. But now he was the same as he had been before. Nothing showed in that bland expression. Nothing at all. She couldn't read him.

"If you want me to," she said quietly.

He leaned back against the pillows. He winced, but this time not because of any physical discomfort. "I've hurt you badly, Sara," he said, his voice deep and tender. "In so many ways. I know it's going to take time. But there isn't another woman in my life. Only you."

She moved a little closer. "There isn't another man," she confessed. "I could...never do those things, with anyone else."

His chest swelled with involuntary pride. She still wanted him, at least. "You can do them with me," he said huskily. "But it will be different next time. Very, very different."

Her eyes were troubled. She thought of a future with the two of them being intimate occasionally, no ties, no commitment. It was dismal.

"What are you thinking?" he asked.

"I was wondering..." She stopped suddenly. She managed a smile. "I was wondering if Grayson is getting impatient. I left her out in the hall."

"Grayson?" he asked. He frowned. "Amelia Grayson?"

Her eyebrows went up. Eb Scott walked into the room before Sara could ask if he knew her companion.

"Amelia Grayson is working for you?" Wolf persisted.

"I told you that," Eb said, and he was making gestures behind Sara's back that Wolf finally understood. "It's not the Grayson you're thinking of. She's in federal prison, remember?" He turned to Sara, lying through his teeth. "She was an arms dealer, of all things. Wolf and I caught up with her in Barbados. He arrested her in an ongoing investigation into money laundering. She led us on quite a chase. But that was Antonia Grayson, Wolf. Not Amelia."

"Oh. Yes." He drew in a breath. "I'm a little fuzzy from the anesthesia and the pain meds, I guess," he said with a sheepish smile. "What's she like, your assistant?"

"She's very sweet," Sara said. "She takes wonderful care of me. I honestly don't know what I'd do without her now." She smiled softly. "She's spoiled me."

"That's going to be my job, when they let me out of here," Wolf said, and his pale eyes were almost eating her.

"I'm so glad that you lived," she whispered. Then her face set, and her black eyes flashed. "Why?" she exclaimed. "Why did you do something so incredibly dangerous? There are all sorts of agencies that deal with people like that, but you went storming in by yourself. They could have killed you!"

"Oh, God, it's the broom and the flying monkeys again," he groaned, lying back against the pillows. "Save me!" he pleaded with Eb.

Eb couldn't. He was laughing his head off.

Sara, torn between amusement and fury, just glared. Her emotions were all over the place. Eb knew why. Wolf didn't.

"I'm going to get a broom and hit you with it," Sara promised. "And if you ever, ever, strap on a gun and try to go back into the field, I'm going to have every cowboy on the place rope you to a fencepost, and I'm going to personally make sure they never untie you!"

He gave her a sardonic look. "Men have to use the bathroom periodically," he said drolly.

She flushed. "We'll find a bedpan or something."

He chuckled.

She smiled sheepishly. "Well, you're not doing it again. Ever."

He smiled slowly. "Okay."

Her heart lifted. He didn't seem to mind if she ordered him around. It was rather intriguing.

"You can enjoy giving me orders. Until I'm out of this bed," he mused, pursing his lips. "And then we'll see who gets to do what."

She lifted her chin. "I can unleash the flying monkeys whenever I like," she warned.

He laughed with his whole heart. His life had been

over when he left the States. He had nothing to come back to, no reason to live. Now, there she stood, the joy of his life, the jewel of his wealth. And he'd never wanted more to live.

"I have to phone Sally and tell her how you're progressing," Eb said. "She likes you."

"I like her, too," Wolf said. "How are the kids?"

"Growing up all too fast," Eb said. He wanted to say something else, but he didn't dare. He couldn't risk letting anything slip about Sara. "I'll be back."

"I don't know what I'd have done without him," Sara said, going close to the bed. "He arranged to fly me up here. I was in such a state, I could never have made it alone."

He caught her hand in his and brought the palm to his mouth, kissing it hungrily. "I didn't know if I wanted to live," he said roughly. "Until they told me you were here. I thought, if she came, it means she cares, even just a little."

"She cares a lot," she managed.

His chest rose and fell heavily. "You're never going to forget that night at the symphony," he said quietly. "I know that," he interrupted when she tried to speak. "I can't make it up to you. But I'm going to try, when I'm out of here."

"Not out of guilt…!" she exclaimed.

"Definitely not out of guilt," he said softly. He searched her eyes. "You still don't know a lot about men. I want you," he added huskily. "Want you, Sara. So badly that it's like losing an arm or a leg. Want you to the point of absolute madness."

She colored as she met his narrow, glittering eyes.

"I can make you want me back," he whispered. "I

can take away all the bad memories, replace them with sweet ones. If you'll let me."

She swallowed, hard, and bit down on her lower lip. Here it was. The bare truth. He wanted to take her to bed.

"Don't look like that," he said. "Don't."

She moved her shoulders restlessly. "I know that I didn't refuse...anything you did to me, and you think I'm, that I don't mind, that..."

"Sara," he said, tugging her closer to the bed, "I want to marry you."

Her eyes were like saucers. "What?"

"I want to marry you." He scowled. "What did you think I was suggesting? Some loose arrangement where I'd spend the odd night at your apartment? Honey, if I even tried, Grayson would put me right through a window!"

"Oh, so you know that she reads a Bible at night," she faltered.

"Does she?" he said, backtracking. "Eb said she was very protective of you," he prevaricated.

"Yes, she is." She searched his eyes slowly. "You want to marry me?"

He smiled sardonically. "I'm too old for you, we both know that..."

"No! Don't you ever say that again!" She went closer, putting a soft hand over his wide, sensuous mouth. "You're not too old." Her eyes went over him like soft, searching fingers. "You're beautiful to me."

He let go of the last fear he had, that she might one day regret what he was proposing. She was fierce. Like a little house wren, protecting her brood. He could see her being that way with a child. He was sad that she'd given up theirs out of a mistaken impression that he didn't want her. But they'd have others. He was certain of it.

"Where do you want to get married?" he asked softly, cradling one of her hands in his.

"Could we do it at the ranch?" she asked, all eyes.

He pursed his lips. "Oh, yes, we could do it at the ranch, but let's get married first, okay?"

"You devil!" she exclaimed.

He chuckled at her expression. It was so easy now, to talk to her like this. He watched her with eyes full of wonder, soft with affection. "Sorry. Couldn't resist it." His smile faded. "But you will need to see the doctor first, Sara," he said firmly. "I won't risk hurting you any more than I already have. You understand?"

She swallowed. "I had it."

"What?"

"I already had it. Before...I went to the symphony." She lowered her eyes. She'd had such plans for that night, when everything had gone wrong. Such beautiful plans.

He drew in a breath, because he knew. He closed his eyes and shuddered. If it hadn't turned out the way it did...

She saw the hurt on his face and quickly erased it from her own. She smoothed over his chest. "Anyway, it's already done," she said firmly.

He looked up at her with anguish on his features. "So much pain," he whispered.

She traced his hard mouth and nodded. "But no more," she said huskily.

He kissed her fingertips. "No more," he agreed.

IT TOOK SEVERAL days for him to get on his feet. They transferred him down to Jacobsville via an air ambulance. He spent only a couple of days in the hospital before Micah Steele released him, with a grin and a warning about trying to overdo too soon.

Sara assured him that Wolf wasn't doing anything he shouldn't on her watch. The big man, who looked much more like a wrestler than a doctor, agreed demurely.

THE COWBOYS LINED up to see the boss brought in by an ambulance, hats to their chests, almost in tears.

"When I get up, I'm swatting the lot of you," he grumbled, glaring at them. "Bullets can't kill me! I've got a cape and a big red *S* on my chest," he added, laughing suddenly and then wincing, because it hurt.

"We're glad you're okay, boss," his new foreman, Jarrett Currier, said, and smiled. "We're just happy to have you…" He looked past the boss at the two women coming up the walkway, and his blue eyes flashed fire. "What in the hell are you doing here?"

"Watch your mouth!" Wolf began, thinking the man meant Sara.

"I'm here looking after Miss Brandon," Amelia said shortly. "And what are you doing here? I don't remember anybody saying you worked for Mr. Patterson!"

"I started last week, when his livestock foreman retired. If I'd known you were anywhere on the place, I'd never have put in an application."

He said it with pure malice.

Amelia just stared at him. "They said you were still in Africa," she said icily.

"I came back," he said flatly.

"How can Eb Scott bear to part with you?" she said with a cold smile.

"If that's a hint, I'm not leaving," Currier shot back, eyes glittering at her. "Not unless he fires me." He indicated Wolf.

"I have just returned from armed combat," Wolf said from the gurney. "And I would appreciate not being landed in another combat zone until I can recover!"

"Sorry, boss," Currier said grimly.

"Sorry, boss," Amelia agreed at once.

Currier nodded to his boss, turned and stomped off toward the barn. The other cowboys murmured, greeted the boss and followed him away.

"So that's the reason you didn't want to come back to Comanche Wells," Sara said while they were unloading Wolf in his bedroom. "I'm sorry, Amelia. If you want to go back to the Wyoming place…"

"I can't," Amelia said gently. But her face was tragic. Whatever had happened between her and the new foreman was obviously still extremely traumatic.

"Yes, you can," Sara replied. "Listen, I'll be perfectly safe here. You know I will." She hugged the other woman. "Go on. I'll be back before you know it."

"But you're getting married."

Sara smiled. "I'm not giving up the ranch. Meanwhile, who knows what might happen? Go on. You haven't even unpacked. Phone the limo company and get a ticket. Business class, Amelia, not tourist. Then you can ramrod Marsden and the others while I'm gone. Okay?"

"You're the nicest boss in the world," Amelia said, thinking that she'd have to talk to Eb Scott covertly and make him aware that she was leaving. But Sara was right. There was enough protection here to safeguard ten threatened people, much less two.

"Call me when you get home, so I'll know you landed safely. Okay?" Sara asked.

Amelia smiled wanly. "Okay."

Sara wondered what in the world had caused the misery she saw in Amelia's face when that handsome cowboy had started raging at her. But it was personal, and she wouldn't pry. She saw her friend off. Then she went to check on Wolf.

"BETTER?" SHE ASKED HIM, noting his color was normal now, and he looked rested and in much less pain.

"Better," he said, his eyes soft and tender on her face. "You sent Grayson back to Wyoming."

She nodded then grimaced. "Your new livestock foreman is a pain in the butt," she informed him. "I don't like the way he spoke to Amelia."

"Neither do I. I'll make sure he knows it. But it's not a bad thing for us to be alone here, at the moment," he added in a deep, soft tone. "Not a bad thing at all, Sara."

She colored, but her black eyes smiled at him. "You aren't that fit just yet," she said.

"I know it." He leaned back against the pillows.

"Can I get you anything?"

"My computer," he said. "It's on the desk. Then grab some pillows and climb in here with me."

"What are we going to do?" she asked.

He gave her a wicked grin.

She caught her breath.

He laughed. "No, not that. Not yet. We're going shopping, precious."

"Shopping?"

"Yes. If Amazon.com doesn't have it, it doesn't exist. Right?"

She laughed. "Right."

THEY PICKED OUT a set of wedding rings for Sara, emerald and diamond, and a plain gold band for Wolf, and had them sent overnight. Sara had blood work done at the hospital while Wolf was there, and Micah had already drawn blood from him for the tests. They had the results before Wolf was released.

"Tomorrow we'll have the rings. I sent Eb off for the marriage license. Two days from today," he said, searching her eyes, "I'm marrying you. Right here, at the ranch. I want you to go into town to Marcella's boutique in Jacobsville. She's making your gown."

"A gown? A wedding gown…" She hadn't considered that.

"I'm going to stuff myself into a morning coat," he chuckled. "And try not to faint at the altar." He shook his head. "I'm not letting you get away." His eyes narrowed. "You're mine."

She met his eyes. "And you're mine," she whispered.

His chest rose and fell roughly. "Can you put this away for me?" he asked. He cut off the computer quickly, before she could see the icons. She might not recognize video gaming, but he didn't want to share that part of his life with her just yet. She might be jealous of the unknown woman he'd been playing with for two years. He would tell her. Just not yet. Even though it wasn't a romantic relationship, it was one of friends. He hoped she'd understand.

She took the computer, set it on his desk and plugged

it back in. She went back to him. "I can fix you something to eat, if you're hungry."

"I'm very hungry," he agreed, looking at her in the black slacks and black turtleneck sweater she was wearing. "Lock the door and let your hair down."

She stared at him. "What?"

"Lock the door and let your hair down. I'm starving to death."

She felt breathless just looking at him. "Wolf, your chest…"

"I don't care if it kills me," he whispered roughly. His face showed the strain. "Oh, God, honey, I'm dying…!"

She went and locked the door. She unplugged the phone. She let her hair down. Then she took off the sweater and the slacks. Her hands hesitated at the bra.

"Come here," he said softly. "I'll do that myself."

She went to him, as hungry as he was. It had been a very long time. Her conversations with Emma Cain had shown her that she'd let a sad incident rule her life for far too long. Wolf wasn't a man bent on hurting her. He was, in a very real sense, her lover. And she wanted him. She wanted to marry him, live with him, love him all her life.

He was wearing pajama bottoms, but he slid those off as she came to the bed. He tossed back the covers and let her look at him. He was painfully aroused already.

"You really are…magnificent," she whispered unsteadily.

"Only for you," he replied, and held out his arms.

She went down into them, shivering a little when her body touched his. He turned her, grimacing a little. The muscles were still sore.

"Are you sure?" she began.

He brushed his mouth over hers. "I'm very sure that I'll die if I can't have you," he whispered back.

"I wouldn't want that," she whispered, arching as he found the clasp of the bra and loosened it, pushing it away from her breasts.

He looked at them, frowning. "You're bigger," he whispered. "Or am I just imagining it?"

"I've gained weight," she lied.

"Is that it?" He smiled. "It's very becoming." He traced the soft flesh down to her nipples and back again, watching her move sensuously against the gentle pressure. "Do you like that?"

"I love it."

He tugged off her briefs and tossed them to the floor. His face was solemn. "We've played at this," he said gently. "But this is the real thing. I have to be slow and careful with you. It may be uncomfortable, even with the surgery. I'm over-endowed."

"I noticed." She flushed, trying to sound sophisticated and failing miserably.

He smiled. "You're nervous. Don't be. I know exactly what I'm doing. This time," he whispered as he lowered his mouth to hers, "there won't be any hurtful remarks. I only want to please you, in every single way I can."

She tried to answer him, but his mouth was on her hard-tipped breasts, and she was lost. His mouth slid up and down her, touching her in new ways, in places she hadn't expected. She fought him a little at first, until the sensuality made her reckless, made her hungry, made her wild.

She cried out softly as he touched her, his fingers probing, teasing, enticing. His mouth burrowed gently into hers while he aroused her to such a pitch that she was moaning long before he began to move over her.

"This is where it might get...complicated," he breathed into her mouth as he slowly, gently, began to enter her.

Her eyes opened very wide as she felt, for the first time in her life, intimate contact with a man.

In the darkened bedroom, there was still enough light for him to see her face, drawn, tense, uncertain.

"Shh," he whispered. He shifted his hips, watching her. "That's it," he murmured when she jerked. "You feel it when I do that, don't you? Lift your hips, just a little...that's it. You're doing fine. Just fine."

She hardly heard him. Something was happening. Something new. Something she'd never felt before, even with him. Her eyes widened, and her mouth opened as a jolt of sensation so excruciatingly painful as death itself lifted her toward him with pure exquisite passion.

"There...!" she cried out. "There. Oh, there...!" Her eyes closed on a harsh moan, her teeth clenched. She lifted and lifted and lifted, pleading, her body straining to hold on to something so sweet that she didn't even know if she could survive it. "There," she choked out, shuddering. "Yes, there, right there, right..."

She cried out, a sound she'd never heard from her own throat in her life. Her body convulsed under his delighted gaze. He watched her, gloried in the fulfillment he could see in the taut arch of her body, in the helpless cries of pleasure, in the shuddering, endless climax that drove her hips up into his with such pressure that he could feel her hip bones digging into him. And still she shuddered, and sobbed, clinging to him, her face rigid with ecstasy, her eyes closed, her breasts arching up against his chest.

She felt him inside her. Felt him swell, felt the power and heat of him. But he was only giving pleasure, not taking it. She fought to get her breath, to stop crying. It had been so sweet, so beautiful…

"Please," she whispered.

He was smiling tenderly. He moved his hips. "Like this?"

"No. For you," she whispered back. "I want what I had, for you," she said. "Tell me what to do. I'll do anything. Anything!"

His face was a study in tenderness. "You don't have to do a thing." His hips moved and his teeth clenched. "Not now."

"I won't watch," she whispered. "I promise." She closed her eyes.

"Don't do that," he whispered back, his voice terse as he moved deeper inside her. "Watch me. Look at me. I belong to you as surely as you belong to me. You gave yourself. Now I'm giving myself. Watch…!"

He went off like fireworks. She saw his body arch over her, his hips grinding down into hers, his face tormented, his throat as taut as rope. He was shuddering. His mouth opened on a harsh, helpless cry as his body convulsed over and over and over again. He sobbed as the passion spent itself in him, as he felt his body explode with pleasure. It was the second time in his life he'd ever had an orgasm. Like this, the first had been with her, with the beautiful, sensual woman under his body, clinging to him, soothing him as he came slowly back down from an incredible height.

"It's all right," she whispered, touching him, kissing

him tenderly, her lips all over his face, his eyes, which were oddly wet. "It's all right, my darling. It's all right."

The endearment, the tenderness of her lips on his face, were tearing him apart inside. He couldn't bear the pain he'd caused her. He'd given her so little, and she'd just given him paradise. He'd never known such joy. Such peace.

He cradled her against him, damp with sweat, still shivering in the aftermath.

"Are you all right?" she asked at his chest, worried. "It didn't hurt you?"

His arm drew her closer. "I never knew what the hell they were talking about when they mentioned orgasms until you came along," he murmured unsteadily. "My God! I think my whole body exploded."

She laughed softly, secretively. "So did mine."

"Yes. I saw. I watched you."

"You did?"

He rolled over and looked down into her wide, soft eyes. "I dreamed of going inside you like this," he whispered. "I ached to do it, to make you feel what I felt that last time we were together. And then Ysera came back into the world and put you at risk. And I..." His voice broke.

"Wolf?"

"I cost you our baby." He buried his face in her throat. His eyes were wet!

"Oh, my darling, no. No! You didn't!"

"You went to a clinic...!"

"Wolf, look at me. Look at me!"

He dashed at his eyes and lifted his head, reluctantly. His expression wounded her. It was taut with anguish.

She took his hand and drew it over her breasts. "Turn on the light, please."

The room wasn't dark, but it was hard to see details. He grimaced as he reached for the light switch and put on the small lamp on the night table.

"Look at me," she said, drawing his fingers over her breasts. "I'm not pale enough for it to show much," she whispered, "but do you see all the little veins?"

He frowned. There were a lot of them. He didn't remember them from before. "Yes."

"They're feeding the milk glands," she whispered. "They're preparing me, so that I can produce milk."

He blinked. His hand was fascinated with her beautiful breast. It was fuller, softer, than he remembered it. He smiled with pleasure. What had she said? Something about milk?

"Sweetheart, breasts only produce milk when there are going to be babies," he said with a faint smile.

"Yes, I know."

He was very still for a minute. His hand pressed down against her breast. He lifted his pale eyes to hers and pinned her with them.

She took his hand and drew it slowly down her body to the small hardness there, and pressed it to her.

"Oh, my God," he breathed reverently. He went pale.

"I went through the front door and out the back door of the clinic," she faltered. "I couldn't. I just…couldn't. I didn't know how you'd react. I thought you might not want the baby, but I did, and…"

His mouth cut off the rest of the hurried little speech. He was kissing her, in a way that he never had before. His whole body was shaking. He gathered her close and just held her, rocked her, his face buried in her throat.

"Wolf?" she asked, surprised.

"Just give me a minute," he whispered gruffly in her ear. "The trip from hell to heaven takes a little time to adjust to."

She couldn't repress a soft laugh. Her arms stole around him and held him tight. "I would have said something sooner," she said. "But I was afraid."

"You thought I wouldn't want a baby."

"I didn't know. I was afraid you wouldn't want something permanent, with me. And I couldn't live somewhere else and have you come to visit the baby…"

His arms contracted. "We got off to a rocky start," he said in her ear. "We didn't know very much about each other, and we were too hungry for each other to take time to talk."

"Yes."

He lifted his head. "I want a baby," he said solemnly. "I want you. I want marriage."

She searched his eyes. "Are you sure?"

"I have never been more sure of anything in my life."

She relaxed a little. "Okay."

Her soft movement triggered a sudden, sharp arousal. He grimaced and started to move away.

"Where are you going?" she asked, pulling him back to her.

"You're pregnant," he began. He winced. "I might have already hurt the baby. I was so hungry for you. I was rough!"

"You weren't rough, and babies are very sturdy," she murmured. She reached down, boldly, and ran her fingers over him. He shuddered. "Now you just come right back here and let me take care of that little problem you've got…"

"Little?" he managed as he rolled her onto her back and went into her.

She gasped. "Ooookkay," she said breathlessly. "Not so little…!"

He laughed wickedly. "And very soon, perhaps not even big enough," he said huskily as his mouth moved down over hers. "Let me teach you something new. Draw your legs in between both of mine."

She gasped again.

"Oh, yes, that's the way," he groaned as he moved down against her.

She shivered. Her body tautened as the pleasure came back, suddenly and very deep. She lifted against him.

"I like that," he whispered into her mouth. "Do it again."

She did. He was more potent than he'd been before. She caught her breath as he moved deeper, slower, into the softness of her.

"You're very, very aroused," he murmured into her mouth, "and sensitized, as well. I'm going to shoot you off like a rocket," he whispered roughly. "And I'm going to watch you go."

She shivered. The pleasure was biting into her like hot nails, lifting her, grinding her up into him. She was frankly afraid, nervous about even being able to survive it, it was so overwhelming.

She didn't realize that she'd whispered that to him, frantically, until she heard the soft, deep laughter above her.

"You'll live," he whispered unsteadily as the sharp, quick movements began to take her right up the spiral into unknown heights. "But you'll blush every time you look at me…for a week," he concluded.

She began to cry out, her voice throbbing in tune with her body as she arched and shivered and then climaxed over and over and over again until she thought she couldn't live through it. At the last, she heard a deep groan from above her, felt a furious shudder, and then driving movements that ended in convulsions so violent that she worried if he was going to survive it, as well.

They shuddered together, sweating all over, trembling in the aftermath of something so powerful that neither of them could even speak.

"The baby," he whispered roughly, his hand going protectively to her belly.

"The baby is fine," she whispered back. He tried to lift away, but she held his beloved weight over her, clinging. "Don't move," she whispered. "I love feeling you on me, feeling your weight."

"I'm heavy," he said.

She smiled against his throat. "No, you're not."

He shivered again as he moved. "Damn," he groaned.

"Damn?" she asked.

He laughed. "I'm sore."

Her eyes were very wide. "You're...what?"

"Sore." He pursed his lips as he looked down at her with possession and affection and pure joy. "Very sore." He drew back, wincing.

She winced, too.

"See?"

He rolled over onto his back, groaning. "That's what we get for overdoing."

She sat up, laughing delightedly. She winced again. "I didn't know people got sore."

He cocked an eyebrow. "What, after reading all those torrid novels?"

"They're romantic novels, not anatomy books," she replied.

He drew in a breath, relaxed, comfortable, letting her look at him with complacent amusement. "Speaking of anatomy lessons," he mused.

She flushed.

"I told you that you'd blush for days," he pointed out. He grinned.

She laughed delightedly.

He caught her hand and pulled it to his lips. "So now we have a real problem."

She stiffened. "We do?"

"Yes. Grayson is going to have to come back down here and live. How do we manage that without firing my new foreman?"

She let go the last bit of her fears. "We go home and tell her about the baby," she said simply. She smiled. "That's all it's going to take."

"The baby." He drew her over and pressed his mouth hungrily to the swell of her stomach. "I wonder if a man can die of happiness."

"Don't you dare try to find out," she said firmly.

He smiled against her belly. "Are we having a boy or a girl?"

"Yes."

He burst out laughing. "Which?"

"We'll find out when he or she is born," she replied. "I don't want to know. Not yet."

He lifted his head. "Neither do I. People will laugh."

"Let them. It's my baby. Our baby."

"Our baby," he whispered. His heart was bursting. He'd never dreamed that out of such tragedy could come such joy.

But the next morning, everything changed.

CHAPTER THIRTEEN

SARA WAS STILL asleep when the phone rang. Wolf reached past her head, pillowed on his shoulder, to get his cell phone off the bedside table.

"Hello?"

"It's Eb. Listen, you have to get Sara out of there, right now," he said urgently.

He sat up, displacing her. She woke up and stared at him sleepily.

"What is it? The man Ysera sent...?"

"No, they've got him in custody. That threat is over," he said. "This is something new, something worse. The reporters got hold of the story. You know where Gabe is, what he's doing?"

"I know where he is. Is he all right?"

"Yes. I've got him stashed, along with his unit, in a luxury hotel in the Middle East. But his ward, you remember her, Michelle Godfrey?"

"Yes," he said.

"She came out to interview me last week. I thought she was going to be fair, to tell the whole story. She didn't," he said coldly. "She told the world that Gabriel and his men led a massacre against women and children. They printed photos..."

"Gabriel would die before he'd hurt a child!" Wolf raged.

"I know that," Eb groaned. "It isn't what it looks like. I have them hidden and I've hired attorneys and a private investigator, but it's going to be a publicity nightmare for a while. They'll find Sara, if they haven't already."

"I'll get her back to Wyoming today," he said.

"You aren't fit to travel," Eb protested.

"I'm going. They have doctors in Wyoming." He looked down at Sara's drawn face, touched it gently. "We'll leave as soon as we're packed. Their ward did this? Michelle?"

"Michelle." Sara's eyes widened. "What did she do?" she whispered.

Wolf put his hand over the phone. "I'll tell you in a minute." He went back to Eb. "Why?" he asked.

"She didn't know Gabe used a different name when he did jobs for me," Eb said shortly. "One of us should have told her. I didn't realize what might happen. She's devastated, but things have gone too far. Get out of there as soon as you can. Satellite trucks are popping up like daisies around here already."

"Thanks, Eb. For everything."

"You're my friend. I'll help any way I can. Hurry." He hung up.

Wolf got out of bed, drawing Sara up beside him. "We'll have a quick shower, then we'll pack. I'll tell you while we're bathing."

He pulled her into the shower and told her what Michelle had done. Tears mingled with soap and water. He held her, rocked her, while she let it all out.

"How could she do that to my brother?" she wailed. "I thought she loved him!"

"She didn't know who Angel Le Veut was," he replied heavily. "Nobody told her."

"I'll never forgive her," she said. "Never!"

"Never is a long time. We have to get moving."

"You're still not recovered," she sobbed. "And the wedding…!"

"We'll take everything with us to Wyoming," he said softly. "I'm absolutely certain they have ministers up there." He pursed his lips. "And we'd better find one quick, because there's no way I'd get past Grayson without a marriage license."

"How do you know so much about her?" she asked.

He kissed her tenderly. "I have spies. Never you mind, jealous heart, the only woman I've ever wanted enough to marry is you. Period."

Because he wanted her? Not because he loved her? She wasn't sure. But she didn't have the strength to walk away from him. She loved him far too much, now more than ever, with his baby growing inside her body.

THEY FLEW TO Wyoming on a private jet.

"I have a property nearby, you know," he reminded her.

"Yes, you went there and stayed for a long time," she recalled.

His hand tightened on hers. "Running away from the memories," he said. "I couldn't run far enough. And then I took you out to the ballet that we never attended." His face darkened, and he averted his eyes. "I wish we could go back and redo that night," he said quietly.

"I don't," she whispered, snuggling close. "That's when we made the baby."

His body shivered. He drew her close, his face buried in her warm throat. "Yes, but still…"

"You made it up to me last night. You made up everything last night," she whispered in his ear, shivering. "It was…indescribable."

"For me, too, Sara," he replied. He kissed her closed eyelids. "For me, too."

THEY HIRED A limousine in Sheridan to take them out to the ranch, but they stopped along the way at a small Methodist church.

Wolf tugged her along with him. "You won't have a proper dress," he said. "Or the rings, just yet. They're en route. But I have the papers we need, if you'll marry me, right now."

"I'd marry you in blue jeans, if that was the only way," she said with breathless delight.

He smiled. "The Reverend Bailey is a friend of Jake Blair, the minister whose church you visited in Jacobsville. He's a friend of mine. So he called the Reverend Bailey and explained things. We're expected."

They walked into the church. The altar had flowers. The reverend greeted them holding out a gray jeweler's box.

"Isn't it amazing what you can find just when you need it?" Wolf murmured, winking at the minister, who'd gone shopping for him. He opened the box. There were two gold rings inside, wide bands. One for her, one for him. "Yellow gold. I noticed that it's all you wear."

"I love it." She touched the rings and looked up at him. "I could wear a cigar band, though. It would be enough."

He bent and kissed her eyelids shut with such tenderness that one of the women standing at the altar had to dash away a tear.

"My wife and mother are going to be witnesses for us," the Reverend Bailey said. "If you're ready?"

Wolf looked down at her. "I've never been so ready in my life."

"Me, either," Sara said softly.

"Then let us begin."

IT WAS A brief ceremony, poignant for all that. Wolf slid the ring onto her finger. It fit perfectly. She slid one onto his, which also fit. They repeated the words of the marriage ceremony, looking into each other's eyes. The minister pronounced them man and wife.

Sara cried silently as he bent to kiss her with aching tenderness.

"Mrs. Patterson," he whispered, and he smiled.

She smiled back.

He kissed away the tears while the minister filled out the marriage license.

"And now," he said after they'd shaken hands and been congratulated, and he'd made sure the minister had a nice memento of his kindness in the form of several large bills for the indigent fund, "we go home. And if we're lucky, after we display the license, Grayson will allow you to sleep with me," he added as they piled into the limousine.

He laughed as he said it. She laughed, too, pressing close.

"Sadly," he said heavily, "sleep is all it's going to be for the immediate future." He leaned close. "I'm still sore."

She burst out laughing and tried not to blush.

Grayson met them at the door. She was all smiles. "I made a cake!" she said. "It's the first time I've ever tried to make one. It may not be very good. But I made quiche and croissants, and they came out perfectly!"

Wolf stared at her. "You feeling okay, Grayson?" he asked.

She glared at him. "I can cook."

He pursed his lips. "Snake, yes. I'm not sure about croissants and…"

"You just come in here and taste it before you start making snide remarks," she scoffed. She smiled at Sara. "How are you?"

"Sad," she said. "My ward sold Gabriel out."

"I heard. It's on the news, everywhere," she said. "They'll probably try to come here," she added with a worried look at Wolf.

"All taken care of," he replied. "I called in markers from every law-enforcement agency I know. Even the U.S. Forest Service. Since this ranch borders their land, we have a few, shall we say, perks."

"Which are?" Sara asked.

"Wait and see." He grinned at her. He pulled her close and kissed her pretty cheek.

"Okay, now," Grayson began.

Wolf handed her the marriage license.

She stared at it, at him, at Sara, with disbelief in her brown eyes.

"I can get married like anybody else," he said defensively.

She felt her forehead. "Maybe I'm hallucinating."

"No, that would mean that you got married," he returned. "And hell would also be freezing over at the same time."

"Do you two know each other?" Sara asked with veiled suspicion.

"Sort of," they both said in unison and then grimaced together.

Wolf looked at Grayson and threw up his hands. "Damn. You can't keep secrets from her. Okay. It was Eb's idea. Grayson is one of his."

Sara's expression was just short of comical. "You're a…a merc?"

Grayson shifted uncomfortably. "I'm a professional soldier," she muttered.

"You're a merc," Wolf muttered.

Grayson sighed. "I'm a merc," she agreed.

"But why, how…?"

"We were afraid Ysera might know about you," Amelia said gently. "None of us wanted to see you hurt, but it wasn't possible to put somebody in the apartment with you unless it was a companion. And we saw your advertisement. Everything fell into place perfectly."

"My brother must have done that," Sara said. "He knew!"

"Yes. It was when he came home for Michelle's graduation," Amelia reminded her.

Sara didn't reply. She looked up at Wolf.

"I'd hurt you so badly," he said, wincing. "I couldn't bear it if anything happened to you. Neither could your brother. So he persuaded you to place the ad and had Grayson answer it."

She let out a sigh. "Well, at least I feel safer now." She glanced at Grayson and then winced. She looked up at Wolf. "Who's going to tell her?"

"You're a woman. So is she." Wolf looked uncomfortable.

"Yes, but you've known her longer than I have."

"Tell me what?" Amelia asked.

"It's not something I feel I should do," Wolf said.

"You're making such heavy weather of it…"

"Tell me what?" Amelia asked again, impatiently.

"If you'd just do it," Sara groaned.

"I don't want to do it," he groaned, too.

"Tell me what, damn it!" Amelia burst out.

"I'm pregnant," Sara blurted out at the same time Wolf said, "She's pregnant."

Amelia gaped at them.

Wolf produced the marriage license and waved it at her.

She drew in a breath. She looked at Sara, whose eyes were clouding. "Oh, come here," she said, hugging the younger woman close. "I'm not judgmental. I go to church, but I don't tell people how to live. And if you got pregnant before you got married, it's all his fault, anyway."

"What?" he burst out.

Amelia glared at him over Sara's shoulder. "I know all about men," she muttered. "I used to work with men. Tough men who didn't want commitment. They talked about the women they lied to…"

"It was an accident," Wolf said in a subdued tone, looking at Sara with eyes that adored her. "But I'm not sorry. I'll never be sorry. Sara, and a baby. It's like Christmas."

Amelia let go of Sara and walked up to the big man. "I'm sorry. I didn't know you very well. I made assumptions." She hugged him, then moved away. "I'm really sorry." She brightened. "I can crochet. I'll make little booties and blankets and… Do you want something to eat?"

"That went well," he whispered into Sara's ear as they followed Amelia, who was still talking, toward the kitchen.

"Coward," she whispered back, and bumped her hip against his.

"Same back at you," he whispered, and bumped her. Then he groaned, because it hurt.

She laughed, pressing close.

BUT WHEN THEY saw the news, later, it was agony for Sara, to watch her brother being barbecued by the media for something she knew he didn't do.

Gabriel managed to get a call through to her later in the day. "The story's going to break like a carton of eggs on pavement," he told his sister. "I don't know how the hell they found out so quickly."

"Our ward told them," she replied coldly.

"Michelle?" he asked, aghast. "No! No, she would never do that to me!"

"She did," came the terse reply. "She was on the news, explaining her position. She told them that Americans who perpetrated such offenses should be publicly hanged."

He was silent. "I wouldn't have believed it of her."

"Nor would I. Not after all we've done for her," Sara said.

"I don't want to see her again. Ever. I want her out of my life, out of yours."

"Yes. I'll take care of that. You be careful," she added gently. "I love you."

"I love you, too."

"There's one little thing I should tell you…"

"What?"

"I'm pregnant."

There was a shocked pause. "Wolf said you went to a clinic…"

"I did. I went in the front door and out the back. And Wolf and I were married this morning."

"I need to sit down."

She laughed softly. "I'm so happy," she whispered, lowering her voice so Wolf wouldn't hear and be embarrassed. "I love him so much I can hardly bear it. He wants the baby, very much."

"I'm sure that he wants you, too," he said.

"He's very fond of me," she said, hiding her sadness that it wasn't more. He'd never mentioned deeper feelings. She hoped they might come, after the baby was born. "And my companion turns out to be a female merc, how about that?" she added with a little venom.

"Guns Grayson isn't going to let anything hurt you," he began.

"Guns?"

"She's the best shot in the unit," he said, chuckling. "One of the guys, and I mean that in the best possible way. She's very religious. We weren't even allowed to curse around her. Gave some of the guys fits."

"I can imagine! Guns, huh?" She chuckled.

"I have to go."

"Eb Scott says they have attorneys for you. It will work out. I know it will."

"Me, too, but it's going to be rough for a while, until the media finds another juicier bone to chew on," he said with resignation. "I'll be in touch, but it may have to be through Eb. I can't risk having anyone trace me."

"Okay. Be safe."

"You be safe. Wolf will take care of you. Good Lord, you should have seen him when he came here, on his way to Ysera. I tell you… What?" There was a pause. "Okay. I have to go. Love you, sis."

"Love you."

She hung up, wondering what he was going to say about Wolf. But then her mind went back to the source of this new misery. Her life was in turmoil all over again. So was Gabriel's.

And she knew who to blame. She called Michelle. She was good for five minutes. When she hung up, she was certain that she never wanted to see or hear from the girl ever again.

Wolf held her while she cried.

"I never thought she'd do this to us. I knew she wanted to be a journalist, I encouraged her. So did Gabriel. But I never dreamed…"

"Shh," he whispered gently, rocking her against him. "Life goes on. People do terrible things. Then they pay for them."

His voice was full of remorse.

She drew back and looked up at him. "I never blamed you."

"I blamed myself." He smoothed back the long, black hair from her beautiful face. "I almost died. But I kept hearing your voice, whispering to me. I held on, because I thought you might care, just a little…"

She pressed close. "A little!" She groaned. She pressed closer.

He was very still. He was thinking, adding things up in his mind. Her eager response to him, with her tragic past. The way she loved his hands on her. The way she reacted when he touched her, giving, always giving…

"You love me," he whispered, awe in his tone.

She drew in a breath. "You big, stupid man. Of course I love you. Why would I ever have let you touch me if I hadn't?"

He chuckled. "Big and stupid?"

She drew back, flushing. "Okay. Not stupid. But big."

His lips drew into a pucker and his eyebrows went up, and his eyes glittered with unholy glee.

She went scarlet. "That is not what I meant!" she burst out.

He just laughed. He pulled her close and kissed her. "Sorry. Couldn't resist it."

"I know where the broom is," she pointed out.

"Don't. I'll reform. Grayson!" he yelled.

She came running. "What?"

"Watch out the window for flying monkeys."

Amelia, who knew about the running joke, saluted. "Sir, I'll find them and bring them down, or give my life in the attempt. I swear." She put a hand over her heart, grinned and left them to it.

JOURNALISTS MOVED INTO TOWN. They took up all the motel rooms, cluttered the local restaurants and pumped the locals for all they were worth trying to find out anything about Gabriel's sister, Sara.

But Billings, Montana, like Jacobsville and Comanche Wells, Texas, were small, clannish towns, and they didn't like outsiders. Not even outsiders who flashed huge bills around fishing for information. They were housed and fed. But they learned nothing.

So they tried to get into the ranch itself. Which

proved an exercise in futility. Wolf Patterson met them himself at the end of the driveway, along with a heavily armed party of cowboys and some federal officials. The reporters were cautioned about taking a single step onto federal land and causing damage. Of course, they didn't know where the Brandon property ended and the federal lands began, and nobody would tell them. Wolf made a few more comments, tongue in cheek, and drove back up to the ranch house.

GABRIEL PHONED THEM a week later, perplexed. "Have you seen the news?"

"No, we're boycotting it," Sara said on Skype, studying her brother's drawn face. "It's bad, isn't it?"

"Actually, Michelle went on national television to defend me," he said. "She found the one witness who knew it wasn't us, and told the whole world. She wrote articles, went on talk shows, even met with the detective who's been working the case for us." He colored. "I guess she really didn't know it was me."

Sara winced. "I said some terrible things to her."

"Did you tell her what I said, too?" he asked.

She just nodded. "She'll never forgive me."

"It just needs time," Wolf said from behind, slipping his arms around her shoulders and planting a soft kiss on her temple. "She'll forgive. So will you. It will be all right. They're dropping the charges, aren't they?"

"Yes. And the real culprits are in custody. But I'm not coming home yet," Gabriel added with a grin. "I got a job offer. You'll never guess from who."

"Whom," Sara teased. "Okay, spill it."

"Interpol," he said. "They like what I did over here.

They said I'd make a nice addition to the staff. So I'm thinking of taking it. For the time being, at least."

"What does Eb think?"

"He's all for it," he replied. "He said I needed a change of pace, and this would be it. He's got plenty of new students who can fill in for me, when he needs help."

"I could go," Grayson said.

"No!" three people shouted.

She held up her hands, grinned with pure delight and went back to the kitchen.

"She's our treasure," Sara said. "She'll never get out the door."

Wolf chuckled. "Not without bolt cutters and a gun, at least."

"She really is a treasure," Gabriel added. "Saved my life once. No, I'm not telling you. It was a classified action."

"Wow," Sara said gently.

"Yes. Grayson is in a class of her own."

"Well, I'd better go. But I'll be in touch. I may be home in a few months. In time for the baby, I hope."

Sara looked up at Wolf. "In the winter," she whispered.

"This winter," Gabriel said with a big smile, "I'll be an uncle. I can't wait. What is it going to be?"

"A baby," Wolf said disgustedly. "Weren't you listening?"

"A boy or a girl baby?" he persisted.

"We have no idea," Sara said with twinkling dark eyes, putting a hand on her husband's arms, cradling her. "We're letting it be a surprise."

"I'd love a little girl with eyes like my best girl here," Wolf mused.

"And I'd love a little boy with eyes like Arctic ice," she replied.

"I'd love twins," Gabriel said.

"What?" Sara asked.

"One of each. And it could happen. We have twins on both sides of the family."

"Well!" Wolf said, and his smile was ear to ear.

"So you let me know how things go, okay?" Gabriel asked.

They both smiled. "Of course," Sara agreed.

THE JOURNALISTS FINALLY went away, but not until the summer flowers were thinning and dropping off their stems.

A new national political scandal drew them all back to Washington, D.C.

"And it's about time," Sara remarked when they watched the news.

"Yes. What did the obstetrician say?" Wolf asked, smiling. "I should have gone with you, but you wouldn't let me."

"It's all women," she said with mock jealousy. "I'm not letting a gorgeous man like you within sight of them."

He pursed his lips. "They're all pregnant, aren't they? Not much risk they'd want to run off with me."

"I want to run off with you every time I see you," she said, with her heart in her eyes.

He drew her close and kissed her. "I'll go anywhere you like. Whenever you like."

She drew a pattern on his shirtfront. "Do you think I'm sexy like this, all swollen and everything?"

"You take my breath away," he replied huskily.

"Grayson went into town to buy groceries," she told his shirt. "She'll be gone for an hour, at least…!"

He'd picked her up in midsentence and carried her straight into the bedroom.

"Well!" she exclaimed as he put her on the bed, locked the door and started throwing off clothes.

"You said the magic words," he told her. He was totally nude. He walked to the bed, magnificent in his arousal, and efficiently stripped her.

"What magic…words?" she managed as his mouth found her.

"Grayson left the house." He smoothed his mouth over the inside of her thighs, loving the soft moans she made. "She inhibits me at night. We need to build her a damned house so I don't have to be quiet when we make love."

"Wolf!" she cried out as his mouth made bright lights explode behind her eyelids. She arched with pleasure.

"That's exactly my point, that sound you just made." He chuckled. "I like it when I can make you scream."

"Oh, my…gosh!" she cried out, arching.

"Another case in point." He slid up her body, his mouth on her breasts. But he jerked back unexpectedly.

She saw why and laughed. "Oh, darling, I'm sorry. I forgot to tell you…they leak sometimes now."

He was brushing a small spray off his cheeks. He chuckled.

"You're not upset?"

He pursed his lips. "I think it's extremely sexy," he murmured. He shifted his hips and moved her long legs aside. "Know something else I think is extremely sexy? Hmm?"

"What?" she asked breathlessly.

He moved down, easing inside her. She made another sound, a high-pitched, shivery one as he shifted his hips from side to side and moved closer.

"That little sound you just made," he whispered. "Would you like to make it again, you think?" He repeated the motion, dragging a moan out of her. He laughed like a devil.

"I can't...match you," she gasped.

"You're getting there," he whispered. He moved closer, loving the way her body clenched around him, intensifying the pleasure. He groaned. "Yes. Do that...!"

"Teach me!"

"I'm...working on it," he bit off. "But not now...!"

"Of course not now," she moaned.

He drove for satisfaction, his body hard and a little rough, his hips moving down against hers in a quick rhythm that sent her right up to the ceiling in an explosion of such joy that she sobbed and sobbed and finally cried out endlessly, her nails scoring down his lean flanks as she endured the agony of fulfillment.

He went with her every step of the way, feeling her pleasure, sharing it, finally stiffening as he felt his own fireworks. He gasped at the last as his body seemed to melt completely down into hers in a welding of passion that never seemed to end.

He was shaking when he finally collapsed onto her.

"It just gets better and better," she whispered, dazed.

"And better." He brushed his mouth over her soft lips. He moved again and groaned.

"You...can?" she asked.

He lifted his head and looked into her eyes, letting her watch them as his body swelled and swelled inside her.

She opened her mouth at the sensations it produced. "You…"

"Yes." He bent and kissed her softly as his hips began to move. "I'm much more potent than I usually am. It's all those little screams," he said wickedly, "that you don't dare let out when Grayson's just down the hall." His hips moved sharply, and he groaned. "Oh, damn," he muttered, shaking. "It's too soon…!"

"No, it isn't." She moved with him, her body attuned to his, feeling his pleasure climb and climb as her own body arched to meet each quick, hard thrust. "Do it," she whispered. "Do it, do it, do it…!"

He cried out as the pleasure took him, drowning, burning, hurting, it was so good. He arched over her and shuddered, feeling her eyes on him. He opened his and looked at her, watched her watching him. The ecstasy was so overwhelming that he almost passed out. He shivered once, twice, and felt her go rigid under him.

A long time later, he rolled over, still joined to her, and fell onto his back, pulling her with him.

"You watched," he teased.

"Yes. It…makes it…I don't know, more…"

He chuckled. "Yes. More. I like to watch you, too."

"No more bad memories?" she asked at his broad, damp chest, where her cheek was pillowed.

"None." He kissed her hair. "How about you?"

"No more bad memories." She sighed and closed her eyes. "I didn't know it was possible to be so happy."

"Neither did I."

She drew in a long breath. "There's a car coming up the driveway."

"Guns is home. Quick, let's get dressed and look like we've been playing checkers."

She laughed out loud. "You wimp!" she accused.

"I'm afraid of Grayson," he teased.

"You are not."

They got up and dressed. When Grayson started inside, they went out the back door to help her bring in the groceries.

Or they started to. Sara got to the lowest step and suddenly went down in a dead faint.

CHAPTER FOURTEEN

WOLF WAS FRANTIC. He carried her to the sofa and started calling doctors in the other room while Grayson ran for a damp cloth and put it on Sara's forehead.

Sara started to fuss for a second, and then opened her eyes and shook her head.

Wolf came back a minute later, looking grim. "I called an ambulance. They'll have her obstetrician meet us at the emergency room."

"I just fainted," Sara protested weakly.

"Better safe than sorry," Wolf replied, brushing back her long hair. "Humor me. I'm terrified."

She looked up, prepared to smile. But his face was pale. His eyes were alive, full of emotion.

"I'll be all right," she said huskily, holding his hand very tightly.

He didn't look relieved. He really did look scared to death.

DR. HANSEN WAS there waiting for them, with another doctor, who also examined her. There were questions and notations taken, while Wolf held her hand and looked scared out of his mind.

"It's going to be all right," Dr. Hansen assured them. "Dr. Butler here is going to monitor her blood pressure and keep a check on that heart issue"

"What heart issue? What about her blood pressure?" Wolf exploded, with blue eyes full of horror.

"Calm down, Mr. Patterson," Dr. Hansen said gently, putting a hand on the older man's shoulder. "It isn't dangerously high blood pressure, and the heart defect shouldn't be a danger at all. She just has conditions that need monitoring, that's all."

"If you think she has serious issues, maybe we should consider going to a bigger hospital in the city," Wolf said.

"No," Sara said icily. "No, I will not!"

"Sara," Wolf groaned, "please, you have to listen to the doctor!"

"That isn't going to be necessary," Dr. Hansen said gently. "I promise you it isn't. We have a wonderful hospital here. It's small, but our obstetrics ward has won awards. We have some of the best nurses in the state. You'll be in good hands."

"She won't be at risk?" Wolf asked tightly, his eyes still showing traces of fear.

"No. You have my word," Dr. Hansen said. "And I don't give it lightly."

He let out a breath. His eyes went to Sara and lingered there. "All right."

"Your blood pressure is quite good," Dr. Hansen said. "Almost textbook readings. And you look radiant." He grinned. "Go home and comfort your husband before we have to admit him as a patient!"

She managed a smile, but she was worried. Was he looking for a way out? Did he want her to have a termination? Was that why he asked the doctor those questions? She was silent and somber all the way home.

Grayson met them at the door. "How are you?" she asked worriedly.

"I'm fine," Sara said, but she wasn't smiling.

"Grayson, can you drive into town to the pharmacy and get one of those expensive blood pressure cuffs?" Wolf asked. "While you're about it, see if you can find a decent salt substitute."

He dug some bills out of his wallet and handed them to Grayson.

"I'll be back soon," Amelia said. She smiled at Sara. "It's okay. We'll take good care of you."

Sara just nodded.

But when Amelia was gone, she turned to Wolf with haunted eyes. "You don't really want the baby, do you? I wasn't smart about precautions. I didn't know anything. I should have…!"

He picked her up and sat down with her on the sofa. His face was hard as stone.

"I'm so sorry," she began, bursting into tears.

He drew her close, shuddering as he felt the tears against his hot throat. He held her very close, his arms enfolding her, cradling her. There was a faint tremor in them.

"Okay," he whispered. "This is where we lay all our cards on the table." His arms tightened. "I want the baby. It will be the joy of my life. But not without you, Sara. I can live without a baby. I cannot, will not, live without you!"

She caught her breath. He was saying something she could barely believe.

"When I thought you had the termination, because you saw me with that woman at the symphony, I was certain that you could never forgive me, for making you do something that would hurt you so much." His arms tightened, almost bruising her. She didn't even feel the pain. "So I strapped on a gun and went to find Ysera. I would have let her kill me, because I couldn't live, didn't want to live, without you in my life."

"Oh, my God," she moaned, shaking.

"I've done nothing but hurt you, from the day we met. It was because you were beautiful and sweet, and I wanted you until my heart ached. But I didn't think you could fall in love with an older man, who had so many scars on his body, in his heart. Ysera had humbled me, used me, humiliated me. I was stinging from all that, the night we were first together." His eyes closed, and he shivered. "I had you, figuratively speaking, over and over again. I made you climax and I watched, then I let you watch me. I had no idea what you'd gone through in the past. I was so drugged on you, so much in love with you, even then, that I couldn't...stop," he ground out. "I'd never felt anything like it. Then you ran, and I knew how far I'd fallen."

She touched his face tenderly, not speaking, just looking at him. His eyes were wet. She kissed them dry.

His cheek nuzzled hers. "So I got drunk. Drunk as any man ever did. I couldn't live with what I'd done to you. Knowing what your stepfather did to you almost killed me." His arms contracted. "I got Emma Cain here, because I was afraid you might do something desperate. And I knew then, that if I lost you, I couldn't live."

"You never...said anything," she began.

He drew in a breath and looked down at her, his eyes naked of camouflage. "I've loved you," he whispered with breathless tenderness, "as long as I've known you.

Wanted you. Needed you. But I hit rock bottom when I had to let you go. Ysera would have killed you. I had to stop her. Any way I could. I hadn't planned to go after her myself, but once I thought you'd lost the baby, and I thought I'd lost you, life had no meaning for me."

She bit her lower lip.

He kissed it, softly. "So I went to war, hoping to die. I don't remember much of it. I felt as if someone hit me in the back, hard, and I started blacking out. I heard my gun go off. I remember seeing a streak of blood on Ysera's mouth…"

"You said I looked like her, once."

He smiled down at her. "No. There was no resemblance at all. I noticed that the minute I saw her again. She wasn't beautiful, or kind, or loving, Sara. She was like a cobra. It amazed her that I didn't respond to her anymore. She couldn't believe it. She knew there was someone. She made threats." He couldn't tell her what they were. His jaw tautened. "I don't think I meant to kill her. But maybe I did. Even from prison, she could have harmed you." He searched her eyes. "She isn't the only person I've killed, Sara. That's part of who I am, what I am. I want you. I love you. But you have to be sure you understand what you're letting yourself in for. I'm not…"

She put her mouth over his, so tenderly that it was like a whisper of feeling. "I will never leave you," she whispered. "I will love you until I die, and forever after. And there is nothing, nothing, you could tell me that would ever change that."

He felt such joy that he was almost drunk on it. He pulled her close and rocked her, his face in her throat, his arms trembling.

"From such terror, hope," he breathed.

"Hope." She clung to him. She laughed. "I've never been so happy in my life!"

"Neither have I. Not even in dreams."

She smoothed over his dark hair. "I hope you gave me a boy," she whispered. "One who'll look just like you."

He drew back. "Sara, the baby..."

"He's going to be beautiful," she said with a smile. "And I'm going to be fine. Really fine. Nobody this happy can die. Honest."

He seemed to relax, just a little. "No more salt," he said. "No more fatty croissants. No more excitement..."

She stopped the words with her mouth. "I won't give up making love to you," she said with a chuckle. "Don't even bother to ask."

"Maybe we can do it less passionately," he murmured.

"Bite your tongue." She nipped his lower lip. "I love how you love me."

"I love how you love me back."

"Besides, Dr. Hansen says lovemaking is healthy and won't hurt the baby. I'm taking my tablets. My blood pressure is stable. And we're having a baby."

He sat back in the sofa and smiled with pure possession. "All right."

"Just like that?"

He kissed her. "I never argue with pregnant women."

"And we'll see about that," she teased.

He grinned and kissed her again.

LATE THAT NIGHT, she got out her laptop computer and plugged it in, in the guest bedroom, one of two that was unoccupied. Grayson had the other one.

"Do you mind?" she asked Wolf. "I need to send an email to Gabriel."

"I don't mind," he said a little too quickly. "I need to send a couple myself. Thirty minutes?"

"Thirty."

SHE FELT GUILTY as she pulled up her game and opened it. She hoped he would be on. Sure enough, he was.

Rednacht whispered her. How has it been?

Very rough, she replied. But things are better. So much better. I never knew it was possible to be so happy and have so much to look forward to.

There was an lol and then a reply. It's the same with me. I have a family now. I can't believe it. I feel like I won the lottery, only better.

She hesitated. I have something sad to tell you.

I know what it is. You're giving up the game.

I feel that I should. I don't want to have secrets from him.

Will you tell him about me? he asked.

Yes. You'll tell her about me, too, right?

Yes, he agreed. Secrets have no place in a good marriage.

I'm very happy for you, she said.

I'm very happy for you, too.

I've enjoyed every minute I've spent with you online,

she typed. Thanks for getting me through some of the roughest times of my life.

You did the same for me. I'll miss you.

I'll miss you. Goodbye, my friend, she typed.

There was the faintest hesitation. Goodbye, my friend.

She logged off, tears rolling down her cheeks.

She shut down the computer and walked into the living room, the peignoir of her pale pink nightgown trailing behind her, her long hair flowing like black silk down her back.

Wolf was standing by the window, in just pajama bottoms; Amelia had long since gone to bed and left them alone.

He turned, broad-chested, beautiful to look at. He was sad.

He moved closer. "You've been crying," he said. "What happened?"

She took his hand and tugged him to an armchair. She pushed him down into it and crawled into his lap. "I have a confession to make."

"You're running away with Psy because you can't stop listening to 'Gangnam Style' on YouTube," he guessed.

She hit him. "No. Pay attention."

"Okay."

She bit her lower lip. "I haven't been honest with you. I do play video games. I haven't recently, because there was so much going on in my life. But there's an online game. You play it with other people. I know you play console games, but this one is played on a PC. It's a fantasy game, sort of, called World of Warcraft."

His eyes were wide with shock.

She thought he might be shocked. She lowered her eyes to his broad chest. "So there's this guy I've played with for several years. We run battlegrounds and dungeons... I told him I didn't feel right to continue in the game because I was married, and my husband might not understand. Besides that, I didn't want to be keeping company with another man, even in a fantasy setting..."

He was sitting stock-still. He didn't even seem to breathe. "I just told...a woman the same thing, in the same game." His eyes searched hers. "Is the toon you play by any chance a Blood Elf warlock?"

Her lips fell open. She searched his eyes. "Rednacht?" she whispered unsteadily.

"Yes." He searched her face. "Casalese?" he whispered back.

"Oh, gosh." Her face flooded with color. She looked at him as if she'd never seen him before and burst into tears. "I've married my best friend!" she exclaimed, and hugged him as hard as she could.

He held her close, laughing, so delighted that he could barely manage words. "I don't believe it! Now I understand why Gabriel didn't want me to tell you Hellie's real name."

She leaned back. "What is it?"

He chuckled. "Hellscream. I named her for the leader of the Horde. Of course I hate his guts, but I love Hellie."

She laughed, too. "All those years, and I never suspected..." She hesitated. "We sympathized about the people who were hurting us, and it was us hurting each other."

"Yes." He traced her cheek. "You got me through some bad times."

"You got me through some, as well."

She curled up in his arms. "We can run battlegrounds together again." She laughed.

"And dungeons."

"I love you," she whispered.

"I love you, too."

THEY PLAYED ALMOST every night after that, delighted to find that they worked even better together since they knew each other's true identities.

But Wolf worried about her pregnancy. As autumn appeared, Gabriel phoned Sara.

"Guess what?" he asked, and grinned.

"What?"

"Michelle and I are getting married!"

"Oh, Gabriel, I'm so happy. Have you told her I'm sorry for what I said, that I didn't mean it?"

"I have. She understands." He hesitated. "I haven't told her about you and Wolf. I mean, she knows you're married. She doesn't know about the baby."

"Don't tell her," she said. "I'm having some problems. Nothing major, but I don't want her to worry. I won't tell her, either. Okay?"

"You'll be all right?"

"The world's most fearsome nanny watches every step I take, and every bite I take..."

"Wolf Patterson?" he exclaimed.

"Him, too. But I meant Guns Grayson," she replied. "They hid the real salt. I can't find it anywhere."

"And you won't, sweetheart!" Wolf called from the next room.

"That's right," Amelia called, too.

"Worrywarts," she muttered.

"We all worry," Gabriel said. "So you behave."

"If I must. Hug Michelle for me. I'm so happy for you both. I wish I could come to the wedding…"

"You'll be there in spirit. Jake Blair's going to marry us."

"I like him," she said, smiling.

"So do I. We'll be in touch."

"Okay. Be happy!"

"I intend to. See you, sweetie."

"Love you."

"Love you back."

She hung up. "Gabriel's marrying Michelle!" she exclaimed, walking into the kitchen.

"Well," Wolf exclaimed. "And here I thought they weren't speaking."

She grinned and kissed him. "Shows what you know. Where's the salt?" she whispered, teasing his broad mouth with hers.

"I have no idea."

"Yes, you do. Come on. Give it."

"This isn't the salt you're looking for. Substitute salt will be fine." He waved his hand, like a Jedi knight doing a mind trick.

She made a terrible face.

"Substitute salt will be fine," Amelia added, waving her own hand in front of Sara.

She glowered at them as she sat down with a long sigh. "It will be fine," she repeated miserably. But inside she glowed, knowing how protective they were.

GABRIEL AND MICHELLE phoned her not a long time later to announce that they were pregnant.

Sara laughed joyously, but she was careful to keep the camera only on her face. It was a little puffy in the final days of her pregnancy, but at least they couldn't see her belly. She congratulated them and made an off-hand remark about being sorry she wasn't pregnant, too.

When she hung up, Wolf shook his head. "My God, you look like a Greyhound bus! Wish you were pregnant?"

"Hush," she said firmly, "or I'll feed you liver and onions for supper!"

He made a terrible face.

She kissed him. "I don't want to worry Michelle. She's having some problems. She didn't tell me, but Gabriel did. We're not going to upset her."

"Whatever you want, sweetheart," he said softly. "Anything at all."

"Anything?" she mused.

"Anything."

She leaned toward him. "Salt!"

He laughed. "Anything but that."

She shook her head and went back into the living room.

HER BABY WAS born in mid-February, not when he was expected, in early February, on a day when snow was drifting into impossible peaks. But they made it safely to the hospital. She wasn't even in labor long. But the result was absolutely shocking. To Wolf, at least. Sara had known for a time, but she hadn't wanted him to worry any more than he already was.

She laughed, exhausted but overjoyed.

"Twins," he exclaimed, fighting tears. "A boy and a girl. A boy and a girl!"

"Yes, my darling. A matched set."

He bent and kissed her. She pulled a tissue from the box by her bed and mopped his eyes, then her own.

"Can we hold them?" she asked the nurse.

"The minute we have them cleaned up. You'll need a gown, Mr. Patterson."

"I look good in red," he remarked. "Something in red silk, maybe, with matching high heels?"

Sara hit him.

THEY BROUGHT IN the twins. She nursed the little girl while Wolf held his son, and stared at him through a mist. "Beautiful," he whispered. "Both of them."

"What are we going to name them?" she asked.

"My grandmother was called Charlotte," he said.

She smiled. "I like Amelia, too."

"For Guns?" he mused. "Yes. I like that, too."

"Charlotte Amelia it is. How about our son? His first name should be Wofford."

"One wolf in a family is enough," he said firmly. "We should name him for your brother."

"Gabriel will want to name his own son after him." She laughed. Her eyes searched his. "Do you have a middle name?"

He nodded. "Dane."

"I like it. And my father's name was Marshall."

"So…Dane Marshall Patterson?"

She smiled. "Done."

He chuckled. "Okay. I'll tell them, for the birth certificates."

INCREDIBLY, GABRIEL AND MICHELLE made it to Wyoming to see the babies when they came home with their parents, despite the snow still piled up everywhere.

Michelle was huge in front. She hugged Sara and cried over the babies. She hugged Wolf, too, a little hesitantly. She didn't know him well.

"I can't believe you didn't tell me!" Michelle fussed. "I'd have been here like a shot to help!"

"I had plenty of help, and I didn't want you worried. How are you?" she added.

Michelle smiled. "It's not what they thought," she said, grinning. "They did all sorts of tests before they found out that I just have an irritable bowel. They're treating me for it. The only problem I have now is heartburn." She sighed. "I would have told you, if you'd called us more often."

"I was worried. They were worried." She indicated Wolf and Amelia. "And I was afraid that I'd let something slip."

"They're so cute," Michelle said, fascinated with them. "Can I hold one?"

"Wolf?"

He turned, smiling, and handed her Dane.

Michelle was awestruck. "He's just perfect. So is Charlotte." She looked up at Gabriel with her heart in her eyes. "We're going to have one of these. I still can't get over it."

"Neither can I, *ma belle*," he said softly. "I can't wait!"

"Neither can I." She laughed, cuddling the little boy close.

WELL, NO CHANCE of that marriage ending in divorce," Wolf said when Gabriel and Michelle had gone back to Texas.

She lifted her eyes to his. "Or ours."

"That goes without saying," he said softly, searching her eyes. His narrowed.

"What are you thinking?" she asked.

"About what a long way we've come together since you backed into me, and I accused you of dropping houses on people."

She was making a fruit drink in the blender. She stopped the machine and stared at him. "What was that?"

"You backed into me. With your car." He smiled.

"You backed out into me without looking where you were going," she countered.

"I did not," he said haughtily. "I am the world's best driver... What are you doing with that thing? Don't you dare...I mean it!"

Amelia, having heard the threat, followed by an amazingly loud slurpy sound, came out of the sitting room, which she was organizing, to see what the commotion was about.

Wolf Patterson was going down the hall toward the bathroom. He stopped just in front of Amelia, with fruit pulp running from his head down his nose onto his shirt and dripping onto the wood floor of the hall. "Just for your information," he said confidentially. "Don't ever upset her when she's using the blender."

He sighed and continued on into the bathroom. Down the hall, hysterical laughter was coming from the kitchen.

Amelia grinned from ear to ear and went back to work.

* * * * *

*Read on for an excerpt from UNTAMED,
Diana Palmer's exhilarating story of a
steely mercenary and his childhood sweetheart...*

It took forever to get anywhere, Stanton Rourke fumed. He was sitting at the airport on a parked plane while officials decided if it was safe to let the passengers disembark. Of course, he reasoned, Africa was a place of tensions. That never changed. And he was landing in Ngawa, a small war-torn nation named in Swahili for a species of civet cat found there. He was in the same spot where a small commercial plane had been brought down with a rocket launcher only the week before.

He wasn't afraid of war. Over the years, he'd become far too accustomed to it. He was usually called in when a counterespionage expert was wanted, but he had other skills, as well. Right now he wished he had more skill in diplomacy. He was going into Ngawa to get Tat out, and she wasn't going to want to let him persuade her.

Tat. He almost groaned as he pictured her the last time he'd seen her in Barrera, Amazonas, just after General Emilio Machado had retaken his country from a powerful tyrant, with a little help from Rourke and a company of American mercs. Clarisse Carrington was her legal name. But to Rourke, who'd known her since she was a child, she'd always been just Tat.

A minion of the country's usurper, Arturo Sapara, had tortured her with a knife. He could still see her, her blouse covered with blood, suffering from the effects of a bullet wound and knife cuts on her breast from one of Sapara's apes, who was trying to force her to tell what she knew about a threatening invasion of his stolen country.

She was fragile in appearance, blonde and blue-eyed with a delicately perfect face and a body that drew men's eyes. But the fragility had been eclipsed when she was threatened. She'd been angry, uncooperative, strong. She hadn't given up one bit of information. With grit that had amazed Rourke, who still remembered her as the Washington socialite she'd been, she'd not only charmed a jailer into releasing her and two captured college professors, she'd managed to get them to safety, as well. Then she'd given Machado valuable intel that had helped him and his ragtag army overthrow Sapara and regain his country.

She did have credentials as a photojournalist, but Rourke had always considered that she was just playing at the job. To be fair, she had covered the invasion in Iraq, but in human-interest pieces, not what he thought of as true reporting. After Barrera, that had changed.

She'd signed on with one of the wire services as a foreign correspondent and gone into the combat zones. Her latest foray was this gig in Ngawa, where she'd stationed herself in a refugee camp which had just been overrun.

Rourke had come racing, after an agonizing few weeks in Wyoming and Texas helping close down a corrupt politician and expose a drug network. He hadn't wanted to take the time. He was terrified that Tat was really going to get herself killed. He was almost sweating with worry, because he knew something that Tat didn't; something potentially fatal to her and any foreigners in the region.

He readjusted the ponytail that held his long blond hair. His one pale brown eye was troubled, beside the one wearing the eye patch. He'd lost the eye years ago, in a combat situation that had also given him devastating scars. It hadn't kept him out of the game by a long shot, but he'd turned his attention to less physical pursuits, working chiefly for K. C. Kantor's paramilitary ops group as an intel expert, when he wasn't working for a covert government agency in another country.

K.C. didn't like him going into danger. He didn't care what the older man liked. He suspected, had long suspected, that K.C. was his real father. He knew K.C. had the same suspicion. Neither of them had the guts to have a DNA profile done and learn the truth, although Rourke had asked a doctor to do a DNA profile of his assumed father.

The results had been disturbing. Rourke's apparent father had been K.C.'s best friend. Rourke's mother had been a little saint. She'd never cheated on her husband, to Rourke's knowledge, but when she was dying she'd whispered to the doctor, Rourke's friend, that she'd felt sorry for K.C. when the woman he loved had taken the veil as a nun, and things had happened. She died before she could elaborate. Rourke had never had the nerve to actually ask K.C. about it. He wasn't afraid of the other man. But they had a mutual respect that he didn't want to lose.

Tat was another matter. He closed his eye and groaned inwardly. He remembered her at seventeen, the most beautiful woman he'd ever seen in his entire life. Soft, light blond hair in a feathery cut around her exquisite face, her china-blue eyes wide and soft and loving. She'd been wearing a green dress, something slinky but demure, because her parents were very religious. Rourke had been teasing her and she'd laughed up at him. Something had snapped inside him. He'd gathered her up like priceless treasure and started kissing her. Actually, he'd done a lot more than just kiss her. Only the sudden arrival of her mother had broken it up, and her mother had been furious.

She'd hidden it, smoothing things over. But then Tat's mother had taken Rourke to one side, and with quiet fury, she'd told him something that destroyed his life. From that night, he'd been so cold to Tat that she thought he hated her. He had to let her think it. She was the one woman on earth that he could never have.

He opened his eye, grinding down on the memories before they started eating him alive again. He wished that he'd never touched her, that he didn't have the shy innocence of her mouth, her worshipping eyes, to haunt his dreams. He'd driven her into the arms of other men with his hatred, and that only made the pain worse. He taunted her with it, when he knew it was his own fault. He'd had no choice. He couldn't even tell her the truth. She'd worshipped her mother. She had passed away from a virus she'd caught while nursing others. Now Tat was alone, the tragic deaths of her father and young sister still haunting her months after they'd drowned in a piranha-infested river on a tour of local villages.

Rourke had been at the funeral. He couldn't help the way he felt. If Tat was in trouble, or hurt, he was always there. He'd known her since she was eight and her parents lived next door to K.C., who was by that time Rourke's legal guardian, in Africa. Since Tat was ten years old and Rourke was fifteen, and he'd carried her out of the jungle in his arms to a doctor, after letting her get bitten by a viper, she'd been his. He couldn't have her, but he couldn't stop taking care of her. He knew his attitude puzzled her, because he was usually her worst enemy. But let her be hurt, or threatened, and he was right there. Always. Like now.

He'd tried to phone her, but he couldn't get her to answer her cell. She probably knew his number by heart. She wouldn't even pick up when he called.

Now she was here, somewhere close, and he couldn't even get information from his best sources about her condition. He remembered again the way she'd been in Barrera, bleeding, white in the face, worn to the bone, but still defiant.

The steward walked down the aisle and announced that the rebels who held the airfield were allowing the passengers to leave after a brief negotiation. He even smiled. Rourke leaned over and unobtrusively patted the hide gun in his boot. He could negotiate for himself, if he had to, he mused.

He called his contact, a man with a vehicle, to drive him to the refugee camp. This man was one of his few friends in the country. It was Bob Satele, sitting beside him, who had given him the only news of Tat he'd had in weeks.

"It is most terrible, to see what they do here," the man remarked as he drove along the winding dirt road. "Miss Carrington has a colleague who gets her dispatches out. She has been most sympathetic to the plight of the people, especially the children."

"Ya," Rourke said absently. "She loves kids. I'm surprised that Mosane hasn't had her killed." He was referring to the leader of the rebel coalition, a man with a bloodthirsty reputation.

"He did try," his contact replied, making Rourke clench his teeth. "But she has friends, even among the enemy troops. In fact, it was one of Mosane's own officers who got her to safety. They were going to execute her…"

He paused at Rourke's harsh gasp.

Rourke bit down hard on his feelings. "NATO is threatening to send in troops," he said, trying to disguise the an

guish he felt. At the same time he didn't dare divulge what he knew; it was classified.

"The world should not permit such as this to happen, although like you, I dislike the idea of foreign nations interfering in local politics."

"This is an exception to the rule," Rourke said. "I'd hang Mosane with my own hands if I could get to him."

The other man chuckled. "It is our Africa, yes?"

"Yes. Our Africa. And we should be the ones to straighten it out. Years of foreign imperialism have taken a toll here. We're all twitchy about letting outsiders in."

"Your family, like mine, has been here for generations," the other man replied.

"We go back, don't we, mate?" he said, managing a smile. "How much farther?"

"Just down the road. You can see the tents from here." They passed a truck with a red cross on the side, obviously the victim of a bomb. "And that is what happens to the medical supplies they send us," he added grimly. "Nothing meant for the people reaches them, yet outsiders think they do so much good by sending commodities in."

"Too true. If they're not destroyed by the enemy, they're confiscated and sold on the black market." He drew in a breath. "Dear God, I am so sick of war."

"You should find a wife and have children." His friend chuckled. "It will change your view of the world."

"No chance of that," Rourke said pleasantly. "I like variety."

He didn't, actually. But he was denied the one woman he did want.

The refugee camp was bustling. There were two people in white lab coats attending the injured lying on cots inside the few big tents. Rourke's restless eye went from one group to another, looking for a blond head of hair. He was almost frantic with worry, and he couldn't let it show.

"She is over there," Bob said suddenly, pointing.

And there she was. Sitting on an overturned crate with a tiny little African boy cradled in her arms. She was giving him a bottle and laughing. She looked worn. Her hair needed washing. Her khaki slacks and blouse were rumpled. She looked as if she'd never worn couture gowns to the opera or presided over arts ceremonies. To Rourke, even in rags, she would be beautiful. But he didn't dare let his mind go in that direction. He steeled himself to face her.

Clarisse felt eyes on her. She looked up and saw Rourke, and her face betrayed her utter shock.

He walked straight to her, his jaw set, his one brown eye flashing.

"Look here," she began before he could say a word, "it's my life…"

He went down on one knee, his scrutiny close and unnerving. "Are you all right?" he asked gruffly.

She bit her lower lip and tears threatened. If she was hurt, in danger, mourning, frightened, he was always there. He'd come across continents to her, across the world, around the world. But he didn't want her. He'd never wanted her...

"Yes," she said huskily. "I'm all right."

"Bob said you were captured, that they were going to kill you," he ground out, his scrutiny close and hot.

She lowered her eyes to the child she was feeding. "A necklace saved my life."

"That cross..." he began, recalling that her mother had given it to her and she never took it off—except once, to put it around Rourke's neck in Barrera, just before he went into the capital city with Machado and the others, for luck.

"No." She flicked open the top button of her blouse. She was wearing a seashell necklace with leather thongs.

He frowned.

"This little one—" she indicated the child in her arms "—has a sister. She was dying, of what I thought was appendicitis. I commandeered a car and driver and took her to the clinic, a few miles down the road. It was appendicitis. They saved her." She took the bottle away from the child's lips, tossed a diaper over one shoulder, lifted the child and patted him gently on the back to make him burp. "Her mother gave me this necklace, the little girl's necklace, in return." She smiled. "So the captain whose unit captured me saw it and recognized it and smuggled me out of the village." She cradled the child in her arms and made a face at him. He chuckled. "This is his son. His little girl and his wife are over there, helping hand out blankets." She nodded toward the other side of the camp.

He whistled softly.

"Life is full of surprises," she concluded.

"Indeed."

She looked at him with eyes that were quickly averted. "You came all this way because you thought I'd been kidnapped?"

He shook his head curtly. "I didn't know that until I got here."

"Then why did you come?" she asked.

He drew in a long breath. He watched her cradle the child and he smiled, without sarcasm for once. "You look very comfortable with a child in your arms, Tat."

"He's a sweet boy," she said.

His mother came back and held out her arms, smiling shyly at Rourke before she went back to the others.

"Why did you come?" she asked him again.

He stood up, jamming his hands into his khaki slacks. "To get you out of here," he said simply. His face was taut.

"I can't leave," she said. "There isn't another journalist in this part of the country. Someone has to make sure the world knows what's going on here."

"You've done that," he said shortly. He searched her eyes. "You have to get out. Today."

She frowned. She stood up, too, careful not to go close to him. He didn't like her close. He backed away if she even moved toward him. He had for years, as if he found her distasteful. Probably he did. He thought she had the morals of an alley cat, which would have been hilarious if it hadn't been so tragic. She'd never let anyone touch her, after Rourke. She couldn't.

"What do you know, Stanton?" she asked softly.

His taut expression didn't relent. "Things I'm not permitted to discuss."

Her eyes narrowed. "Something's about to happen…?"

"Yes. Don't argue. Don't hesitate. Get your kit and come with me."

"But…"

He put his finger over her lips, and then jerked it back as if he'd been stung. "We don't even have time for discussion."

She realized that he knew about an offensive, and he couldn't say anything for fear of being overheard.

"I'm taking you home," he said, loudly enough for people nearby to hear him. "And no more argument. You've played at being a photojournalist long enough. You're leaving. Right now. Or so help me God, I'll pick you up and carry you out of here."

She gave him a shocked look. But she didn't argue. She got her things together, said goodbye to the friends she'd made and climbed into the backseat of the car he and Robert had arrived in. She didn't say another word until they were back at the airport.

He seated her beside him in business class, picked up a newspaper in Spanish, and didn't say another word until they landed in Johannesburg. He bought her dinner, and then she got ready to board a plane for Atlanta. Rourke had connections back to Nairobi, far to the northeast. They got through passport control, and Clarisse stopped at the gate that led to the international concourse. "I'll get on the next flight to DC from Atlanta and file my copy," she told him as they stood together.

He nodded. He looked at her quietly, almost with anguish.

"Why?" she asked, as if the word was dragged out of her.

"Because I can't let you die," he bit off. "Regardless of my inclinations." He smiled sarcastically. "So many men would grieve, wouldn't they, Tat?"

The hopeful look on her face disappeared. "I assume that I'll read about the reason I had to leave Ngawa?" she asked instead of returning fire.

"You will."

She drew in a resigned breath. "Okay. Thanks," she added without meeting his eye.

"Go home and give parties," he muttered. "Stay out of war zones."

"Look who's talking," she returned.

He didn't answer her. He was looking. Aching. The expression on his face was so tormented that she reached up a hand to touch his cheek.

He jerked her wrist down and stepped back. "Don't touch me," he said icily. "Ever."

She swallowed down the hurt. "Nothing ever changes, does it?" she asked.

"You can bet your life on it," he shot back. "Just for the record, even if half the men on earth would die to have you, I never will. I do what I can for you, for old time's sake. But make no mistake, I find you physically repulsive. You're not much better than a call girl, are you, Tat? The only difference is you don't have to take money for it. You just give it away."

She turned while he was in full spiel and walked

slowly from him. She didn't look back. She didn't want him to see the tears.

He watched her go with an expression so full of rage that a man passing by actually walked out of his way to avoid meeting him. He turned and went to catch his own flight back to Nairobi, nursing the same old anguish that he always had to deal with when he saw her. He didn't want to hurt her. He had to. He couldn't let her get close, touch him, warm to him. He didn't dare.

He flew back to Nairobi. He'd meant to go to Texas, to finalize a project he was working on. But after he had to hurt Tat, his heart wasn't in it. His unit leader could handle things until he got himself back together.

He drove out to the game ranch with his foreman from the airport in Nairobi, drooping from jet lag, somber from dealing with Tat.

K. C. Kantor was in his living room, looking every day of his age. He got to his feet when Rourke walked in.

Not for the first time, Rourke saw himself in those odd, pale brown eyes, the frosty blond hair—streaked with gray, now—so thick on the other man's head. They were of the same height and build, as well. But neither of them knew for sure. Rourke wasn't certain that he really wanted to know. It wasn't pleasant to believe that his mother cheated on his father. Or that the man he'd called his father for so many years wasn't really his dad…

He clamped down on it. "Cheers," Rourke said. "How're things?"

"Rocky." The pale brown eyes narrowed. "You've been traveling."

"How gossip flies!" Rourke exclaimed.

"You've been to Ngawa," he continued.

Rourke knew when the jig was up. He filled a glass with ice and poured whiskey into it. He took a sip before he turned. "Tat was in one of the refugee camps," he said solemnly. "I went to get her out."

K.C. looked troubled. "You knew about the offensive?"

"Ya. I couldn't tell her. But I made her leave." He looked at the floor. "She was rocking a baby." His eyes closed on the pain.

"You're crazy for her, but you won't go near her," K.C. remarked tersely. "What the hell is wrong with you?"

"Maybe it's what the hell's wrong with you, mate," Rourke shot back with real venom.

"Excuse me?"

The pain was monstrous. He turned away and took a big swallow of his drink. "Sorry. My nerves are playing tricks on me. I've got jet lag."

"You make these damned smart remarks and then pretend you were joking, or you didn't think, or you've got damned jet lag!" the older man ground out. "If you want to say something to me, damn it, say it!"

Rourke turned around. "Why?" he asked in a hunted tone. "Why did you do it?"

K.C. was momentarily taken aback. "Why did I do what, exactly?"

"Why did you sleep with Tat's mother?" he raged.

K.C.'s eyes flashed like brown lightning. K.C. knocked him clean over the sofa and was coming around it to add another punch to the one he'd already given him when Rourke got to his feet and backed away. The man was downright damned scary in a temper.

Rourke had rarely seen him mad. There was no trace of the financial giant in the man stalking him now. This was the face of the mercenary he'd been, the cold-eyed man who'd wrested a fortune from small wars and risk.

"Okay!" Rourke said, holding up a hand. "Talk. Don't hit!"

"What the hell is wrong with you?" K.C. demanded icily. "Tat's mother was a little saint! Maria Carrington never put a foot wrong in her whole life. She loved her husband. Even drunk as a sailor, she'd never have let me touch her!"

Rourke's eyes were so wide with shock and pain that K.C. stopped in his tracks.

"Let's have it," he said. "What's going on?"

Rourke could barely manage words. "She told me."

"She who? Told you what?"

Rourke had to sit down. He picked up the glass of whiskey and downed half of it. This was a nightmare. He was never going to wake up.

"Rourke?"

Rourke took another sip. "Tat was seventeen. I'd gone to Manaus on a job." Rourke's deep voice was husky with feeling. "It was Christmas. I stopped by to see them, against my better judgment. Tat was wearing a green silk dress, a slinky thing that showed off that perfect body. She was so beautiful that I couldn't take my eyes off her. Her parents left the room." His eyes closed. "I picked her up and carried her to the sofa. She didn't protest. She just looked at me with those eyes, full of… I don't even know what. I touched her and she moaned and lifted up to me." He drew in a shaky breath. "We were so involved that I only just heard her mother coming in time to spare us some real embarrassment. But her mother knew what was going on."

"That would have upset her," K.C. said. "She was deeply religious. Having you play around with her teenage daughter wasn't going to endear you to her, especially with the reputation you had in those days for discarding women right and left."

"I know." Rourke looked down at the floor. "That one taste of Tat was like finding myself in paradise. I wanted her. Not for just a night. I couldn't think straight, but my mind was running toward a future, not relief."

He hesitated. "But her mother didn't realize that. I can't really blame her. She knew I was a rake. She probably thought I'd seduce Tat and leave her in tears."

"That could have happened," K.C. said.

"Not a chance." Rourke's one eye pinned him. "A girl like that, beautiful and kind..." He turned away. He drew in a long breath. "Her mother took me to one side, later. She was crying. She said that she'd seen you one night at your house, upset and sick at heart because a woman you loved was becoming a nun. She said she had a drink with you, and another drink, and then, something happened. She said Tat was the result."

"She actually told you that Tat was your half sister? Damn the woman!"

Rourke felt the same way, but he was too drained to say it. He stared at his drink. "She told me that. So I turned against Tat, taunted her, pushed her away. I made her into something little better than a prostitute by being cruel to her. And now I learn, eight years too late, that it was all for a lie. That I was protecting her from something that wasn't even real."

He fought tears. They played hell with the wounded

eye, because it still had some tear ducts. He turned away from the older man, embarrassed.

K.C. bit his lip. He put a rough hand on Rourke's shoulder and patted it. "I'm sorry."

Rourke swallowed. He tipped the last of the whiskey into his mouth. "Ya," he said in a choked tone. "I'm sorry, too. Because there's no way in hell I can tell her I believed that about her mother. Or that I can undo eight years of torment that I gave her."

"You've had a shock," K.C. said. "And you really are jet-lagged. It would be a good idea if you just let things lie for a few days."

"You think?"

"Rourke," he said hesitantly. "The story she told you was true," he began.

"What! You just said it wasn't...!"

K.C. pushed him back down on the sofa. "It was true, but it wasn't Tat's mother." He turned away. "It was your mother."

There was a terrible stillness in the room.

K.C. moved to the window and stared out at the African darkness with his hands in his pockets.

"I got drunk because Mary Luke Bernadette chose a veil instead of me. I loved her, deathlessly. It's why I never married. She's still alive and, God help me, I still love her. She lives near my godchild, her late sister's only living child. I told you about Kasie, she married into the Callister family in Montana. Mary Luke lives in Billings."

"I remember," Rourke said quietly.

He closed his eyes. "Your mother saw what I was doing to myself. She tried to comfort me. She had a few drinks with me and things...happened. She was ashamed, I was ashamed...her husband was the best friend I ever had. How could we tell him what we'd done? So we kept our secret, tormented ourselves with what happened in a minute of insanity. Nine months later, to the day, you were born."

"You said...you weren't sure," Rourke bit off.

"I wasn't. I'm not. I don't have the guts to have the test done." He turned, a tiger, bristling. "Go ahead. Laugh!"

Rourke got up, a little shakily. It had been a shocking night. "Why don't you have the guts?" he asked.

"Because I want it to be true," he said through his teeth. He looked at Rourke with pain in his light eyes, terrible pain. "I betrayed my best friend, seduced your mother. I deserve every damned terrible thing that ever happens to me. But more than anything in the world, I want to be your father."

Rourke felt the wetness in his eyes, but this time he didn't hide it.

K.C. jerked him into his arms and hugged him, and hugged him. His eyes were wet, too. Rourke clung to him. All the long years, all the companionship, the shared moments. He'd wanted it, too. There wasn't a man alive who compared to the one holding him. He respected him. But, more, he loved him.

K.C. pulled back abruptly and turned away, shaking his head to get rid of the moisture in his eyes. He shoved his hands back into his slacks.

"Don't we have a doctor on staff?" Rourke asked after a minute.

"Ya."

"Then let's find out for sure," Rourke said.

K.C. turned after a minute, looking at the face that

was his face, the elegant carriage that he knew from his own mirror.

"Are you sure?"

"Yes," Rourke said. "And so are you."

K.C. cocked his head and grimaced as he looked at Rourke's face.

"What?"

"You're going to have a hell of a bruise," K.C. said with obvious regret.

Rourke just smiled sheepishly. "No problem. It's not a bad thing to discover that your old man can still handle himself," he chuckled.

K.C. glowed.

Need to know what happens next?
UNTAMED is available wherever print
and e-books are sold!